Oliver Optic

Up and Down the Nile

Young Adventurers in Africa

Oliver Optic

Up and Down the Nile
Young Adventurers in Africa

ISBN/EAN: 9783743385054

Manufactured in Europe, USA, Canada, Australia, Japa

Cover: Foto ©Andreas Hilbeck / pixelio.de

Manufactured and distributed by brebook publishing software (www.brebook.com)

Oliver Optic

Up and Down the Nile

All-Over-the-World Series

UP AND DOWN THE NILE

OR

YOUNG ADVENTURERS IN AFRICA

BY

OLIVER OPTIC

AUTHOR OF "THE ARMY AND NAVY SERIES" "YOUNG AMERICA ABROAD" FIRST
AND SECOND SERIES "THE BOAT–CLUB STORIES" "THE GREAT WESTERN
SERIES" "THE WOODVILLE STORIES" "THE ONWARD AND UPWARD
SERIES" "THE LAKE SHORE SERIES" "THE YACHT–CLUB SERIES"
"THE RIVERDALE STORIES" "THE BOAT–BUILDER SERIES"
"THE BLUE AND THE GRAY NAVY SERIES" "THE BLUE AND
THE GRAY ARMY SERIES" "A MISSING MILLION" "A
MILLIONAIRE AT SIXTEEN" "A YOUNG KNIGHT-
ERRANT" "STRANGE SIGHTS ABROAD"
"YOUNG AMERICANS AFLOAT" "THE
YOUNG NAVIGATORS" ETC.

BOSTON
LEE AND SHEPARD PUBLISHERS

Up and Down the Nile

ILLUSTRATIONS

PREFACE

"UP AND DOWN THE NILE" is the third volume of the second series of the "All-Over-the-World Library," in which the voyage of the Guardian-Mother is temporarily suspended at Alexandria, while the excursionists make their trip up and down the great river of Egypt in another steamer more suitable for inland navigation. Although the story, which has been a prominent feature in its predecessors, is somewhat abbreviated in this book, for the reason that more space was required for the remarkable history of the oldest existing nation of the world, and for the wonderful monuments of its ancient people, the thread of it is still continued, and will form the basis of some exciting adventures in the next volume.

The exploration of such a country as Egypt, with its delicious climate, its rainless skies, its extraordi-

nary testimonials of ancient grandeur, revealing the
artistic taste, the astonishing mechanical skill, and
the wonderful patience, perseverance, and persist-
ency in overcoming almost incredible difficulties in
generations of the human race that existed thousands of years ago, would seem to furnish abundant interest ever for young readers without the
stimulant of the story.

One young lady, and the quartet of young men
from fifteen to eighteen years old who have called
themselves the "Big Four," are students. They
attend to regular studies a portion of the time, especially when the ship and her little consort are
at sea; and when the party are engaged in sight-
seeing, which forms most of their occupation in
this book, they are still students, and the commander takes the greatest pains to have them well
instructed. All the excursionists are students in a
less technical sense, and all of them are employed,
not only in gratifying their curiosity, but also in
acquiring knowledge. Through lectures and conversation the history of Egypt, ancient and modern, is
brought out to a considerable degree, as well as the
geography, resources, and religion of the country.

While it was impossible to give in detail the wonders of the Museums of Bulak and Gizeh, some of their prominent curiosities are mentioned, particularly some of the latest, and perhaps most important discoveries which have been placed on exhibition, including those of hardly a dozen years since they were brought forth from the gloom of their ancient tombs. It seems hardly credible that the remains of the particular Pharaoh who persecuted the children of Israel, of whom the young people have read in the Bible, should be still present in his mummied flesh on the face of the earth, as our party gazed upon them.

The pyramids, the rock-tombs, and the ruins of the temples, more or less decayed by the stroke of three thousand years or more of time, have been described so far as space would permit. Cairo and Alexandria have not been neglected, and the manners and customs of the medley of people in Egypt have received attention.

WILLIAM T. ADAMS.

DORCHESTER, MASS., April 11, 1894.

CONTENTS

UP AND DOWN THE NILE

CHAPTER I

A DELIGHTFUL OCCASION

"I suppose Captain Royal Ringgold knows where he is, and as long as we follow the Guardian-Mother the Maud will be all right," said Louis Belgrave, the sole owner of the larger steamer, though he was serving in the capacity of a deck-hand on board of the smaller one.

"And perhaps I know where we are just as well as Captain Ringgold does," replied Captain George Scott Fencelowe, a young man of eighteen, who was at the wheel in the pilot-house of the Maud. "I suppose when a fellow knows a simple fact, he knows it as well as anybody else can."

"If you absolutely know where you are, you are correct," added Louis.

"I absolutely know where we are; I mean that I am certain of our position, and I should be a fool if I did not know it," argued Captain Scott, as he directed his spy-glass to the south, where the land

1

was in plain sight. "You can see that fort on an island, which is Fort Adjémi; and off to the east north-east you can see the principal lighthouse, though there are two more of them within the harbor."

"I see that you are reading the substance of what you say from the plan of the harbor of Alexandria, which you have cut out of your chart," suggested Louis with a laugh.

"I don't claim that the knowledge of this locality was born into me when I came into this world; and what I know about it I obtained from hard study of the chart, the plan of the harbor of Alexandria, and the book of sailing directions," replied the captain, a little nettled at the remark of the deck-hand.

"I know you have been the most diligent of students, Captain; and after I have seen you poring over your charts, measuring on them, and figuring out the results of your inquiries, I am not a bit surprised that you absolutely know where you are. After sailing three or four thousand miles with you in the Maud, I have never known you to be off the track even in a fog," said Louis earnestly.

"Thank you, Louis; that is hearty, and pleasant to my sense of hearing. I can only say that, if I haven't gone wrong, it is only because I love navigation, and have given my whole head to the study of it," returned Captain Scott.

"The Guardian-Mother has stopped her screw!" exclaimed the millionaire, suddenly dropping the subject of conversation.

"We will run up a little nearer to her before we follow her example," added the young commander of the Maud.

"Of course this is the coast of Egypt," continued Louis, as he gazed at the low shore, hardly more than a couple of miles distant.

"No doubt of it. You have not seen your mother for a week, and, as the sea is smooth here, I will run alongside of the ship, so that you can go on board of her at once. Morris will be as glad to see his mother as you will be to see yours," said the captain, as he headed the little steamer for the Guardian-Mother.

"We are neither of us babies, though I shall be happy to see my mother again, as I always am."

"I wish I had a mother," added the captain, with something like a sigh. "If I had had one the last dozen years, I am sure I should have been a better fellow."

"You are as good a fellow as any of us now; and we have three ladies on board the ship, who are all the same as mothers to you, for they think the world of you, to say nothing of a sweet sister in the person of Miss Blanche," replied Louis lightly, as the captain rang the speed bell to slow down the engine.

"She is too lovely a girl to be any fellow's sister except Morris's. You would not be quite willing to have her for your sister," answered the captain with a significant chuckle. "Stand by to heave the bow line!" he added sharply.

Louis hastened to obey the order; and he was always

as obedient as though he had been a beggar instead of a millionaire.

"Stand by the stern line, Flix!" called the commander at the door of the pilot-house.

"Oy, oy, sur!" responded the Milesian, who was the other deck-hand.

Morris Woolridge, who was the first officer of the Maud, came forward at this time. Pitts, the cook and steward, came out of the galley to assist if needed. Seated on the rail, near the engine-room, was John Donald, the second engineer, whom all called "Don," with a book in his hand, whose pages were covered with strange characters, which attracted the attention of the first officer as he passed him.

"Are you reading Chinese, Don?" asked Morris.

"Not a bit of it; I am not up to that, sir," replied the engineer.

"But what you are reading looks like the tracks of a fly that had escaped from an inkstand," added Morris.

"It is Arabic," said Don. "I have not had to talk or read it much lately, and it slips away from me like an eel from my hands."

"I should think it would; for it seems to be made up of hooks and eyes, including that 'hump,' sickles, and fish-hooks."

"But they all stand for sounds."

"Never mind; I don't want to learn such a lingo as that."

"I bought this book in Cons'ti'ple when I was told that we were coming to Egypt, and I have been studying it the last three months."

" Then you will be able to do my talking for me on
the Nile," said Morris, as the captain struck the gong
to stop the screw.

On board of the Guardian-Mother all the cabin
party had gathered on the upper deck, and the ladies
were vigorously waving their handkerchiefs, while
the gentlemen flourished their sea caps. It had been
the longest separation of the members of the round-
the-world excursion since they sailed from New York,
about a year before.

" Get out the bunters, if you please, Pitts," called
the captain. " Heave up the bow line, Louis ! "

The line was promptly caught by the seamen of
the ship, and made fast. The little steamer had come
up under the lee of the other, and the bunters pro-
tected both of them from any injury in the slight
swell. The gangway steps were lowered before the
Maud was made fast.

" Come on board ! " shouted Captain Ringgold.

The " Big Four " understood to whom this order
applied, though no names had been mentioned. Louis
led the way, followed by Morris, for both of them had
mothers on board, and the two others were close behind them. Mrs. Belgrave folded her son in her arms,
and kissed him as though he had been a baby ; but
the stalwart young man, though he weighed one hundred and fifty pounds, did not rebel at this maternal
demonstration ; on the contrary, he returned the
kisses of his mother as heartily as they were given.

Morris Woolridge was rather more afraid of being

called a "baby," and though his mother was hardly less demonstrative than Mrs. Belgrave, he was somewhat chary of his labial endearments; but he appeared to satisfy his maternal parent that he had not parted with his affections during his absence. Louis's mother wanted to see more of him before she resigned him to the commander, who stood ready to take his turn with his owner; and the lady was reasonable enough to turn her boy over to him.

"I am glad to see you, Mr. Belgrave," said Captain Ringgold, as he warmly grasped the hand of the young man.

In the presence of the ship's company he always gave him this simple title, though he addressed him by his given name when they were alone, for he made a great deal of the dignity of the owner of the steamer.

"I believe you have been growing fat since I saw you last, Mr. Belgrave," he added.

"We have had excellent food on board of the Maud, and Pitts is a good cook. I hope my physical condition will be regarded as a sufficient testimonial to the skill of the worthy fellow who presides in our galley," replied Louis. "But I don't think I have gained over fifty pounds, and am in no present danger of outweighing Uncle Moses."

"I cheerfully give you my permission to kick the beam of the scale against me," interposed Uncle Moses, who was the young man's trustee, the keeper of his million and a half, which had made him a millionaire at sixteen, as he thrust in his great fat hand where his ward could grasp it, which he did with energy enough to make himself felt. "I really believe you have added something to your avoirdupois since I saw you last in the harbor of Malaga."

Mrs. Blossom, the companion of his mother, was the next of the party to present herself before the young millionaire. She had been Squire Moses Scarburn's housekeeper, with whom Felix McGavonty had been brought up; and she had subjected him to more embraces and kisses than the subject of them cared to endure, causing him to break away from her before she had satisfied the longings of her affectionate nature.

"O Louis, how glad I am to see you and Felix!" she exclaimed; but the owner of the ship fell back before she had an opportunity to hug him as she had his crony. "It makes me feel like home."

"I hope you are not homesick, Mrs. Blossom," replied Louis, as he saw Dr. Hawkes, the surgeon of the ship, and rushed towards him to avoid being a victim of the good lady; for he thought she rather overdid the business of hugging and kissing, which was all right to any extent with his mother. "I hope you are very well, doctor," he continued, as he took the proffered hand of the medical gentleman.

Uncle Moses had insisted that Dr. Hawkes and himself were on board of the steamer in the capacity of ballast; for there had been a difference of only a quarter of a pound in their weight when they sailed from New York, the trustee weighing two hundred and twenty-six pounds and a half, the surgeon exceeding this weight by four ounces. Both of them were exceedingly jolly, as full of fun as boys of twelve. The doctor called the lawyer Brother Avoirdupois, while Uncle Moses had named the other Brother Adipose Tissue; and in the cabin they rarely used any other names.

"I am very happy to see you in such excellent condition, Mr. Belgrave," replied the doctor. "Do you know, I have been in a sort of terror ever since we sailed from Malaga?"

"Indeed! I am very sorry for that, and I hope I am not responsible for it; for I should have jumped overboard if I had thought I had done anything to excite a fear in the mind of a gentleman as courageous as I know you are, doctor."

"Courageous!" exclaimed the surgeon. "I haven't courage enough to fit out a small-sized mosquito."

"You have done what no other person on board of this ship would dare to do," protested Louis.

"What was that?" demanded Dr. Hawkes, suspecting that his meditated joke had gone wrong.

"You have cut off a man's leg; and I am sure any other man would rather fight a snake forty feet long than do such a thing."

"I have cut off a hundred of them, and it required no courage. But you are responsible for my terrors, and I am grateful to you for coming on board in such a vigorous condition of body," said the surgeon. "We

have had some rough weather during the last seven
days, and I have been in mortal terror lest the millionaire owner of the Guardian-Mother should get sick,
tumble down a hatchway, be wounded by Algerine
pirates, or that some such calamity should happen to
you."

"Any of these things might have frightened me,
but why they should disturb one who has the courage
to cut off a man's leg, I can't see."

"Don't you see that I should have been obliged to
go on board of the Maud to attend to your case; and
that would have compelled me to climb down the
gangway into a little boat, and be jerked about by the
angry waves. I am not as nimble as I was when I
was of your age, and I would rather have cut off a
dozen legs than risk my corporosity in the first cutter,
or even in the barge. I am truly grateful to you for
keeping well, and not tumbling down the hatchway,"
said the surgeon as he retreated to the rear of the
group.

Louis went to the Woolridges, sorry that the rather
far-fetched joke of the doctor had kept him so long
from meeting them. He took the hands of the heads
of the family, and as he rushed to Miss Blanche,
there was a blush on her cheeks which Captain Scott
noticed if the young millionaire did not. But Louis's
cheeks were quite as red as those of the beautiful
young lady. If her parents wondered whether or not
the owner and Miss Blanche were not becoming too
fond of each other, they never said anything on the

subject. Even the young man's mother, who had carefully warned her son not to think too much of Miss Blanche when he was comparatively a poor young fellow, had never alluded to the matter during the voyage.

Everybody shook hands with everybody else, and had some pleasant words to say; and even Mrs. Blossom, though the outpourings of her abundant affection had been rejected by Felix, declared that it was a "delightful occasion."

CHAPTER II

"THE VILLAIN OF THE STORY"

AFTER Louis Belgrave had shaken hands with all the officers of the Guardian-Mother, Captain Ringgold called him into his private cabin. The seamen had cheered him the moment he put his feet on the deck, and he was treated as though he had been a lord instead of a simple American boy, as he regarded himself, made a millionaire by his grandfather before him, and without any effort on his own part.

"What are we doing out here, Captain Ringgold? I see you are flying the signal for a pilot; why don't he come on board and take the ship into the harbor?" asked Louis, as the commander seated himself at his desk.

"I suppose you have to-day's ship's time in your pocket, my boy; what is it?" asked the captain.

"Quarter-past five, sir."

"Where does the sun happen to be just now?"

"The sun has gone down; and it was a beautiful sunset, only we had not time to look at it."

"Nobody in the Orient is ever in a hurry to do anything, as you have learned before this time. Besides, the pilot will not come off this evening, and it would

do no good to do so, for we can go into port only by
daylight. There are three passes, or channels, by
which the harbor may be reached, and all of them are
narrow, rocky, and dangerous. We can't go in before
to-morrow morning."

"I thought we should see something of the city of
Alexandria to-night, at least what could be seen from
the deck of the ship. It is rather stupid lying off
here, where nothing is in sight but a lighthouse and
the tops of several towers," added Louis.

"For my part, I was rather glad that we should
have a little breathing-spell before we enter upon
the business of sight-seeing again," replied the commander with a pleasant smile, of which he always
had a bountiful supply for the owner.

He was almost as fond of the young man as though
he had been his own son. Louis was a model youth
in every respect, and he could not help respecting
him; for the commander was a very high-toned gentleman himself. He had been led into intimate associa-
tion with his young companion by a mere accident,
and together they had fought their way through
some perilous adventures. He had found that Louis
was as brave as a lion in danger, and as peaceable as
a lamb in his ordinary relations with everybody.
They were the strongest of friends.

Mrs. Belgrave was now hardly thirty-five years of
age, and she was accounted a very attractive woman.
She was as good, high-toned, religious, as she was
handsome. She had been a model mother to her son

and only child, and had brought him up in the "way he should go." Mother and son were wholly devoted to each other; in fact, the degree of affection subsisting between them was something remarkable. Even some of the party in the cabin had whispered pleasantly that the commander loved the son for the mother's sake.

They were mistaken. Captain Ringgold was fond of the boy because he was his ideal of what a young man ought to be. Millionaire as Louis was, he never put on any airs, was always respectful and kind to others, and never willingly hurt the feelings even of the humblest who came into relations with him. Mrs. Belgrave was little given to the vanities of this world, had been a church-member from her girlhood, though she was not a bigot nor a fanatic. She believed that religion was enjoyment, and that it could be carried even into innocent amusements; so that she was one of the liveliest members of the cabin party.

It was generally believed in Von Blonk Park, the town in which she had lived all her life, that Mrs. Belgrave could marry any man she pleased. While the widow of Louis's father, she had thrown herself away upon a man who was utterly unworthy of her, and had been redeemed from her infatuation by her son; but she gave no one an opportunity to approach her on this delicate subject. If anything could be judged from appearances, Captain Ringgold had a very high respect and regard for her, and his attentions to her were constant and earnest. But neither he nor the lady ever said a word or gave a hint that would enlighten others on this interesting question. Certainly Louis had no suspicion that the attentions of the captain meant anything at all.

"I think we have had considerable breathing-time the last week," said Louis. "But I have no doubt we shall have a good time in the cabin this evening. By the way, Captain Ringgold, has it occurred to you that there are just thirteen of us when all are present at the table?"

"I have had occasion to count them more than once; but what of it?" inquired the commander.

"It is an unlucky number to sit at table together," replied Louis with a smile which was intended to acquit himself of being unduly impressed by the fact.

"Fiddledy dee!" puffed the captain.

"But I knew a gentleman in Von Blonk Park of fine education and high standing in society who would no more sit down at table in a party of thirteen than he would jump into the sea," replied Louis.

"Of course it is all nonsense; and I believe there is a club of thirteen in New York City who dine together regularly for the very purpose of proving that the superstition is simply ridiculous, though I have met educated men who cling to the belief. I could tell you enough in my own experience to convince you that the idea is absurd and ridiculous," answered the commander. "I once commanded a steamer in the cabin of which thirteen persons sat down to table together three times a day for sixty days. The ship went into port all right, and I have not yet heard of the death of any one of this 'baker's dozen.'"

"I don't believe in any superstition, not even that the tenth wave of the sea is bigger than any other," added Louis.

"That is a profitless subject to talk about; and if any or all the thirteen should die within a year, the number would not have anything to do with their decease. To change the subject, before we left Malaga, as you know, I assigned an Egyptian subject to every gentleman and one lady on board of the Guardian-Mother, and to the 'Big Four' on board of the Maud, and each one was to be prepared to deliver himself of his information as soon as we anchored in the harbor of Alexandria. I had to excuse Mr. Woolridge, though I have seen him looking over the books and maps in the library. We shall doubtless be in port to-morrow, and I hope the 'Big Four' have attended to this matter."

"They have, sir; and even Flix, who pretends that he is no scholar, though he had a very good standing at the Academy, has given considerable attention to study," replied Louis.

"I advised both your mother and your trustee, the latter to purchase this steamer, and the former to engage in this voyage round the world, more as a means of education for you than as an extended frolic, and my conscience would reproach me for doing so if we neglected the instruction it is capable of giving to you and the rest of the party."

"I can say that I have attended closely to my studies all the time except when we were engaged in actual sight-seeing."

"And then quite as much as when you were engaged in study with the book in your hands. What may be called our unconscious study is quite as important in our intellectual progress as that which we pursue systematically. In fact, we are learning something during all our wakeful hours."

"I believe that with all my might, though I never thought of the matter before. My subject was 'The Nile,' and I have searched all the books within my reach for information in regard to this river, and some of the facts in regard to it have surprised me. I hope the pilot will come on board early enough in the morning to get us into the harbor before noon."

"I hardly expect to come to anchor inshore before noon, though the pilotage fee for the ship may hurry up the pilots, and give us one in good time, and possibly one may come on board to-night. But I called you into my room to speak about another matter. We have seen nothing of the Pacha or any of his minions since we left Zante, and I hope he will not come down upon us here, though I acknowledge that I expect to see or hear from him in Egypt; for he must be to some extent at home here, where the Mohammedan religion prevails, and there must be some sympathy between this country and Morocco. The Pacha " —

"Excuse me, Captain, but how do you spell that word ? " interposed Louis, who had been somewhat exercised in regard to the orthography of the word.

"You pay your money for your dictionary, but you don't have to pay anything for choice in spelling such words as the one I mentioned," replied the commander. "I have always written it P-a-c-h-a, perhaps because I read Captain Marryatt's book, 'A Pacha of Many Tales,' when I was a youngster, and it was so spelled in that work. I suppose the author intended this title as a pun, for Turkish magnates had their rank indicated formerly by one, two, or three horse-tails borne before them in public, on a sort of cross surmounted by crescents. My dictionary prefers Pacha, Webster inclines to Pasha; but all of them leave you to take your choice. It is also written Pachaw, Pashaw, and Bashaw ; and if there is any other possible way to spell it, you may include that in the list."

" My French dictionary has it in your way."

" Then of course it must be right," added the captain with a laugh ; for his owner was a good French scholar, and spoke the language fluently after years of study with native teachers. "Now, to leave the shadow for the substance, I am really afraid Ali-Noury Pacha may step on the stage of action again either in these waters or on shore."

" I suppose we needn't mince the matter in speak-

ing of it, Captain Ringgold," said Louis very seriously. "Do you believe the Pacha is really in love
with Miss Blanche Woolridge?"

"I do not believe he is capable of the emotion of
love, as we understand it," replied the commander
quite as seriously; for he knew, though he never mentioned it, that the young man was deeply interested
in the direction of the beautiful maiden, who had
been his fellow-passenger on board of the Guardian-
Mother, and sometimes in the Maud. "I do not
believe he is in love with her, and have never believed
it. He is an immensely wealthy Moor, has served in
high civil and military positions, I was informed in
Madeira and Gibraltar."

"We can have no doubt that he is a very powerful
Pacha," added Louis; "but his character is villan-
ously bad; and for that reason we could have nothing
to do with him; and certainly I could not allow him
to come in contact with our lady passengers, least of
all with Miss Blanche. I have run away from him
not less than three times, for which I have been a
little ashamed of myself, though I may find it advisable to do so again if it can be done without any sacri-
fice of our plans and purposes."

In the course of the voyage round the world the
Guardian-Mother had visited Mogadore, an Atlantic
port of Morocco. Mr. Woolridge was accompanying
the steamer in his sailing yacht, with all his family
on board. The powerful Moor had visited the ship
while the yachtman's family were on board of her.

He had come in state, in a magnificent barge. He was not known then, and as he spoke English fluently he was introduced to all the party.

It was soon observed that he was very devoted in his attentions to Miss Blanche, who was really an innocent child of sixteen. The Pacha invited the party to his palace, and promised to obtain a firman that would enable them to visit mosques and other places ordinarily closed to "Christian dogs." But Mrs. Woolridge did not like the attentions bestowed upon her daughter, and was alarmed. She talked with her husband, and he shared her fears. He spoke to the commander about the matter. He had not kept his eyes closed, and he "took the bull by the horns," and at daylight the next morning the steamer towed the yacht to sea, and they sailed for Madeira.

The Pacha followed in his steam-yacht of four hundred tons. Among the Portuguese friends the party made at Funchal, Captain Ringgold learned the true character of his late Moorish guest; and before the Fatimé, as the Pacha's yacht was called, had been a day in port, the Guardian-Mother and the Blanche went to sea. The Mahommedan magnate followed to Gibraltar, where the information in regard to the character of "His Highness" was fully confirmed. He approached the commander there in a conciliatory manner; but the captain, while treating him in a polite and gentlemanly way, refused to have anything to do with him, or to permit him to meet his lady passengers.

The commander spoke plainly, and bluntly gave the reason for his action, which so enraged the Moor that he attacked him in a street of Gibraltar, backed by four of his servants. But the stalwart seaman upset him and his minions, pitching the magnificently dressed Pacha into the muddy gutter. The Maud, with the "Big Four" on board, was sent to sea at midnight, and the ship followed her in due time. The Moor seemed to be animated by a feeling of revenge now rather than by any other motive.

At Constantinople he had employed a Moorish captain to persecute the party, with the especial purpose of capturing Miss Blanche or Louis, or both of them, as fully related in a preceding volume. This was the " villain " of the story, — the Pacha, assisted by Captain Mazagan and other agents, whom the commander did not wish to encounter again.

CHAPTER III

PRECAUTIONS FOR THE FUTURE

SEVERAL attempts had been made by Captain Mazagan and his accomplices to obtain possession of the persons of the young millionaire and the houri, as " His Highness " called her ; but the vigilance, energy, and decision of Captain Ringgold, assisted by Scott, Louis, and Felix, had defeated the schemes of the conspirator, who had been shaken off three months before when the ship and her puny consort sailed from Zante.

It was really marvellous that in all the plots and conspiracies through which the party of thirteen had passed, only four persons were aware of the purposes of the conspirators. Mr. and Mrs. Woolridge, Morris and Miss Blanche had no suspicion that the object of the attacks by the felucca or the armed men on shore was the capture of the fair maiden and Louis, one or both. Mrs. Belgrave had no idea that her son was in particular danger. If she had known the whole truth, probably it would have brought on a recurrence of her nervous malady, of which Dr. Hawkes appeared to have cured her.

It was not the " Big Four" that possessed this momentous secret, for Morris Woolridge was one of them,
and it was feared that he might tell it to his father
or mother. The commander believed that if Mrs.
Belgrave and the Woolridges knew of the peril that
surrounded them, they would all be very miserable,
and the knowledge of it on their part might bring the
cruise as projected to an end. The party had been
anxious to visit the Holy Land, from Jaffa to Beyrout.
The captain had full confidence in his ability to protect his passengers under all ordinary circumstances,
and had fully justified this feeling; but in such a
journey as that through Syria, he realized that his
resources would be likely to fail him, and he had
promptly vetoed the project.

But he did not give his real reason for refusing to
entertain the idea; but, as the wise physician conceals
from his nervous patient the nature of his malady,
he was silent as to his real motives. It was already
the month of December when the Guardian-Mother
approached the shores of Egypt, and the Syrian tour
would make them too late to go up and down the Nile
at the best season; besides, two of the ladies were not
accustomed to riding horseback, and it would be quite
impossible for such bulky personages as Uncle Moses
and Dr. Hawkes to travel in this manner.

The captain's reasons seemed to be sufficient to
compel them to abandon the trip, and it was very
reluctantly postponed to some future period. The
secret was still kept inviolably; for the three members

of the "Big Four" band fully realized that a whisper of it might break up the voyage, and their personal interest fortified their discretion. But the consideration of the wish of the party had brought the Pacha and his agents to the captain's attention at this early stage of the visit to the land of Egypt.

During the three months' cruise of the steamers from port to port on the Mediterranean, the four who were in possession of the secret kept a vigilant look-out for the Fatimé, and for the Pacha himself. But the cities of Europe were not favorable for the operations of "His Highness" and his agents. Mussulmans were rather at a discount when they interfered with enlightened civilization, and they were all efficiently policed; and nothing had been seen of the Fatimé, and no one had been identified as his agent. But the party were going to a region more favorable to the Pacha's tactics, and the most diligent watchfulness must be exercised. No one could imagine in what form a new attempt to carry out the purpose of the enemy might be made, and the commander deemed it necessary to charge anew his only assistants in warding off an attempted attack to renew and increase their vigilance.

"Perhaps you have discovered that one of your 'Big Four' has considerable talent in the capacity of a detective," continued the commander.

"Of course you mean Flix, for I have noticed that he has a taste in that direction," replied Louis. "He was the first to discover the Pacha in Constantinople, and the first to determine that the Samothraki meant mischief."

He alluded to the fast-sailing felucca which had followed the party through the Dardenelles and through the Archipelago, her crew, under Captain Mazagan, attempting to board the Maud when she had all the passengers on board.

"And he was the first to snuff that French detective in Athens," added the captain. "Before we left Malaga I had some talk with him in regard to the Pacha and his movements. He had seen nothing of him or any of his gang. I told him that Egypt would be especially favorable to his operations, and I warned him to keep a close lookout for the Fatimé on the voyage, and especially as we approached these shores."

"He said nothing to me, but I think he has obeyed his orders; for every time a sail hove in sight, he rushed for his spy-glass. I have seen him doing the same thing since we came on board of the ship."

"I have wished a dozen times that Captain Penn Sharp, now of the Viking, were on board of the Guardian-Mother," continued the commander.

"He is doing better now," replied Louis with a smile.

"So he is; but his coming on board of the ship as a quartermaster was the beginning of his fortunes. He had been a very skilful detective for many years in New York, and nothing but the failure of his health would have tempted him to leave his profession. He worked up your mother's case, and then married the divorced wife of Scoble, after she had inherited a princely fortune from her uncle."

"Six o'clock, and there is the dinner-bell," interposed the owner. "You have not told me yet what you are driving at on this detective business."

"Time enough yet, for we have to lie here all night, and the 'Big Four' will sleep in their own state-rooms," added Captain Ringgold, as he rose from his chair, and led the way to the boudoir, from which the grand staircase descended to the state cabin, as they were called on the original plan of the steamer.

"Where is Flix?" asked Louis, as he met Scott in the gangway.

"He is fooling with a spy-glass on the upper deck; and I should think the fellow was studying to be an optician from the amount of time he gives to the glass," replied Scott, laughing.

Louis understood the matter better, and he went to the upper deck instead of to the cabin. He found Felix very busy with the glass, though it was getting rather dark to see anything.

"What are you about, Flix? Didn't you hear the dinner-bell?" he asked. "You know that punctuality is enjoined upon all of us."

"I heard it; but just now I am busy, and you will have me excused for a few minutes," replied Felix, still straining his eye at the instrument in his hand.

"You are engaged in your mission, Flix, and you shall be excused," added Louis in a low tone.

" What mission ? Who told you I had any mission except to keep praties from spoiling ? " demanded Flix, apparently startled by the question.

" Captain Ringgold. But I think you can come to dinner now, for your absence will provoke some questions, especially from Mrs. Blossom, who is a mother to you."

" She is one of the best women in the world; but she overdoes her mothering. I will go with you, darling; but I have a mighty request to make of the captain, and you must make it for me, for you are the millionaire and a half that owns the ship."

" Never mind the mighty request now, and we will talk about it after dinner."

" Just as you like, and I will go with you," replied Felix, as he returned the glass to the brackets.

The party were not yet seated at the table, but were standing behind the chair; for the captain had been detained by one of the officers in the boudoir. But he appeared in a few moments. Every person knew his place, for all the chairs were numbered the same as the staterooms, and the same figures were on the napkins; an arrangement made by Mr. Melancthon Sage, the chief steward. Sparks and Sordy, the stewards in the cabin, welcomed the " Big Four," who had been absent a whole week, as they seated them. The commander said a very brief grace; for Mrs. Belgrave and Mrs. Blossom could not have eaten their dinners if this grateful acknowledgment had been omitted.

The dinner was an excellent one, as it always was, though the accomplished head steward had not had access to a market for seven whole days. With the soup came abundant conversation. The captain sat at the head of the table, with the back of his revolving chair against the mainmast. Louis was on his right, the place of honor, though he always resigned it when distinguished guests were present. On the owner's right sat Mrs. Belgrave, who had two thousand questions, or less, to ask her boy, as she was very apt to call him. The commander had arranged the places at table in accordance with his own ideas of etiquette.

While Louis appreciated his seat at the side of his mother, who was more to him than any other human being, he sometimes envied Felix, who sat at the left of Miss Blanche; but he would not have hurt the feelings of his mother by changing places with his crony, even if the opportunity had been presented to him. Mrs. Blossom would have been happy to change places with anybody if it would put Felix at her side; but the Milesian would not have enjoyed the situation then, in spite of his respect and regard for the good lady. She was too lavish in her endearments to suit his taste, and she would not have permitted him to keep a secret from her if any amount of teasing could have drawn it out of him. Felix was not exactly a "mother-boy," as Louis was, though his maternal parent was more reasonable in her requirements.

"I hope all the lecturers I appointed for the symposium, if our meeting is entitled to this modern name, though I find it means a party engaged in a drinking bout — "

"I don't think the conference for which we were to prepare ourselves will admit of that name," interposed Professor Giroud, who, though a Frenchman, was an authority in English. "A symposium, as used in recent years, means a collection of opinions on a given subject, generally given in print, though I suppose they may be expressed verbally."

"Thank you, professor; and I will not give my meeting that name again," added the captain. "But I hope you are all ready."

"I am for one," said Mr. Woolridge, to whom no subject had been assigned, as he asked to be excused. "As you gave me no topic, I selected my own."

All the company applauded; for the gentleman had formerly been a sporting character, and had very little taste for literary matters, though he was well educated.

"I am glad you have changed your mind, Mr. Woolridge," added the commander, when the applause subsided.

"I did not decline to take part because I was not willing to do my share in the meeting, but because I feared you would give me a subject beyond my capacity to treat. If you had given me the Arabic language, I should have broken down under the load. My subject is horses, mules, donkeys, and camels."

"I will add it to the list of subjects; and I am sure you will treat it as an expert."

"Where have you been all the time since you landed on board of the steamer, Felix McGavonty?" asked Mrs. Blossom.

"Oi've been coaxin' the main to' gallant hatchway to shut up, for fayer some lady moight fall overboard into it, and brake her schkull agin the main r'yal keelson."

The party laughed heartily at this sally of the Milesian, who could talk English as well as his companions, but he had a great affection for his brogue, which he claimed to have inherited from his mother, and occasionally used it to amuse his companions.

"You know I can't understand that sea talk, Felix; and why won't you speak so that I can tell what you mean," pouted Mrs. Blossom.

"Faix, I cudn't oonderstand your say slang ony betther than you cud moin, not a bit, thin," replied Felix, very quietly.

"I don't use sea slang, for I don't understand it," retorted the lady.

"Didn't ye's say I landed on boord this staymer? I app'ayl to the cap'n to get the m'aning of the sintince."

"I think you must have meant that Felix fell overboard down the hatchway," laughed the commander, as he rose from the table, and the others followed his example.

The good lady wanted to get hold of the Milesian to explain matters, but he rushed to the deck in spite of her calls, and Louis followed him.

CHAPTER IV

THE MIGHTY REQUEST OF FELIX McGAVONTY

Felix thought he was mildly persecuted by Mrs. Blossom. He was thoroughly devoted to her, and would do almost anything to please her; but he felt that he had sacrificed his dignity as a young man in permitting her to treat him like a small boy. In a word, he thought it was necessary to give her a little gentle discipline. She was not his mother, his grandmother, or even his aunt; if she had been, the situation would have been entirely different, and in that case he believed he should have enjoyed her caresses.

With the feeling that she had no right to treat him as Mrs. Belgrave did her son, he fled to the upper deck, and again obtained the spy-glass he had so persistently pointed out to sea. Louis took his mother's hand as he kissed her, and did not feel that he was "a great calf," as Felix called himself after he had submitted to Mrs. Blossom's lusty embraces.

"You will come down again soon, Louis?" said Mrs. Belgrave. "I have hardly seen you since you returned to the ship."

"I will, mother, if I am not ordered to some duty

"Now, what in the world are you up to, Flix?" Page 31.

on board the Maud," he replied, with the idea that the
movements of Felix meant something, as he followed
the Milesian.

Felix had glued his right eye to the sight of the
glass, when the owner found him on the upper deck,
though it was too dark to see anything clearly.

"Now, what in the world are you up to, Flix?" he
asked, as he placed himself behind his crony, and
looking in the direction in which the glass was
pointed.

"Whisht, darling; there comes the second officer,"
replied Felix, as Mr. Gaskette passed them.

Louis thought his friend had eyes in the back of his
head as well as in the front, for he had not noticed
the approach of the officer, and wondered how Felix
could have seen him with one eye closed and the
other gazing out on the broad Mediterranean; but he
had before observed that the Milesian always saw
everything before any other person, as the commander
had suggested.

"What do you see, Flix?" asked Louis when the
officer had passed out of hearing.

"I don't see anything; and I wish I did," replied
Felix, without removing the glass from his eye.

"Well, what do you wish you saw?"

"See here, my darling, what has Captain Ringgold
been saying to you about me?" demanded the observer, turning his attention this time to the inquirer.
"What did you mean by my mission, before dinner?"

"Of course I meant your mission. The captain

said he told you to keep a sharp lookout for a certain steam-yacht of four hundred tons, especially as we approached the shores of Egypt."

"Did he tell you that?"

"How could I have known it if he had not? You keep as close within your shell as a snail, though I have seen you fooling with a glass all day."

"All right; then you know that I am looking for the Fatty," as Felix always called the Fatimé, the Pacha's steam-yacht. "I wish I could make her out."

"I don't wish so, and I hope we shall never set eyes on her again," added Louis heartily. "She seems to me like the craft of which Milton writes in Lycidas, 'rigged with curses dark.'"

"She's schooner-rigged," said Felix gravely. "I don't want to see her any more than you do, darling, if she isn't here; but if she is sculling about in these waters I want to get my right eye on her."

"I suppose if you could see her with your left eye, it would do just as well."

"Perhaps it would; but I am not left-eyed any more than I am left-handed. To come down to a point that makes the business practical, I believe upon the honor of my dawning mustache, that the Fatty is off there somewhere, though I can't see her just at this precise moment," replied the observer, as he placed the glass at his eye again.

"But it is too dark to see anything to-night, Flix," added Louis as he gazed out into the gloom that hung over the water.

"But this is like the watchman's grog; it is a night glass. To come down to hard frying-pan, I saw a craft off there just as it was getting dark that looked something like the Fatty. I could not make her out exactly; but I had a suspicion that weighed two hundred and forty pounds."

"That's a heavy suspicion, and I wish it did not weigh as many ounces."

"I don't want anything of her; but the captain of the ship told me to look out for her, and I'm going to do so."

"You have faithfully obeyed your orders; but what makes you think you have seen the Fatimé, Flix?"

"Well, it isn't because I have seen a full-rigged four-master out there in the distance, but " —

"But because you have seen a vessel that you thought looked like the Fatimé," interposed Louis.

"Well, my darling, I have a faint recollection of having seen the Fatty something less than five hundred times, and I think I know a mill-stone when I see the square hole through the middle of it," returned Felix, who flared up a little when he supposed his judgment was called in question. "I don't believe I should mistake a P. and O. steamer for the Fatty, even in the night."

"I don't believe you would, Flix; but I was only suggesting that it was rather difficult to identify a vessel when she is from three to five miles distant, either in a fog or in the night. I did not mean to call the accuracy of your perception in question " —

"That's metaphysics!" interrupted the Milesian. "If ye's can't shpake Oirish with the proper brogue, talk good old United States to a fellow like me. Why couldn't you say I couldn't see what was in it?"

"Because all cats are black in a dark night," laughed Louis. "Well, you couldn't see what was in it when it was too dark to see anything."

"Besides, nevertheless, to the contrary notwithstanding, I believe the Fatty is off there, though I can't put the tip of my finger on her at just this particular moment," persisted Felix.

"Then I believe you have good grounds for your belief," added Louis heartily.

"Now you talk like a Christian as you are, my darling; and they are not coffee-grounds, either, on which I pin my faith."

"Then suppose you cease your struggle to be funny, in which you always succeed beyond peradventure, and come down to bed-rock," suggested Louis.

"No bed-rock for me; I prefer a hair-mattress. But we will come to the point, and I hope it will stick you," continued Felix, putting his mouth close to the ear of the other. "I have been looking for the Fatty ever since we left Malaga, as Captain Ringgold told me to do, but I didn't see a taste of her till this afternoon."

"Where was she then?" asked Louis, deeply inter-

ested, too much so to take advantage of the Milesian-
ism of his friend.

"She was away down to leeward, and not less than
five miles off. I could hardly have seen her at all
without a glass. As the Guardian-Mother headed in
for the coast, she veered to the southward; and that
helped me to believe that she was the Fatty."

"But how could you make her out when she was
five miles off?"

"I didn't measure the distance she was from the
Maud, and she may have been eight or ten miles
from us. But you put me out with questions, and
don't let me spin out my yarn. How could I make
her out?" pouted Felix.

"I won't interrupt you again," added Louis.

"I took the measure of the Fatty at Funchal and
at Gibraltar. We had time enough to study her up
when she was chasing the Sally Hay, as the Maud
was called then (Salihé), from Tangier to the Rock.
I am not much of a drawist, but I made a picture of
her as I sat in the standing-room, for I thought we
had better remember just how she looked. I have
her fixed in the back of my eye as cleanly as I have
my mother, who is no longer in the flesh."

Louis only nodded.

"Faix, ye're houlding your tongue like a fish that
can't shpake."

"Go on," added Louis, true to his promise.

"I saw enough of the craft — I forget how you
said she was rigged —

"Go on."

"I saw enough of her to make me believe she was the Fatty, without regard to her rig, and I kept on spying her through the glass. When the ship came to anchor, the steamer, with the rig Captain Milton gave her, came about and headed to the eastward. She went off till I could see nothing but her black smoke against the sky. This was before dark, you mind. Half an hour later I found her headed to the westward. To make a long story no longer, she has been standing back and forth, east and west, for the last two hours."

"Off and on," suggested Louis.

"Not a bit of it, my darling!" exclaimed Felix, who, in spite of the objections he had made, rather liked Louis's comments. "You are off in your nautics, fellow deck-hand. Off and on means running towards the shore and then from it."

"Go on," replied Louis laughing, for he did not pride himself upon his "nautics."

"I have got to the end of my story. I believe the Fatty is keeping just near enough to the Guardian-Mother to see where she is going," replied Felix.

"May I speak now, Flix, as you have finished your yarn?" asked Louis.

"You may, my darling; but don't speak loud enough for His Highness to hear you on board of the Fatty."

"You said you had a mighty request to make just as we were going down to dinner."

"I had, and I have it still."

"Perhaps you will not object to mentioning it to me."

"Not the least in the world, for I want you to make the request of the captain. You are the owner of the ship, and you would have more weight than I should, as you kick the beam at one hundred and fifty pounds, while I can't hit that figure by fifteen pounds."

"What is the mighty request?" asked Louis, disregarding the argument.

"It is a fine night, though it is a bit dark; but the stars haven't turned in yet."

"To the point, Flix, for my mother wants me in the cabin."

"I want to take the Maud and run out to sea far enough to enable me to make out that craft with Captain Milton's rig," said Felix in the ear of his companion.

"But I can't go, for my mother wished me to go back to the cabin and spend the evening with her," pleaded Louis.

"The mighty request doesn't include you and Morris; for no Woolridge must have the ghost of an idea what we are about. We are going a-fishing after some sort of polywogs that bite best in the night, though we may not catch any."

"I understand you, Flix. Now come with me to the captain's cabin, and we will give voice to the mighty request," said Louis, as he started for the main deck.

"No, you had better talk it over together alone," Felix objected.

Louis yielded the point, and hastened to the cabin of the captain, expecting to find him smoking his cigar there after his dinner. But he had finished his smoke, and gone back to the cabin. He rang the electric bell, and Sordy presently appeared, whom he sent with a polite request for the commander to visit his cabin. He appeared in a few minutes, as the message came from the owner. Louis reduced the long yarn of Felix to its "lowest terms," and then enunciated the mighty request.

Captain Ringgold hardly asked a question, and granted the request at once in spite of its magnitude, as Felix viewed it.

"Where is Captain Scott, for he must go with you?" asked the commander.

"I am not going, for mother wants me to spend the evening with her in the cabin. Of course Morris must not go, and if I remain behind, he will ask no hard questions. I suppose Captain Scott is still in the cabin."

"You are quite right, Louis," replied the captain, as he touched his bell and sent Sordy to request the presence of the captain of the Maud.

Captain Scott was one of the four who were in possession of the momentous secret, and the request of Felix was repeated to him. The Milesian was sent for, and gave his views of the management of the affair, and the details were very soon arranged.

The commander and Louis went to the cabin while Captain Scott and Felix hastened on board of the Maud. Captain Ringgold proposed to send several seamen on board of the little steamer, but they were declared to be unnecessary, and would be in the way. Scott had no mother to call him into the cabin, and Felix was glad to escape from the endearments of the good woman, which were an infliction to him, except when he was sick.

CHAPTER V

A NIGHT CRUISE TO SETTLE A QUESTION

THE Maud was a "juvenile steam-yacht," as Felix had been known to call her, which had formerly been the property of Ali-Noury Pacha. Her engineer was a young Spaniard from the Canary Islands, who had been ill-treated when he objected to some of the purposes for which the craft was used, and he had run away from Mogadore, proceeding first to Funchal, and then to Gibraltar when he found the Pacha was there.

He had picked up Louis, Felix, and Scott, who were adrift in a open boat, and they had proceeded on the voyage together. Felipe Garcias, the engineer, was a very conscientious young man of eighteen, had not intended to steal the little steamer, and when he found the Fatimé at Gibraltar, he had caused the craft to be made fast to her and left there. The Pacha had recovered his property, but she seemed to be an elephant on his hands at that distance from his residence, and he had sold her for a song to a person of whom Uncle Moses and Mr. Woolridge had purchased her.

The little vessel, under the command of Scott, had made the voyage to the Orient, and had twice traversed the Mediterranean, and her young captain had proved himself to be not only a good seaman, but a well-informed and skilful navigator. Morris was his first officer, and Louis and Felix served in the humble capacity of deck-hands, or seamen. Felipe was first engineer, and the second was a man who had fled from the Fatimé at Gibraltar, and was not only valuable in his position, but he spoke Arabic, which had been of great service to Louis when he was doing detective duty at Gallipoli. Pitts, the cook and steward, completed the complement on board, consisting of seven persons.

In the cabin of the ship, as she was called to distinguish her from her consort, the party had become very animated after dinner, and the two real mothers had taken possession of their sons, who were relating the details of the voyage from Malaga, as they occurred on board of the Maud. It so happened that Mrs. Blossom had placed herself near the Woolridges, and she had already begun to ask for Felix; but Morris did not know. The commander said he and Scott were on duty, when he was interrogated, and that was all he would say.

" We can get off without anybody in the cabin knowing anything about our movements," said Scott, when he and Felix had reached the pilot-house of the Maud.

" But we must instruct the engineers and the cook before we do anything," suggested the leader of the movement.

" We needn't tell them anything except what they

are to do. I will attend to that. Felipe must run the engine, while Don and Pitts act as deck-hands, and both of them are willing to do all kinds of work."

"All right," replied Felix, as he took the night glass he had brought with him from its leather case.

He resumed his former occupation of using the glass, and swept the horizon with it at once. In a few moments he had apparently fixed his gaze upon an object which he continued to scrutinize till the captain returned to the forecastle. The fire in the furnace had been banked, and Felipe was starting it up. Pitts and Don obeyed the order to report on deck without asking any questions. Scott had followed the example of Captain Ringgold in keeping his own counsels as a rule, and the officers and seamen of both vessels were thoroughly schooled in the sailor's duty to obey orders without inquiring for reasons.

"Do you make out anything, Felix?" said the captain, when he saw his associate still making diligent use of the spy-glass.

"I think the Fatty is out there still; but she has gone so far to the eastward that I can only just make her out. But I believe she is making her runs a mile or two nearer the shore than when I saw her last," replied Felix.

"We shall have to wait a little while for Felipe to get up the steam, but it will not be long, he says. I think we had better cast off the fasts on board here, and then we shall not have to call on the watch on the deck of the ship for anything. We can drop them into the water, and pick them up when we return."

" I don't meddle with the navigation, Captain Scott," replied Felix.

" But the commander told me I was to consult you," added the captain.

" We will manage the affair together. You know that all we want is to ascertain if the steamer in the offing is the Fatty; and I don't think you need any assistance from me in carrying out the idea," answered Felix with becoming deference.

"All right, Flix, and we will talk it over as the occasion may require. If you will handle the glass, I will handle the steamer," replied Scott, who had not quite liked the idea of being placed under the orders of one of his deck-hands ; but the words and the manner of Felix had fully conciliated him.

In a little while Don brought word from Felipe that he had steam enough to move at half speed. The deck-hands were directed to cast off the bow and stern lines, and buoy them with sticks of wood from the fire-room. The order was executed without noise, so as not to attract the attention of the watch on the deck of the ship. The ports opened from the state-rooms, and all the party were in the cabin, so that they were not likely to discover that the Maud was in motion.

There was current enough to carry the steamer astern of the ship. Some of the watch discovered the smoke from her funnel, and reported that the Maud

was going astern. Mr. Gaskette mounted the taffrail,
and hailed her. Captain Scott reported that he was
acting under the orders of the commander, and the
second officer said no more; but he was a little
troubled. He had heard of such a thing as boys running off with a vessel, and it occurred to him that
Scott and Felix were engaged in such an enterprise.
He went to the boudoir, and sent down for the commander, who assured him that it was all right, and
thanked him for his vigilance.

The Maud was permitted to drift about half a mile
before Captain Scott rang to start the screw; and by
this time she had a full head of steam. Then he
sent the two acting deck-hands to keep a lookout in
the standing room, as the open space abaft the cabin
was sometimes called, though it was provided with
cushioned seats extensive enough to seat a dozen persons. This was done so that the captain and Felix
could talk more freely than they were willing to do in
the presence of any other of the ship's company; and
this phrase is as properly applicable to the people of
a small as a large vessel, if she is something more
than a mere boat.

" Do you make out anything more in regard to the
vessel, Flix ? " asked the captain.

" Nothing more; she is too far off," replied the
observer.

" Can you make out which way she is going ? "

" She is headed to the westward. When I first
made her out she kept growing smaller and smaller."

"That proved that she was increasing her distance."

"Precisely so; I took that in; but since that she has been increasing in size, which proves that she is coming nearer."

"Right you are. Now, if she is headed to the westward, we shall be likely to go astern of her on our present course. If you don't object, I will head her so as to come near her by intercepting her," suggested the captain. "I am sure we can get near enough to her to make out what she is."

"Of course I don't object to anything you do, Captain Scott. We are both working in the same holy cause, and you know far better than I do just what to do to enable us to find out what that steamer is."

This speech pleased Scott, as Felix intended it should, and he shifted the helm so that the bow of the Maud was pointed to the north-west. The suspicious craft did not appear to be sailing at full speed, so that the Maud was likely to come out ahead of her. For half an hour the captain held her as she had been pointed, and Felix continued to use his glass. Although the Maud must have been well known on board of the Fatimé, no notice was taken of her, which at first gave the observer some uneasiness, and led him to suspect that he had mistaken the identity of the vessel.

It would have been a happy mistake, though Felix did not like the idea of acknowledging that he had made a blunder. Scott, of course, kept a close watch over the object of the pursuit; but at the distance of a quarter of a mile he could not make her out, though he had a more nautical eye than his companion.

"Can you make her out, Flix?" asked the captain, after he had scrutinized the craft very thoroughly.

"I cannot; and I'm bound to say that she don't look like the Fatty," replied Felix.

"I'm glad to hear you say so; and Louis and the commander will be glad they sent you out here to settle the point."

"But I don't say it is not the Fatty; though if it is she, her appearance is changed. She has two sticks across her foremast, like the Guardian-Mother," added Felix, who was not altogether sure on all the nautical terms; and on this subject he was afraid of the captain.

"A fore yard and a fore topsail yard," said Scott, supplementing the reply. "It seems to me that settles the question. I never saw the Fatimé when she carried such spars; and if the steamer we are looking after carries them, she can't be the Pacha's craft."

"But the Guardian-Mother sent down these sticks in a heavy gale on our voyage to the Canaries," argued the Milesian.

"But she don't send them down in a calm, for it is not much better than Paddy's hurricane just now," returned the captain.

"Perhaps you are right, Captain Scott, though it is possible that she may have changed her rig for some reason," added Felix. "But I want to see

something more of her before we give up the inquiry."

"You shall see all you wish of her, for she is not
running more than eight knots an hour, and we will
go alongside of her if you say so."

"I should like to go as near her as it is prudent to
go."

"No trouble at all about it; we are going ten knots,
and we shall come out ahead of her, so that we can
take any position we choose."

The Maud continued on her course for another half
hour, and was then directly in the course of the
stranger, as she still appeared to be. If the eyes of
those on board of her were as sharp as the observers',
they would have been likely to recognize the Maud,
though she carried her two masts as she had seldom
done when in the service of the Pacha.

"I wonder if the Grand Mogul is on board of her,
if it should turn out that she is his craft," said the
captain, after both of the observers had been silent
for some time.

"He is a fast crab, that Pacha; and if he is on
board, he stays in the cabin. We learned at Funchal
and at Gibraltar, that, though he is a Mussulman, he
drinks wine and even brandy like an old toper; and
probably he is having a good time in the cabin of
the Fatty, wherever she may be, for they say he
spends most of his time in the winter on board of
her," replied Felix.

"But here she comes," added the captain, as he

rang the gong to stop the screw, having come down to half speed some time before.

Scott rang again to back her, and secured just the position he desired. The stranger was within a cable length of the Maud, when Felix went aft and very carelessly asked Don if the Fatimé ever carried yards on her fore mast.

" She always carried two of them on her deck in case the engine was disabled, but I never saw her wear them," replied Don.

Felix did not wait to hear any more. The movements of the stranger were almost enough to convince him that she was the Pacha's steamer; for why, he asked himself, should any honest vessel be running back and forth three miles or more from the shore.

The captain was still manœuvring, for the other steamer had sheered off a little, though she was now about to pass across the bow of the Maud. Both of the observers had a good chance to see her alow and aloft, and Felix was as certain as he was of his own existence that she was the Fatimé. Not a little to his astonishment, the captain hailed her in plain English; and she stopped and backed, holding a position with her stern on a line with the bow of the Maud.

CHAPTER VI

A FISHING EXCURSION UNDER THE STARS

"Ship, ahoy!" shouted Captain Scott with all the force of his lungs.

" On board the steamer!" was the return in quite as good English.   " What steamer is that?"

" The Viking, from the Bahama Islands," answered Scott, who had prepared this fib beforehand.   "Have you seen a large man-of-war steamer, flying American colors, coming up from the eastward?"

" I have not," replied the officer on the deck of the steamer; and he did not appear to recognize the Maud.

" Have you seen all you wish of her, Flix?" asked the captain.

" I have," answered the other.

" Thank you; I am very much obliged to you," shouted Scott.   "I wish you a pleasant voyage."

"Same to you," replied the unknown officer. "Where are you bound?"

" On the lookout for the American cruiser, Spread Eagle.   She is wanted at Rosetta," replied the captain.   "If they are not Hottentots on board of that

steamer they would know that my reply is humbug,"
he added in a lower tone to his companion.

At the same time he rang the gong to start the screw,
heading the Maud to the eastward when it began to
give her headway. The officer of the other steamer
appeared to be satisfied. Felix lighted a match as
soon as the little steamer began to move, and touched
off a Roman candle, which he had placed on a board
for use if needed. It fizzled up promptly, and bril-
liantly illuminated the scene. By its light he could
distinctly see and read the name on the stern of the
suspect, Fatimé. More than this, the officer who answered the hail had mounted the taffrail when he did
so, and still remained there, looking at the Maud.

"By the powers of mud, that man is Captain Mazagan!" exclaimed Felix, as the fireworks went out,
leaving the scene in greater darkness than before to
the half-blinded eyes of the observers in both vessels.
" I will wager all the leather in my old shoes against
a Turkish para that it is he."

"I thought I had heard the voice before," added
Scott.

Felix hastened to the standing-room to observe the
movements of the Fatimé, as the Maud had left her
astern. The two acting deck-hands, faithful to the
discipline, had not left their places, and could have
seen but little of what had just transpired. But the
change in the course enabled them to see the Pacha's
craft; and their eyes were not dazzled by the fireworks.

"That steamer is the Fatimé, Mr. Felix!" exclaimed Don, the engineer. "I hope you will not take us any nearer to her. Felipe would be shaking in his shoes if he knew we were within hail of her; and I don't feel altogether easy when I am so near to her."

"You need not be alarmed, Don John; if the officer who spoke to us is the captain, he does not appear to smell any mice near him," replied Felix. "But what makes you think that is the Fatty?"

"I spent most of my time in her stoke-hole when I was on board of her, but I reckon I know the craft when I see her," replied Don rather doggedly. "She's the Pacha's steam-yacht."

"You are mistaken, Don; that was not the Fatty. Did you hear what the captain said to the officer on the taffrail?"

"I did."

"Then you understand that we are looking for the American man-of-war Spread Eagle."

"You may make a spread eagle of me if that isn't the Fatimé, as her captain did of me once when I expressed my mind."

"I tell you that you are mistaken, Don John. You are a free born British citizen, and you have a perfect right to your own opinion in religion, politics, and steamers; but don't you tell any mortal body or immortal soul that you have seen the Fatty on this cruise. If it should get to the ears of Captain Ringgold, it would frighten him out of his wits."

"I should like to see the commander when he is

frightened out of his wits," interposed Pitts, with a very vigorous laugh.

"At any rate it would make him very uneasy and uncomfortable. As to the ladies on board of the ship, if they knew the Fatty was anywhere in the Mediterranean Sea, they would go into fits, and compel the commander to hurry back to New York as fast as he could make the ship go. Then some of you would be out of a job. You see that the Grand Mogul means to kill Captain Ringgold if he can get at him in a quiet place, and all the women that have no husbands are in love with him. They are bound to save him, even if they have to give up the voyage round the world. You can see through a brickbat when there is a hole in a mill-stone."

"I won't tell any person, living or dead, that we have seen the Fatimé, or any other steamer for that matter," protested Don.

"Nor I either," added Pitts.

"Good, Don; I am glad to have you acknowledge that you were mistaken, for any false rumor that the Fatty was in these waters would breed the biggest row you ever heard of," added Felix.

"I did not know the steamer, and I don't believe now, of course, that it was the Pacha's craft," Pitts declared.

Felix was satisfied, and went forward. Neither of the men aft knew anything at all about the momentous secret, or even that there was a secret. In common with all the uninitiated, they believed that the attacks which had been made upon the party in the Archipelago, and at Zante, were the work of pirates and brigands. The Fatimé had started her screw again, resuming her course to the westward. Captain Scott went at full speed in the opposite direction as a blind to the officer of the other steamer. In less than half an hour the two vessels were practically out of sight of each other, and the Maud, with her lights doused, made for the shore.

Felix explained his interview with the deck-hands, and then, in order to make the stories consistent, he insisted upon doing some fishing. The steamer was stopped, and all hands threw overboard the lines, the hooks baited with salt pork. Half a dozen large sardines were hauled in, though Don called them pilchards; but almost any fish of the herring kind is called a sardine, which takes its name from Sardinia, in whose waters they are abundant.

It was found that not one of the fish had bit at the bait, and all of them had been "hooked." The number was sufficient to establish the consistency of the story, and the Maud ran for the ship, coming alongside after an absence of not more than two hours. The buoys of the fasts were picked up, and the deckhands were left to moor the steamer. The fish were put in a small pan, and Felix mounted to the deck with it, following Scott. It was only nine o'clock in the evening, and the cabin party had gathered in the music-room, where the piano was located.

The two absentees marched into the **apartment**,

and Felix deposited the pan of fish on the table, and waited for the hymn to be finished, for most of the singing was of sacred music. All the party looked at them, for they had been missed, and Mrs. Blossom had had a great deal to say about the non-appearance of the one she insisted upon calling "her boy."

"Where under the sun have you been, Felix McGavonty?" demanded the good lady as soon as she had an opportunity to speak, though she had stopped singing when the truant entered.

"Nowhere," replied the Milesian without a blush.

"Nowhere!" exclaimed the lady. "Why, Felix, I always thought you were a truthful boy."

"So Oi am whin it's convaynient," answered he, switching into his brogue, as he was apt to do when he intended to tease the worthy lady.

"You ought always to tell the truth, whether it's convenient or not, and even to your own injury," a sentiment that was approved by all the party, though no one said anything.

"Wud I tell a sick mahn he's go'n' to doie?"

"But I'm not a sick man."

"Faix, ye're not, nor a sick wuman ayther. But when we had Spearman, the one what was hurted in the wreck of the Bunyan, you tould him he wudn't die, forinst the wurruds of Docthor Hawkes, long loife to him and his adipose tissue, who tould you he cudn't live the day out, and he didn't. Sary Blossom, you ought allus to tell the truth whether it's convaynient or not."

The entire party laughed heartily, and Mrs. Blossom joined them, though there was a telltale blush on her cheeks, as much at the manner of the speaker as at the moral he was illustrating.

"'The letter killeth, but the spirit giveth life,'" returned the lady.

"A good answer!" exclaimed the doctor, clapping his hands.

"It wasn't the letther at all that killed Spearman, but the broken ribs he got aboord the Bunyan; but the spirit you guv him out o' the brandy bottle guv him loife for some hours," added Felix.

"You didn't answer my question, Felix McGavonty, said the lady, returning to the assault. "I asked where under the sun you had been."

"And Oi answered it on the instant."

"But you said 'Nowhere.'"

"Which was thrue as though Oi had taken it from the New Tistamint."

"Oh, Felix! how can you tell such an abominable falsehood? I asked you where you had been, and you said" —

"Oi beg your pairdon, but that wasn't the question at all at all."

"I asked you where you had been."

"I appayl to the company. You asked me something more than that. Won't you repayt the question jist as you put it fursht?"

"Where under the sun have you been, Felix McGavonty? That's just the way I put it," protested Mrs. Blossom.

"That's thrue for ye's; and I said I had been no-where under the sun, and I say so now, and Oi'll shtick to't till the river Noile droies up," said Felix warmly.

Then the company saw the point, and they all laughed heartily.

"What a tease you are, Felix!" exclaimed the victim of the joke.

"Oi'm no tayse whin it comes to speaking the thruth. How could I go anywhere under the sun, whin there's no sun out to-night to go under?"

"Flix has the best of the argument, Mrs. Blossom; that expletive clause in your question ruined you," laughed the surgeon.

"Perhaps you will be willing to tell me now, Felix, where under the stars you have been," continued the good lady.

"Wid all the pleasure in loife. Captain Scott and Oi have been a fishing. We expected to catch some say-serpints; but here is all we could gather in, for the villains wudn't boite at all at all, and we hooked these," answered Felix, as he took the pan from the table, and carried it to the lady.

"What are they?" she inquired.

"They are Sardinians, called sardines for short, and they are all waiting to be b'iled in ile, and packed in a tin box, as they do it off the coast of Maine, and sometimes on the coast of France and Italy. These air the rale Oytalian fish."

"Mr. Gaskette wishes to see you at the door, sir," said Sparks in the ear of the commander.

It was the pilot who had just boarded the ship. The captain made him show his branch, and then engaged him, giving him a berth in the hospital, which had rarely been used since the ship left New York. Calling one of the stewards, he told him to invite Felix to his cabin, for he was somewhat impatient to learn the result of the Maud's mission to seaward. Scott thought he was entitled to be present at this conference, and he soon followed his fellow-voyager.

He was promptly admitted when he gave his name at the closed door. Felix was relating the details of the cruise. The commander knew how easy it was to be mistaken in the identity of a vessel miles distant, and he hoped that such had been the case with the amateur detective. The evidence that he had not been in error was all-sufficient, to the great regret of the commander. It was fortified by the testimony of Don, and the name of the steam-yacht had been read on the stern. Captain Penn Sharp could not have done any better if he had been on board of the ship.

"I suppose the villanous Pacha is still intent upon capturing either the ' houri ' or Louis," said Captain Ringgold, after Felix had given in all his evidence. "We shall go up the Nile after we have visited Alexandria and Cairo, and we shall be peculiarly exposed to the machinations of the Moor and his agents, for here he will be at home, as it were, while we are total strangers."

"I am of the opinion that Captain Mazagan is in

command of the Fatimé; at any rate I think it was he that answered Captain Scott's hail," said Felix.

" Very likely; but we will let the matter rest for to-night. The pilot will take the ship in early to-morrow morning, and we shall have plenty of time to consider the situation."

The boys retired from the cabin, and soon after were sound asleep in their staterooms.

CHAPTER VII

THE HARBOR OF ALEXANDRIA

As soon as it was fairly daylight in the morning, Boatswain Biggs was walking the men around the capstan in heaving up the anchor, though it was generally done by steam. The pilot spoke English very well; but in the variety of races in this region no one could tell whether he was a Turk, Arab, or Egyptian; but he was clothed in the ample garments of the Orient.

Captain Scott had been called by the cabin watch; he had roused the other members of the " Big Four," and they had gone on board of the Maud, ready to follow the Guardian-Mother into port. The young captain had studied the chart and the plan of the harbor so thoroughly, that he believed he could take his little craft into port without any help from the Mohammedan, who had taken his place on the bridge of the ship.

From Eunostos Point on the north-east to Marabut Island on the south-west, a distance of not quite five miles, was a line of reefs and shoals, which made the passage very intricate, though the Maud could have gone in almost anywhere, for there was hardly less

than three fathoms in the shoalest places. But Scott
had prepared himself to take in a vessel drawing over
twenty feet of water.

The coast of the mainland was low and flat, and it
could not be seen from the anchorage where the ship
had lain over night. Scott took his place in the pilot-
house of the little steamer, and brought out his plan
of the harbor, on which he had drawn out the bearings that would enable him to go safely through the
Boghaz Pass, which is the central channel through the
reefs. Louis, the only available deck-hand on board,
though Pitts was ready to lend a hand if needed, had
cast off the stern line, and was standing by the bow
line, awaiting further orders. Felix had directed his
spy-glass to seaward as soon as he came on board,
and the captain was not inclined to interrupt his
observations.

"Do you make out anything, Flix?" asked Scott,
for the amateur detective stood directly in front of
the windows of the pilot-house.

"There are half a dozen steamers coming in from
the north-west, and I can't make out the sheep shears
on the tablecloth flag of Morocco yet; but they are
all headed in shore, and I shall soon be able to see
which is which," replied Felix.

"Captain Ringgold appears to have appointed you
the chief detective of the fleet, Flix," added Scott,
with a pleasant laugh to indicate that he was not jeal-
ous of the promotion of his companion.

"Nonsense!" exclaimed the observer, dropping his

glass long enough to look the captain in the face. "He has not appointed me any more than he has the rest of us fellows. He can't say a word to any one except the three who have had the secret for over three months, and he is mighty short-handed in the matter of detectives."

"But he depends more on you, Flix, than on any other of the fellows," suggested the captain.

"But it was Louis who did most of the work in getting possession of the secret of what the Pacha intended to do," Felix objected.

" You were with him all the time, and it was only because Louis spoke and understood French that he was enabled to get at the purposes of the conspirators. Captain Penn Sharp could not speak a word of French any more than you can, and he is the man after the commander's own heart as a detective."

"We were on English ground then. I am not a philosopher or a metaphysician ; but I am willing to grant that I rather like the business of a detective," replied Felix, with a sort of deprecatory smile, as though he had confessed to what he sometimes called a "strong weakness."

"Then you have a taste for the business."

"Perhaps I have in a mild way; but I should certainly never think of following it to get my bread and butter, and go into the business of picking up every-day rogues."

"You can go into it in a very genteel way in getting the weather-gage of the Moor — of Venice," added

Scott, uttering the last two words in a loud tone, just as Morris Woolridge came forward.

" Which of you is going to play Othello ? " asked the new-comer.

" Flix thinks of becoming a tragedian. Cast off the bow line, Louis ! " he called, as the screw of the ship began to turn, and afforded him an opportunity to change the subject.

The Maud dropped astern as the ship started, and then went ahead at half speed. Pitts wanted to know if the ship's company would dine on board ; the captain thought not, as there was to be a conference on board the Guardian-Mother, in which parts had been assigned to the " Big Four," and the cook retreated to the galley. Felix would not devote himself to his spy-glass in the presence of Morris, for it might suggest hard questions, and Felix was decidedly opposed to lying, though he could do some of it "in case of sickness," as he had explained it.

" You may be on the lookout forward, Morris," said the captain, in order to give Felix an opportunity to continue his investigation, which must now be done in the standing-room, as the steamer was headed for the harbor.

The amateur detective moved about in an indifferent manner as though he had no possible object in living ; but when Morris was gazing ahead with all his might, he took the glass from the brackets very slyly, and went aft. As Louis had nothing to do on the forecastle, he sauntered after him ; and it soon became his business to see that Felix was not interrupted in his occupation.

It was a very quiet time on board the Maud; but the cabin party made it more stirring on board of the Guardian-Mother. The upper or hurricane deck was the favorite resort when there was anything to be seen. It was the top of the house on deck, extending nearly the whole length of the ship. The pilot-house was elevated three steps above the upper deck, so that the quartermasters could see over the top-gallant forecastle. The captain's cabin was next to it, and the top of it was on a level with that of the pilot-house, which gave the commander's quarters a ceiling about two feet and a half higher than the other apartments on the same deck.

This higher part of the upper deck formed what had been called first the officers' promenade. Since the passengers used it more than any others, it was known simply as the "promenade." Over the forward part of it was the bridge, which was used by the lookout, and by the pilots in going into port, as well as by the officer of the watch in thick weather. Both the bridge and the promenade could be reached by stairs from the pilot-house.

It was only six o'clock in the morning, but all the cabin party were seated on the promenade, which commanded an excellent view of everything in sight; but hardly anything was yet visible. Mr. Boulong, the first officer, was on the bridge with the pilot, and the captain was devoting himself to the passengers.

He had been to Egypt before, as he had been to nearly every country on the face of the earth. He had been to Alexandria several times, and he was fully prepared to act as the cicerone of the tourists.

"You have seen the lighthouse before," said he, when the ship had advanced far enough for him to begin his task. "A couple of miles to the north-east of it you can just make out the fort which occupies the point where stood the ancient Pharos, which means a light; and the French still call it a *phare*. Alexandria has two harbors, most of the city lying between the two."

"I should think we had got back into Holland by the number of windmills in sight," suggested Mrs. Belgrave.

"There are many of them in the waste places about the city; but they are not used here, as in Holland, to pump out the country," replied the commander, who never failed to answer when the owner's mother spoke. "Away off to the eastward, eight or nine miles distant, like a speck, you can just make out the château of the Khedive, at Ramleh."

"What under the sun is that?" asked Mrs. Blossom, whose education had been more limited than that of the other members of the party, and whose store of information was even more limited; but she had learned a great deal on this voyage.

"I should like to ask at the same time how you pronounce the name of the ruler of Egypt," added

Mrs. Belgrave; and of course this question was the first to be answered.

"Make the first syllable *k-e-d*, with a short, or obscure *e*, to rhyme with 'head,' and the second is just the same as the name of the lady in the Garden of Eden who was somewhat mixed up in the apple question," replied the commander.

Every one of the eight pronounced the word according to the directions given, and all but Mrs. Blossom did it correctly. She contrived to get it wrong, but the captain did not deem it advisable to use his time in correcting her, for she was usually incorrigible in such matters. "The Khedive is the ruler of Egypt, Mrs. Blossom, and his château is his palace, his summer residence in this instance; but we shall have more to say about this young gentleman at the conference. We are now just entering the harbor, you can see a buoy on either side of us; and the water under them is only about twenty-two feet deep, which is not enough for the large steamers that come in here."

"There is some sort of a tower directly ahead of us," said Dr. Hawkes.

"That is on the fortifications called Bab el-Arab, which means the Bedouin Gate. Arabs in all this part of the world are generally called Bedouins."

"Perhaps you wouldn't mind pronouncing that word for me, for I suppose all the others know how to do it," asked Uncle Moses. "I hear some call it Bed-yew-ins, and others as you spoke it."

"My dictionary gives it Bed-oo-ins, accent on the

first syllable, and the *e* in it short; and I think that is the way to do it. As you can see, there are plenty of windmills in that quarter. The fortifications extend across the tongue of land a little less than a mile wide, lying between the West Harbor and Lake Mareotis, of which more will be said at the conference. Now you can see the light at the end of the breakwater, which protects the inner harbor from the north winds from the sea. We shall go around it, and come to anchor near the red light we can see across it. We have got through the shoals, and now the water is from eight to ten fathoms deep where we are. Mr. Gaskette!" called the commander to the second officer, who was pacing the upper deck.

"On deck, sir," reported the officer, touching his cap, as all did when addressing the commander.

"You will station the boatswain with two seamen on the top-gallant forecastle, and all the rest of the hands along the bulwarks all around the ship," continued Captain Ringgold. "There will be a swarm of boats come off as soon as we are in sight from the landing-place, and the natives will come on deck without leave or license if you permit them to do so. You will see that no one is allowed to come on board, — I mean the beggars, boatmen, dragomans, and such people. But you will use your judgment in regard to others."

Mr. Gaskette touched his cap, bowed, and retired. The party heard the boatswain's whistle, and the call for all hands.

"Are you afraid of an invasion, Captain?" inquired the surgeon.

"I have been here before, and these fellows who want a job to put you ashore, or to furnish you with donkeys, or to take the party up the Nile, are an intolerable nuisance, and they would worry the life out of you."

"But it would amuse us," suggested Mrs. Woolridge.

"You will have an abundance of that sort of amusement at the city here and at Cairo, and all along the Nile. But if you desire it, I will permit the beggars to come on board," said the commander.

"No, Captain; I prefer to leave the matter to your judgment rather than to my own, for I never was here before," replied the lady.

In a few minutes more the ship passed the breakwater light, and turned to the north-east, headed directly for the custom-house. Early as it was in the morning, a multitude of boats began to put off from the landing-place near the end of the inner breakwater. The anchor was all ready to drop in six fathoms off the inner light, and hands were stationed for the purpose.

"Let go!" shouted Mr. Boulong, when the pilot gave him the word, and the ship soon swung round to her cable.

Then began the efforts of the swarm in the boats to get on board, but the seamen were obedient to their orders. The Arabs and Egyptians were angry, for they were admitted on board of the steamers from Marseilles, Brindisi, and the Archipelago. The sailors used their fists when necessary ; but only a couple of custom-house officers came on board, admitted by order of Mr. Gaskette.

CHAPTER VIII

THE ONSLAUGHT OF THE ORIENTAL BEGGARS

THE Maud did not follow the Guardian-Mother very closely, for Captain Scott had a great deal of faith in his ability to pilot the little steamer into the harbor. But he knew there was not less than twenty-two and a half feet of water anywhere in the Boghaz Pass, and he couldn't have taken the bottom if he had tried to do so; so there was no great virtue in his piloting, and he did not claim any.

"Well, Flix, what do you make out?" asked Louis, as the Maud approached the entrance to the Pass, and the long silence had become rather monotonous. "Do you see anything?"

"I see lots of steamers, and among them one you have seen several times, so that you know her by heart," replied the detective, as the inner ring of the "Big Four" soon began to call him; and this number simply excluded Morris.

"You have seen her?" exclaimed Louis.

"I have indeed; and I have been following her with my right eye since the screw began to whirl. She is so much smaller than the other steamers that I had no trouble in making her out just as soon as

I discovered her. She sailed with the crowd for a while, and then she went off to the eastward again. But she didn't go more than a couple of miles before she headed to the south again. I can't make out yet what her little game is; but I am satisfied that she means to make a port in Egypt, and is only off here now to keep the run of the Guardian-Mother and her consort. That's my opinion, whether you agree with me or not."

"I haven't any opinion, except that if you are right, and the Fatimé is in these waters, she is looking for our party," replied Louis. "And I have no doubt you are right."

"Of course I am right," exclaimed Felix, dropping the glass from his eye. "Didn't I read her name on the stern, 'La Fatimé'; and I knew French enough to read it, since it was the same as in English."

"I haven't doubted any of your statements; and I told the commander you were the best detective in the inner ring."

"The inner ring isn't a big one, and only means three out of four," replied Felix, laughing.

"But there is one thing on which I do not feel so well satisfied."

"What's that, darling?" demanded the detective.

"Don't you believe they recognized the Maud on board of that steamer?"

"No, I don't; but of course I can't be sure of it. If they had made her out, I am confident they would have sent a dozen or twenty men on board of the

Maud and captured her, for there was no other vessel near us at the time. Even Captain Mazagan knows that you sail in this boat, and he must naturally have supposed you were on board of her; and they would have expected to do half their business over here by making a prisoner of you."

"That would have been bad business for me," added the young millionaire, with a smile, though he did not quite believe the banditti on board of the Fatimé would have been able to capture him: for the half dozen breech-loaders which had been sent on board of the Maud in the Archipelago were still in the lockers under the seats in the cabin.

"That's one reason why I believe Captain Mazagan, who, I think, commands her now, did not make her out. Both vessels were thoroughly painted at Malaga, and at the request of Captain Scott, they changed the color to white; for she was black when Mazagan saw her."

"That indeed."

"He did not ask me what steamer this was; perhaps because I omitted to put the same question to him. Captain Scott did his best to fool the officer who answered his hail, and I believe he fully succeeded. I am sure the Fatimé would have chased us if they had smelled anything like a mouse," argued Felix; and Louis believed he was right in the main.

"Don't you think it would be rather reckless of them to bring that steamer into the harbor of Alexandria while the G.-M. is there, Flix?" he asked.

"The Pacha would understand that Captain Ringgold would take to his heels again if her saw her, as he has done three times before."

"I haven't the remotest shadow of a spectre that he intends to come into the harbor of Alexandria; on the contrary, he don't mean to do anything of the kind. His Highness is a villain, but he is not quite a fool except in the sense that all villains are fools."

"What will he do, then?"

"He will make a port at Rosetta or Damietta, both of which are connected by railroad with Alexandria and Cairo. That is what I should do if I had made a contract to carry out his job," replied Felix, as he fixed the glass at his eye again. "There she is, still going to the eastward; and she is nearly hull down, as though she had been stirring up the fires in her furnaces and making more steam. Mazagan could make out with his glass that the Guardian-Mother has gone into the harbor of Alexandria, and that's all he wanted to know. What he has to do just now is to set his snares and traps, and you and the houri may fall into them."

Felix was evidently satisfied with what he had done, and with the conclusions at which he had arrived. He closed up the implement with which he had done good service, and started to go forward. The Maud was in the Boghaz Pass, and the captain did not seem to be at all worried about the task of taking the steamer through the perils in her way. He said nothing to Felix about the mission in which he was engaged, for Mardis was within hearing.

Instead of doing so, he began to describe the various objects which were in sight by this time, reading the names from the little plan of the harbor and its surroundings, which he had placed before him on the binnacle. As soon as the Maud had rounded the breakwater light, he saw the boats that were hurrying to the side of the Guardian-Mother. A little later he saw the sailors beating off the occupants of them, as they would an enemy that was boarding the ship.

"Captain Ringgold evidently understands the way they do things here, and I will take the hint," said he. "Call all hands except the first engineer, Morris."

"Let no one on board except officers!" shouted Captain Ringgold from the upper deck, as the Maud approached the ship.

"Ay, ay, sir!" replied Scott.

He had observed how the seamen of the ship were managing the business, and he instructed his crew to act in like manner. There was a vast number of boats on the starboard side of the Guardian-Mother, and Scott decided to scatter them as he came alongside. He rang the gong to stop the screw, and steered for the berth he had chosen.

"*Imshi! Imshi!*" shouted Don, who was the only person on board of either vessel who could speak Arabic.

"What does that mean, Don?" asked Felix, as he tumbled an Egyptian over backwards into his boat.

"It means go away, get out, or anything of that

sort," replied the engineer. "But these fellows have no right to come on board till the doctor's boat has boarded the ship. That's the rule in all these countries."

"Stand by the fasts!" called Captain Scott, as he steered the steamer so that she cut in between the boats and the ship, shoving them away from her.

As she came alongside half a dozen sailors dropped down aboard the Maud, evidently sent by the commander to assist in keeping off the intruders; but all of a sudden the latter pushed off and retired a short distance from the sides of the vessels. The cause of this movement was immediately apparent, for a boat pulled by six oarsmen dashed through the small craft, which were careful to keep out of its way. In fact, they all fled to a considerable distance from the scene, for an officer in the new-comer poured some vials of wrath upon them for their disregard of the sanitary regulations of the port, which allow no one to board a vessel till after the medical inspection.

"*Bon jour, Messieurs*," said the sanitary officer, after the captain had ordered the gangway steps to be placed for him.

"Answer him, Louis," said Scott.

"*Bon jour, Monsieur le docteur*," replied the owner.

"Well, you speak French very well," added the visitor with a pleasant smile, still using the polite language, and he was evidently a Frenchman. "Have you any sick persons on board?"

"Not one on either vessel," replied Louis. "But

this little steamer is only the tender of the ship, which is a yacht from New York, last from Malaga, and the bill of health is on board of her."

The Frenchman asked a few more questions, and was exceedingly polite, though probably the surrounding boatmen did not think so. Captain Ringgold spoke French only indifferently, though like most persons who have little or no practice, he had forgotten a considerable portion of what he had formerly known. He stood on the landing of the gangway, and heard the brief conversation on the deck of the Maud. He asked Louis to come with the doctor, though he had a Frenchman on board in the person of Professor Giroud, and Mr. Gaskette spoke French fluently.

"Good-morning, Captain," said the medical gentleman in tolerable English.

The commander was relieved, produced his papers, and the inspection proved to be a mere matter of form, though the doctor was conducted through the lower part of the ship to enable him to see for himself that all was right. As politely as he had come, he took his leave, and was ceremoniously conducted to the gangway by the commander, from which Louis attended him to his boat.

As soon as it had pulled away from the ship, the swarm of boats renewed the onslaught. The men who were so persistent to get on board were runners from the hotels, carriage-drivers, guides, dragomans, with a few donkey boys, who had procured places from others, for their business was not large enough to enable them to run boats to procure customers. They were dressed in all sorts of costumes, not excepting a few in the European, though most of them wore Turkish garments. Several of them could speak a little English, but most of them jabbered in Arabic.

The order of the commander was again enforced, and the men were told to say that no one would go on shore at present, which the sailors did in nautical English, not much of which could have been understood. The officers did it better, though no one but Don John, the engineer, could make an effective impression upon them. In the midst of the confusion a custom-house boat made its way through them, and a couple of officers mounted the deck of the Maud. The principal one spoke French, though he answered Captain Scott in fair English. Louis explained that the ship was a yacht and the Maud her tender, and that neither was a merchantman or passenger steamer. Then he conducted both of them to the deck of the Guardian-Mother.

Mr. Gaskette explained more fully the character of the two vessels, assuring the officers that no goods would be landed, and that the passengers would remain on board for the present. The commander repeated the substance of what had been said in English. But the officer said that he and his associate must remain on board during the stay of the vessels. He was invited to breakfast in the cabin, and requested to make himself entirely at home.

It required some time to convince the occupants of

the boats that no one was going on shore from the ship or her consort. Most of them returned to the landing-place at last, but a few, evidently of a better class than the others, still remained, begging and pleading to be permitted to come on board : but the officers and seamen were immovable.

The cabin party were still on the promenade, amused by the scene alongside. The commander joined them as soon as he had discharged his duties on deck, and pointed out some of the prominent objects that were now in sight, among them Pompey's Pillar, the custom-house, several mosques and churches, and some old palaces in a ruinous condition. The gong sounded for breakfast, and the party descended to the cabin. On the way he called for Don, and sent him ashore to procure certain books he desired, and had not been able to obtain elsewhere. The engineer had been here before in a Spanish steamer, and knew his way about the city. Both of the custom-house officers appeared to be gentlemen, and seats were given them at the table.

CHAPTER IX

A PATRIOTIC ORATOR ON HIS FEET

" THESE beggars which one meets in Egypt are a great nuisance, Mrs. Belgrave," said Captain Ringgold, as he seated himself at the head of the table, with Louis on his right, and his mother next to her son.

" I have not seen any beggars," replied the lady.

" Because I have not allowed them to come on board. They are not really beggars, though I call them all so, for they all ask for something, though it may not be for alms. When a passenger steamer comes in, hordes of these fellows swarm on board of her as soon as the health inspection is finished, and they make life a burden to visitors to the land of Egypt.

" They desire to improve their fortunes at the expense of the European and American travellers who come here, and all of them are considered fair game to these sharpers. The largest and noisiest part of the crowd are the boatmen, who want the job to take you on shore. There are half a dozen hotels in Alexandria that are available for foreigners, and each of them has one or more touters on board to look out for the interests of their employers."

"I think I should be glad to take one of them," suggested the lady.

"It would be wise for you to do so if you had decided what hotel you would patronize," continued the captain. "I went to the Khedivial when I was here the last time. If you employ a hotel runner, he will do everything for you, and it is not for the interest of his hotel to cheat you, especially in the beginning; then he will take you under his protection, and rid you of the importunities of the vagabonds."

"He is rather a good fellow, then," suggested Louis.

"He is indeed. Most of these fellows will cheat you out of your eye-teeth; and the fact that you have made a bargain with one of them is not always a protection, though you will find many Egyptians and Arabs who are as honest as the people of any other country. Once, when I was here, I hired a boatman to pull me down to El-Meks for a certain sum, I forget what it was now; but when he had made half the distance, he stopped and demanded double the sum upon which we had agreed.

"I knew a few words of Arabic then, and he had a few of English. I tried to reason with him, but he insisted on double the price arranged. He insisted on robbing me, threatened to upset the boat, and to stay where we were all night. I could not stand the threats, and I took from my pocket a small revolver I always carried, and pointed it at his head. He did not like this kind of argument, and he pulled for our destination. When we got there, I paid him what I had agreed, and gave him no *bakshîsh*, as I should have if he had not tried to rob me."

"*Bakshîsh* — that is a very common word here," said Louis. "How do you spell it, Captain?"

"It is Arabic, and you can spell it any way you please, and pay nothing for the privilege. B-a-k suits me best for the first syllable, though a *c* is often inserted before the *k*; but the easiest way that does the business is the best. S-h-î-s-h for the second;" and the captain wrote it on the back of a letter.

"What is the effect of the circumflex accent over the *i*?" asked Louis.

"I have studied what Arabic there is in the guide book, though I have forgotten almost all of it. *I* in this language is pronounced like *e*, and the accent lengthens the sound so that it is double *e*; and for this reason Webster gives the word *backsheesh* for one form of it. The circumflex has the same effect on all vowels when you see Arabic words written in English letters.

"You will learn the word by heart before you get out of Egypt, and however they may spell it, they all pronounce it the same."

The meal was finished, and all the party hastened on deck. Three of the "Big Four" had taken their breakfast on board of the Maud, with one of the custom-house officers as a guest. The awning had been spread on the upper deck of the ship, and a sufficient number of armchairs had been placed for the whole company, and those on board of the consort were sent for. When the party were seated, Captain Ringgold stood up before them.

"Ladies and gentlemen, I have taken the liberty to call this occasion a Conference, as you may have noticed during the last three months. I borrowed this word from Professor Giroud, because I do not like to have any of you accuse me of having given a lecture, when I have told you what little I know about some of the countries we visit, and the term had another meaning, a " —

" *Une mercuriale* " prompted the professor, when he saw that the commander had forgotten the French word. " It means a speech, a lecture, such as we sometimes have to give the boys when they neglect their lessons, a reprimand, a rebuke."

"Thank you, Professor; you have given just the idea with which I was struggling. In a word, what some of you insist upon calling a lecture shall now be a Conference, for the word seems to me to be less formidable and less ceremonious than lecture," replied the commander. "I have given out subjects to every member of the party. But I am afraid if all of you treat them at full length, it will take a week to go through them all. I hope all will be reasonably brief.

"I have placed the topics in what I regard as their proper order, after consulting the several learned gentlemen on board, and asked them to suggest subjects to me. That of geography was given to me; and

as it is the first on the list, it devolves upon me
to open the ball — I don't mean the dance, Mrs.
Blossom, but the ball which contains needed information.

"The country in the north-east of Africa, taking in
about all the territory watered by the Nile, is called
the Egyptian Empire; and it is as big as two-thirds
of Russia in Europe. But a considerable part of this
vast region is hardly more than a myth, and much of
it consists of sandy deserts, and all the southern part
is very loosely held, the Khedive's armies having
sometimes been driven out of it. While the whole
area of the empire is a million and a quarter square
miles, the real, substantial, cultivable Egypt all lies
between the Mediterranean Sea and the first cataract,
in latitude about twenty-four north, and consists of
only 11,373 square miles, about the same as Maryland
and Delaware united.

"In the Libyan Desert, which is a part of Sahara,
are several oases which are very productive, especially
The Fayûm. From east to west, the country extends
from about twenty-eight to thirty-eight east longitude,
'aking in most of the Libyan Desert and the Penin-
ula of Sinai. The part north of the first cataract
s called Lower Egypt, while that part south of it is
Jpper Egypt, though some of the guide-book makers
'ay the divisions ought to be called the other way.
In the southern part are the Soudan, bordering on
the kingdom of Abyssinia, Dongola, Berber, Darfur,
Sennar, and other divisions. But as I said before, all

this southern part around the sources of the Nile are still rather indefinite divisions."

To be consistent with the hint he had given, he made his portion of the Conference much briefer than he might have done. As he was about to take his chair, he discovered Don standing near him with a roll and a bundle in his hand, which he handed to the commander as soon as he saw that he was disengaged.

"I am glad you have come, Don John," said he, as he took the roll, and spread it out, and then secured it to a stanchion with the assistance of the engineer, so that it could be seen by all the members of the party.

It was a map of Upper and Lower Egypt, about six feet square, with some of the adjoining territory. The captain sent to the pilot-house for a brass curtain rod he had used in his cabin for a pointer. With this in his hand he proceeded to review what he had said, pointing out the various localities and boundaries on the map; and certainly he made his remarks much plainer to his audience.

"The next topic is the Nile, and it was assigned to Mr. Belgrave. I have endeavored not to steal any of his thunder in what I had to say, though the temptation to do so was difficult to resist," said the commander.

"I am sorry you resisted the temptation, Captain Ringgold, for you could have done my part much better than I can," Louis proceeded, as he rose and took from his breast-pocket a rather bulky manuscript. "I beg you will not be alarmed, for what I have to say about what some call the longest river in the world will be mainly extemporaneous, and I shall endeavor to act on the hint in regard to brevity which has been given."

"But don't leave out too much of it. Take the pointer, and let us see as well as hear," interposed the captain.

"The Nile, according to a guide-book I picked up in Athens, is one of the three longest rivers of the world, which are stated to be four thousand miles long. The Mississippi, with the Missouri, which is as much a part of it as the White and the Blue Nile are a part of the Nile proper, is entirely ignored. The Amazon, the Congo, and the Nile are called the three longest rivers; and I take it upon myself to defend the national honor of the United States of America."

This introduction was greeted by an enthusiastic burst of applause, started by Scott and Felix, and taken up by every member of the party, not excepting the commander and the ladies. But a general laugh accompanied it, and Louis's smiling face indicated that he was not entirely serious.

"Without a blush, inserted in parenthesis, my book proceeds to style the Nile the 'Father of Rivers,' thus practically robbing the Mississippi of its long-acknowledged title of the 'Father of Waters.' I submit that this is an outrage (violent applause), and little short of an insult to the flag of the Union, which floats majestically at the peak of the G.-M."

"This is the fifth of December, and not the fourth

July," interposed Captain Ringgold, laughing so heartily that he could hardly speak.

"But patriotism is not an attribute of the fourth of July only, and every true American is as much bound to defend the honor of his country on the fifth of December as on the fourth of July," continued Louis, making a spread eagle of himself, much to the merriment of the party; and his last remark was received with another storm of applause.

Possibly the officers and some of the seamen of the ship thought the denizens of the cabin had gone mad or wild, but they immediately sought positions where they could ascertain what was going on upon the upper deck.

"But I wish to be reasonable," pursued the fervid orator, suddenly elongating his smiling face, so that his expression was consistent with his words. "I could not be satisfied with the statements of the work from which I have quoted; but if they were true, I felt obliged to accept them, even if they washed all the stars out of the flag I reverence as the emblem of my country and its liberty. I examined an English work, for I wish to be impartial, and especially uninfluenced by patriotic considerations, and I found the lengths of the rivers mentioned as follows: Mississippi, 4096; Amazon, 3545; Nile, 4000. The work that gave these three did not mention the Congo at all; and I went to another English volume published only last year, which gave the Congo at 'over 3000.'

"According to these figures the Mississippi is still

entitled to be regarded as the ' Father of Waters ; ' and ' long may she wave ! '   In order to be wholly and entirely fair, as I believe my British authorities are, I ought to add that the Nile and Congo have not yet been sufficiently explored to fix their lengths definitely.   When the Royal Geographical Society of England decides without a peradventure upon the lengths of these two rivers, I for one very humble person interested in getting at the truth, shall be happy to ' acknowledge the corn,' and admit that the Nile is bigger than the Mississippi.   I have something to say about the Nile, Mr. Commander, for it is a very interesting stream in spite of the assumption put forth in regard to it; but if I have exhausted my time, I will take my seat."

" Go on ! Go on !" shouted all the boys and most of the gentlemen.

"It seems to be the pleasure of the company that you proceed, Mr. Belgrave," replied the commander.

But just at this moment Mr. Boulong placed himself at the side of Captain Ringgold, and appeared to have something to say.   He touched his cap when the commander looked at him.

" An Egyptian gentleman alongside exhibits a letter, and says he is instructed to deliver it to the captain in person," said Mr. Boulong.

" I cannot be interrupted now ; but if he is willing to wait till I am disengaged, you may permit him to come on board," replied the commander, turning his attention to Louis. "You may proceed, Mr. Belgrave."

Louis had been looking at his manuscript while the commander was occupied ; but he closed it, and took the pointer in his hand. After a glance at the map, he began to give his account of the Nile.

CHAPTER X

THE INUNDATION AND THE CLIMATE OF EGYPT

"To the ancient Egyptians the Nile was the sacred river; and the service it rendered to them well entitled it to be so regarded, to say nothing of the fact that it was the only one known to them," Louis began. "It gets most of its water from the two great lakes, the Albert Nyanza and the Victoria Nyanza. There are other large lakes south of these which may be connected with them. The Victoria is the larger of the two, and the equator passes through it. It is said to contain 30,000 square miles; and patriotic geographers may add a couple of thousand miles to it in order to give it a greater area than Lake Superior, which has 41,200 miles, and is the greatest body of fresh water on the earth. Some rivers from the south flow into the lakes, and doubtless the length of these will be added to the Nile in due time."

The "twins," as Uncle Moses had sometimes called Dr. Hawkes and himself on account of their aldermanic proportions, shook their great bulk with suppressed mirth at the satire of the speaker; and the boys were disposed to indulge in more applause, which the commander prevented by raising his hand.

"These lakes have been discovered within the memory of those present who are older than the 'Big Four,' and European and American geographers, including Stanley, have been searching over this region within my time. The source of the Nile was a mystery for about two thousand years, the Emperor Nero having begun the search; and since that time Speke, Baker, Dr. Livingstone, Stanley, and other explorers have continued it, and the question has been settled. I have not time to follow them, and our affair at present is with the Nile in Egypt proper.

"The great river is formed by the junction of the White and Blue Nile at Khartum, latitude about sixteen. The White comes from the region of the equator, and, besides the lake, is fed by a multitude of streams from the south-west. The Blue rises in the mountains of Abyssinia, and the greater portion of its water comes from Lake Tana, on a plateau 5,658 feet above the sea. This stream takes its name from the color of its water, which is true also of the White. After getting down from the mountains, the Blue passes through Sennar, an exceedingly fertile region, where it gathers some of its mud. Two hundred miles below Khartum, the" — Louis had to stop and refer to his manuscript, which made the boys laugh.

"I don't bother with the Arabic words, for I can't remember them; but two hundred miles below Khartum, the Atbara flows into the Blue Nile; and I hope you will all remember this name better than I did. This stream is also called the Bahr-al-Aswad," continued the speaker, reading from his manuscript. "I give you this Arabic name because you will all know that it means the Black Nile. Like the other Niles, it takes its name from its color; and here is where the most of the mud comes from. The rich black soil is floated down on the fields of Lower Egypt, and gives them their remarkable fertility.

"About twenty miles below the Albert Nyanza the river takes a leap of one hundred and twenty feet down into a rocky gorge. It drops twelve feet after leaving the Victoria. The navigation is piecemeal until the river reaches the first cataract, though there is a run of nine hundred miles below Khartum where the river is slow and sluggish. In some parts of the distant regions, it almost dries up in the hottest season. There are six cataracts below Khartum, through some of which boats are hauled by the skilled boatmen; and I suppose you will see at least the first of them.

"The breadth of the valley of the Nile — please to notice, Mrs. Blossom, that I say the valley of the Nile, and not the Nile itself — is from four and a half to ten miles in Nubia;" and the commander shook his head at this bit of personality.

"Ten miles!" exclaimed the lady whose name had been mentioned. "That's nothing, even for the width of a river. Isn't the Amazon a hundred and fifty miles wide at its mouth?"

"I stand corrected," replied Louis, with a graceful bow to the lady, correctly interpreting the gesture of of the captain, "though I was speaking of a region nearly a thousand miles from the mouth of the river. The breadth of the valley of the Nile between the hills and the mountains on each side of it, and taking in the barren strip that borders the stream on both sides, is from four and a half to ten miles in Nubia, and from fourteen to thirty-two in Egypt proper. The hills on the Libyan side are sometimes a thousand feet high. The width of the arable region varies greatly, as does the valley of the river; but it does not exceed nine miles in any place."

"Only nine miles!" exclaimed Uncle Moses.

"So the books say, and I never measured it," replied Louis. "But if we call the river three thousand miles long, this would give an area of arable territory of 27,000 square miles, almost as many as there are in the whole of the State of Maine."

"Big enough," chuckled the trustee. "But the captain said Egypt was about as big as Belgium."

"He spoke of Lower Egypt only. The soil brought down by the Nile is from thirty-three to thirty-eight feet deep, piled up for centuries on a bed of sand. This rich earth is unlike any other known, and the deposit is increased every year. The annual inundation is caused by the rains in the Abyssinian mountains, and the rise is not therefore always the same. It always comes at the same season, and the trade winds have something to do with it, for the rains from the equatorial regions contribute to the rise of the waters.

"About the first of June the river begins to rise slowly, and six weeks later it increases very rapidly. Near the end of September it reaches its height, and remains so for a couple of weeks. In the last part of October it rises again, and then it attains its greatest level. Even after it has begun to subside, it gives another spasmodic jerk, and has been known to mount higher than before. Then it drops steadily at first, and after a while it goes down faster and faster. On this fifth day of December the inundation is subsiding, though it is still high water, comparatively speaking.

"During the first three months of the year, the regions from which the water has gradually receded dry up (as it is time for me to do), and the river is lowest about the first of June. This subject of the inundation has been faithfully studied by native and foreign *savants*, and it has been found that a rise of forty-one feet two inches is the most favorable to the agriculture of the country, for a rise of two feet more makes mischief in the Delta by covering the land for the important autumn crops with water; and a deficiency of four feet causes a famine and drought in the upper regions.

"In the time of Herodotus, 16 cubits, or 28.7 feet, was enough; and the God of the Nile was represented with sixteen children about him for this reason. The water sent down by the inundation is economized at the present time by modern appliances in the shape of canals and reservoirs. There are machines in use for raising water for the purpose of irrigation, from those run by steam to simpler ones worked by hand. The *Barrage*, about twelve miles below Cairo, is something like a big bridge, fitted with locks like a canal for holding back the water. It was intended to distribute the water as it was needed, and also to improve the navigation below it, for the larger craft were stopped by shoals at the season of low water.

"This immense structure was begun by Mohammed Ali, of whom you will learn more later; but it was a failure at first, and for twenty years it was an impediment to navigation. Less than ten years ago a couple of English engineers examined the work, and concluded that it could be utilized. The pressure of the water had burst through the gates, and ruined some of them. The engineers experimented with the gates, and then lowered them inch by inch, and succeeded in producing a decided effect upon the level of the stream. It would require a million dollars to complete the work, and only time can tell whether or not it will be completely successful.

"If I should read all that I have written, I should keep you on deck all the rest of the day; and therefore, as the Nile is doing at the present time, I will subside," Louis concluded, and resumed his chair.

A liberal portion of applause was bestowed upon him, in which the boys appeared to be the prominent factors, though all the party joined, and the commander did him the honor to say that he had done very well.

"Perhaps the subject next in order is properly the

history of this marvellous country; but as the Professor may need more time than we can afford this forenoon, I shall call upon Dr. Hawkes to give us his information in regard to the climate of Egypt. This Conference is entirely informal; and those who prefer to sit while speaking are entirely at liberty to do so, and will not be regarded as in the least degree impolite," said the commander at this point.

"Thank you, Mr. Commander, for your kind consideration," replied the surgeon, chuckling in concert with Brother Avoirdupois. "I suppose it is considered a more difficult matter for the heaviest man on board of the ship to stand, than for light bodies like that of the entertaining young gentleman who has just taken his seat."

"But you outweigh me, Brother Adipose Tissue, by only four ounces," interposed Uncle Moses. "You make altogether too much ado about your quarter of a pound."

"I admit that Brother Avoirdupois is my twin fellow-voyager in spite of the difference in our weight. Four ounces of strychnia would kill thousands of men; and therefore it is not an insignificant quantity."

"But four ounces of wheat would not keep a man alive for any great length of time; and therefore it is an insignificant quantity," retorted Uncle Moses. "But climate is the topic just now."

"Not till I have declared that I am keeping my seat solely and simply as a precedent for my worthy Brother Avoirdupois, for he is exceedingly bashful, and would not have stood up during his disquisition without one," returned the doctor. "But my learned legal friend would talk all day if I permitted him to do so; and while I recommend him to cork up his vials for his discourse, I will go on with mine.

"The climate of Egypt is in some degree influenced by the great river which our young friend has so effectively described; but they say that the desert, which we generally regard as a very hot and disagreeable region, is its principal regulator. I suppose you can all understand the immense absorbing power of a vast quantity of dry sand. The rains that fall in the winter on the country about the Mediterranean are eaten up, so to speak, by the dry air of the desert, which extends nearly across the continent. Otherwise these rains would extend far up the Nile valley. They would also convert 2,500 square miles of low lands about the Delta into a region so unhealthy that it could not be inhabited; and this is a tract half as big as the State of Connecticut.

"The air from the desert in this region is agreeably cool, and my old friend Bayard Taylor called it the 'elixir of life.' This air contains a modicum of salt from limestone rocks, which is beneficial to respiration. Add to this the purity of the water of the Nile, which is excellent in spite of the mud it brings down, though I think a filter would sometimes come into needed use.

"Throughout the greater part of Lower Egypt, rain is almost as rare as snow is in the West Indies. At Cairo in five years the average was an inch and a half; in fourteen years at Alexandria it was eight inches, while it is about thirty inches where we come from. In Upper Egypt rain is practically unknown; and natives may be met who have never seen such a thing as a shower.

"I will not go into the matter of the various winds that blow, or look too closely into the causes of the climate of Egypt. Gauged by the temperature, this country has really but two seasons. One, the season of hot weather, lasts about eight months, from April to November; the other is the cool season, from December to March. They sometimes have a north-west wind in this city which modifies the heat. In the Delta the greatest heat is about 95°, while in Upper Egypt it mounts to 109°. At Cairo the glass sometimes goes up to 114° during the Khamsin, as a certain south wind is called. Strange as it may seem in the exception, the mercury very seldom goes down to freezing, except in the desert, and there at night. The mean temperature here and at Cairo is 58° in winter, 78° in spring, 83° in summer, and 66° in autumn. Wishing to be reasonable, I will stop here, Mr. Commander."

Hearty applause, which appeared to have become a matter of politeness, followed, and all eyes were turned to the captain for the next announcement.

CHAPTER XI

AN ORIENTAL VISITOR IN THE BOUDOIR

As soon as Dr. Hawkes had finished his remarks on the climate, the commander consulted his watch, which he had refrained from politeness to do while any one was speaking.   He was satisfied that the surgeon had omitted a great deal that might have been profitably said on his topic, though he had given all that was essential to a mixed audience.

"As it wants only half an hour of lunch time, I shall not call upon Professor Giroud for the history of Egypt, especially as I have a matter of business on my hands," said the captain.   "I have no doubt you can profitably use the time in observing the various objects on shore, and what is going on in the harbor. I have four copies of the latest and best guide-book for Egypt, which I sent for, and I will hand them to you;" and he tendered one of them to Louis.

"Thank you, but I have one I found in Athens," replied the owner.

They were given out to the party, and they mounted the promenade to see what was to be seen.   They were placed where they would do the most good, and holders of them opened to the plan of Alexandria, and pointed out Pompey's Pillar. But the names on the map were in French, and they were passed to those who knew something of that language.

Captain Ringgold went to his cabin, and sent for Mr. Boulong, who presently appeared.

"Where is the gentleman of whom you spoke to me, Mr. Boulong?"

"I invited him to the boudoir, and asked him to help himself to any book in the case," replied the first officer.

"What sort of a person is he?"

"He is dressed in Turkish costume, and is a very elegant looking person. That is really all I know about him, for I asked no questions of him."

"I will go down and see him," added the commander, as he rose from his chair.

"Perhaps I ought to add, Captain Ringgold, that I suspect I have seen the gentleman before," said Mr. Boulong. "It is only a suspicion, and maybe I ought not to have mentioned it. I have been trying to place him since I saw him, but without success."

"Was it Ali-Noury Pacha?" asked the commander, deeply interested in what the officer had said.

"Whoever he may be, I am sure it is not the Pacha," replied Mr. Boulong very decidedly.

"Have you no idea where you have seen him before?"

"Not the least; and I have been over all the Orientals I have met from Algiers to Zante."

"I have had just such instances in my own experience, and I am glad you spoke to me about the matter," replied Captain Ringgold.   "Will you please to ask Felix to come to my cabin?"

Mr. Boulong left the apartment, and the commander dropped into his chair.   The suspicion of the officer, even if it was nothing more than a suspicion, recalled the information that Felix had procured the night before.   He was certain that the Fatimé was on the coast; but it did not seem to him probable in any degree that she could have made a port, and sent an agent of the Pacha to the Guardian-Mother since she had been last observed, for the amateur detective had reported that he had seen her going to the eastward that morning.

Captain Ringgold was determined to use the most extraordinary precautions to defeat any possible plot of the Moor.   The bugbear of childish fears did not disturb him in the least degree; for he preferred to be charged with over-prudence rather than with the lack of it, if any disaster should happen to one of the persons in his care.

Felix came to the commander's room, and the latter proceeded to inform the other what he had just learned from the first officer.   It was not the Pacha, and that was all the mate had dared to affirm.

"Was it Mazagan?" inquired Felix.

. "I did not think to ask about him.   He is on the upper deck; ask him to come in again;" and presently Mr. Boulong presented himself.

"You remember Captain Mazagan, who was in the Samothraki?"

"I do, Captain; for we made a prisoner of him, and kept him for some time on board of the ship," replied Mr. Boulong.

"Was it he who has come on board to see me?" asked the captain, fixing an anxious gaze upon the officer.

"I should say not, Captain; at any rate, it did not occur to me that it was Captain Mazagan," replied the mate.

"Is the visitor a tall or a short man?"

"Rather tall."

"Mazagan was above the average height of Turks and Moroccans," suggested the commander.

"But there was nothing about this man that reminded me of Mazagan. The gentleman is elegantly dressed, with a general air of refinement that was utterly lacking in the Moorish captain," Mr. Boulong explained.

"He was not dressed up when we met him on the felucca," added the captain. "Dress sometimes makes a wonderful difference in the appearance of a man."

"I cannot believe this visitor is Mazagan; but I could tell better if I saw him again, with a particular object in view."

"I will see him for myself, Mr. Boulong. That is all;" and the first officer retired. "We must find out who this man is before he has time to do any

mischief.   You were present in the *café* at Gallipoli,
Felix, when Louis overheard the conversation between
the Pacha and Mazagan."

"I was ; but I could not have understood a word of
it, if I had been near enough, for the talk was all in
French ; and Louis's knowledge of that lingo no
doubt saved his bacon."

"Ask Louis to come to me, Felix."

"Have you done with me, Captain ? "

"No, Felix ; I may have a week's work for you in
connection with this matter."

"A week's work," repeated Felix to himself, as he
left the cabin.   In a moment more he returned with
Louis, and the situation was rehearsed to him.

"I am going to ascertain who this man is if I don't
do anything else," said the captain.   "The first thing
I wish to know is whether or not he speaks French."

"Even if he speaks it as fluently as Mazagan did
at Gallipoli, it would not prove that he was that
worthy," replied Louis with a smile.

"I am aware of it; but it is one point in the
inquiry," answered the captain.

"Perhaps he will refuse to speak it if he can do
so," suggested the owner.

"Then we will do what we can to bring him out.
Go down to the boudoir, and don't utter a word of
English.   I appoint you to learn his business with
me ; and you can do it in French as well as in English.   You may go with him, Felix ; but be prudent,
both of you," said the captain.

They descended to the main deck and stopped
there for a conference in regard to the situation.
Louis suggested that his crony should pass through
the boudoir, take a look at the stranger, and then go
into the cabin, where he was to remain till he was
wanted. Felix assented to the plan, and proceeded
to carry it out. He found the Mussulman busily
engaged in reading a book with a red cover, which he
knew very well was French, for he had seen Louis
reading it, and he had translated a page of it for him.
He thought this was something gained, and went back
to the main deck to tell his friend what he had seen.
Then he made his way through the boudoir, stopping
there long enough to scrutinize the form and features
of the stranger.

He took no apparent notice of the visitor, and bus-
ied himself in arranging the curtains at the windows.
If the Mohammedan gentleman looked at him at all,
he did it in a furtive manner, and kept his attention
fixed on the book. Louis allowed Felix time enough
to observe the stranger, and then came into the
boudoir himself.

" *Bon jour, Monsieur*," Louis began. " *Monsieur le
capitaine est tres occupé, et il m'a envoyé vous de-
mander votre affair avec.*"

" I speak English; I don't speak Italian," replied
the visitor very politely from the sofa; and Louis
noticed that he made an effort to conceal the book he
had been reading.

" Italian; I don't speak Italian," replied Louis,

still using his favorite language, to which he had given a great deal of attention for several years. " I speak only French and Spanish (on the present occasion)," the last clause in too low a tone to be heard. "*¿Habla V. Espagnol?*"

"Arabic, Turkish, English," added the visitor, with an abundance of smiles.

"*Français*," said Louis.

They did not get ahead a particle in speech, though Louis had reached the obstacle he suggested he might encounter. If the stranger was Mazagan, though he had not recognized him, like the first officer, he suspected that he had seen him before. It was no use for either to talk, as the other obstinately refused to do so, and Louis went to the cabin staircase, and shouted quite loudly : —

"François," continuing to use his French. "The villain is here!"

Felix mumbled something that seemed like an answer to the announcement his crony had made ; but he took good care that he should not hear it.

"Bring up my revolver, François, and I will shoot him before he has a chance to kill another man!" added Louis, even more vigorously than before. "Hurry up, or he may escape me!"

Felix rattled off some "hog Latin" he had learned at school.

"We will put a weight to his body, and drop him overboard at the stern," replied Louis, as if in answer to an objection made by 'François.' "The revolver, quick!"

Felix procured the weapon from his stateroom, and passed it up to his companion. The visitor had ceased to smile, and he looked worried as Louis glanced at him.

"*Que voulez-vous dire?*" demanded the stranger. "*Je n'ai jamais tué un homme!*" (What do you mean? I never killed a man.)

"Oh, you can speak French!" exclaimed Louis, as before. "The captain sent me to ascertain your business with him."

"I have a very important letter for Captain Ringgold, which I can deliver only to him in person," replied the gentleman, in French again, whom the representative of the commander now had an opportunity to observe.

Though the Mussulman spoke fluently, there was something peculiar about the pronunciation, as well as the idiom, of his French, which struck the listener, and it was not unfamiliar to Louis.

"I have not the pleasure of knowing your name, sir," added the owner of the Guardian-Mother, speaking now in English.

"Ibrahim Abdelkhalik is my name," replied the visitor, changing his speech to English, as Louis had done; and there was a smile on his handsome face, as though he was happy to find that he was not to be murdered, and his body sunk to the bottom of the harbor. "Will you do me the honor to give me your name?"

"Certainly, with the greatest pleasure. My name

is Jean Bagatelle," replied Louis promptly. "If you will give yours to Captain Ringgold" —

"I have no card with me," replied Ibrahim, after fumbling about his Oriental garments.

"Then you will write one," added Louis, handing him one of his own cards, on which the visitor wrote the name he had given in Arabic or Turkish.

"Will you please to write it in English?"

"I can speak English, but I cannot write it," replied Ibrahim.

Louis asked the name again, and then wrote under the pot-hooks the name, "Ibrahim Abdelkhalik," though he did not spell it in just this manner. Bowing politely to the Oriental, he went to the captain, reported what had transpired, and gave his opinion. The commander then went to the boudoir, and fixed his most piercing gaze upon Ibrahim; and he had an eye like a hawk when he found it necessary to bring it out.

Both of them were polite, the visitor being even obsequious, and the important letter was handed to the captain. He opened it, and found it was in Arabic. Doubtless the Mussulman expected to have the recipient of the epistle ask him to translate it for him; but he did not. The gong for lunch rang just then.

"I am very busy to-day, and you must excuse me from giving immediate attention to this matter; but I will read the letter at my leisure, and give you my reply by letter," said the commander. "I wish you a very good morning;" and he abruptly left the boudoir.

As he went out on the main deck, he directed Mr. Boulong to show the visitor to his boat; and probably the obsequious Ibrahim did not believe he had made much out of his visit.

CHAPTER XII

THE MISSION OF THE AMATEUR DETECTIVE

THE company gathered immediately at the table; but Captain Ringgold could not speak a word about Ibrahim and his mission to Louis, for Mrs. Belgrave and the Woolridges were within hearing distance of them. The party were in excellent spirits, and were beset by none of the weariness of travel which sometimes overtakes tourists, for the scenes about them were more novel and strange than in the European surroundings through which they had been passing during the preceding six months.

None of them except Louis and Felix had even seen the Oriental visitor, for they were on the upper deck when he came on board, and they had no difficult questions to ask. They were exceedingly merry, and talked about what they had seen, and what they had found in the guide-books which had been given to them. They all had lively anticipations of the scenes that were before them in Cairo, at the Pyramids, and up the Nile.

The captain announced that the Conference would be continued on the upper deck at two o'clock. Louis was with him when they left the cabin, and on their way Louis discovered that Ibrahim's boat was still alongside the Maud. It was a shore craft, and he was seated in the stern sheets, evidently troubled because he had made so little progress in his mission, whatever it was, for that had not transpired, except in the Arabic characters of the letter, which neither the commander nor the owner could read.

"This affair of our visitor seems to have been all a farce," said Captain Ringgold, as he seated himself at his desk in his cabin, and took the Arabic letter from his pocket. "The fellow has not gone yet, and he evidently intends to accomplish something more. But he will get tired of waiting for me."

"Of course Ibrahim is a humbug; and I think we fooled him very nicely," replied Louis, laughing.

"It was a tragic scene that you acted; but it was of your own invention, and I am not responsible for it, though I have no fault to find with it. Where is Felix?" demanded the commander, suddenly springing from his chair as though a new idea had struck him very forcibly.

"He is on deck, I suppose."

The commander struck the electric bell, and, when Sordy appeared, he directed him to send Felix to him. In a few minutes he entered the room.

"Mr. McGavonty," the captain began.

"Is it me you mean?" asked Felix.

"I mean you."

"You don't mister me, Captain, as a rule."

"Leave the joke till another time, Flix."

"Now I know whom you mean," laughed the Milesian.

"You have a taste for the calling of a detective, and you have shown some little skill at the business," continued the commander.

"Thank you, Captain; but Louis can do it quite as well as I can."

"Now be silent if you can for two minutes, and I will tell you what I want. You are the only detective we have, and I wish you to follow the fellow you saw in the boudoir; 'shadow' him, I believe you call it in your profession. You will take John Donald, dressed in his orientals, with you; for he is the only man we have that can speak Arabic, and you will need him. I am sorry to send you away just as the Conference begins again."

Felix shrugged his shoulders with a meaning smile on his face, which was as much as to say that he could get along without the lecture the professor was about to give, for he was not a very earnest student; but he was silent.

"That is all the instruction I have to give you. Shadow him wherever he goes," added the captain.

"Excuse me for speaking; but suppose he should take a train?" asked Felix.

"That depends; you needn't follow him to Cairo; but if you find that he is going to any other place, Rosetta for instance, go with him. One thing more: I want you to buy a new suit of orientals for John Donald, if you have time to do so. Here are two hundred francs in French gold; and this money passes in the cities of Egypt;" and the captain took the coins from his purse and handed them to him.

"What is the fellow's name?" asked Felix as he transferred the gold to his own purse. "I heard Mr. Bumblegrubbins give his name to Louis; but I could not make it out any more than I could the lingo of a cock-turkey when he gobbles."

"Here is his card; but you must walk by sight rather than by faith in names. Don't lose it, for I may want it."

Felix took the card, tipped his head from one side to the other, and squinted at the characters on it.

"You are holding it upside down!" exclaimed Louis.

"What difference does that make? Sure a cuttle-fish wiggled across this card, and shed his sepia on it as he hitched along. Oh, this is it in English," added Felix, as he turned the card right side up. "I will keep it safely, and spell it out when I have a quarter of an hour to spare."

"I will set Mr. Boulong to watch Ibrahim's boat, and he will notify you when it leaves the Maud. Let John engage a shore boat when he is rigged, and stand by it. That's all; now go and find Donald, and let him get ready."

The captain and Louis talked a while longer, and both of them had decided opinions in regard to the identity of Ibrahim. What his method of proceeding was to be might be indicated in the Arabic letter, which was a sealed book to them for the present, though Don could translate it when he could be spared from his present mission.   In regard to the engineer, the commander had some new views and intentions, and for this reason he wished him to be clothed in more becoming "orientals," as he called the Turkish garb, than those he had worn when he came on board of the ship at Gibraltar.   As the time for opening the Conference approached, both of them went to the starboard rail, and found that Don was already in possession of a boat.   Mr. Boulong was instructed as arranged, and presently Felix appeared on the promenade deck.

"You needn't lose the whole of the history of Egypt, Felix," said the commander, in a sort of a condoling tone.

"I think I shall be able to get along without the whole of it, for I read a little of it (it was a very little), in Louis's book; and if I am going to make any money by it, I will read what the professor don't tell me," chuckled Felix.

"I shall have to yoke you and Mr. Woolridge together, for he does not take much interest in the Conference and the events of the past," replied the captain with a smile.

"All right; I shall be in good company then," added Felix, as the commander took his place in the circle of ladies and gentlemen who were already in their armchairs.

The amateur detective took his chair to a place

where he could easily make his escape when the first officer summoned him, and where he could creep down to the main deck without being noticed.

"I have the pleasure of announcing that our learned fellow-voyager was assigned to the department of history, and I have the honor to present to you Professor Giroud," said the captain.

"Ladies and gentlemen," the professor began when the applause subsided, "I am not exactly called upon to make bricks without straw, but I am required to put a gallon of fluid into a pint pot, for it would take a week to tell all that might be said about the history of Egypt, for no record of past events can be traced so far back as that of the country we are now visiting. The records of the ancient Egyptians have been cut out in stone, baked in clay, and written in strange hieroglyphics on skins of animals or scrolls of papyrus; and the marvellous dryness of the air in this almost rainless valley of the Nile has preserved them to be read or deciphered by the *savants* of modern times."

"What's papyrus, Professor?" interposed Mrs. Blossom.

"I beg your pardon, madam, but I shall never get through if I stop to answer questions on the way, for they throw me off the track, and take more time in that way than would be required simply to answer them. Papyrus is an Egyptian plant that grows to the height of about ten feet, from the pith of which a kind of paper was made, upon which many of these ancient records come down to us. Now, if you will make a note of any questions you wish to ask, I shall take the greatest pleasure in answering them when I have finished my remarks," said the professor with all his abundant suavity.

"In the reign of one of the Ptolemys a learned man was employed to collect and collate all the historical works of various kinds preserved in the temples as the records of the country. This man was a priest, and his researches were made nearly three hundred years before the time of Christ. This history, as compiled by the priest, was in great repute after its completion ; but it was afterwards lost, with the exception of his chronology of the kings, which has been handed down to us in the work of Josephus, which I have seen in popular form in the houses of many American people. The priest gave the names of the kings by dynasties, with the date of the reign of each.

"This list is still the basis of our knowledge of ancient Egyptian history. Modern discoveries and researches have elaborated this catalogue, confirming and supplementing the data thus transmitted to us. In the Scriptures you read of Pharaoh as though he were a particular king of Egypt; but it was really the official title of the ruler, though some difficulty has been experienced in determining whether the name applied to a single king or a dynasty of them.

"Learned men in modern days have diligently studied these old records. Mariette was a Frenchman, Wilkinson an Englishman, and Lepsius a German, who have been distinguished Egyptologists; and each of them has given a chronology to the world, though they differ very widely.   Menes was the first king, and is believed to have founded Memphis, the site of which you will see when you go up the river. The date of this monarch is given by the three authorities I have named respectively as 5004 (before Christ, of course, in every instance), 3892, and 2700. After you have studied the subject, each of you can decide for himself which he will accept as the most correct.

"As I have said before, the reigns of kings were given by dynasties; and there are thirty of them down to the time of the first Ptolemy, 324 B.C.   It would be absurd for me to repeat the names of these, with their dates, and I shall not do it; and if any of you wish to read them you will find them in Baedeker's 'Lower Egypt,' a most excellent work, of which the commander has been kind enough to provide several copies for your use. But I will mention a few salient points taken from the list.   Khufu and Khâfrâ, called by the Greeks Cheops and Cephrenes respectively, were the builders of the three great Pyramids of Gîzeh."

At this point it was observed that those who held the book mentioned in their hands, and were following the discourse on its pages, made notes, in accordance with the speaker's request.

"We may safely set down the date of these Pyramids as at least 3000 years before Christ, which makes them nearly 5,000 years old. The ruler that followed the builders of the Pyramids is sent down to posterity as a wicked despiser of the gods, while Khufu and Khâfrâ are glorified on the monuments as worshippers of the gods, as industrious and persevering, and consequently prosperous and wealthy. The arts reached their highest ancient perfection in these reigns.

" Ramses II., or Sesostris, whose kingly ancestors had made some conquests of countries, carried his arms to the south into Dongola, and in the direction of Asia Minor. He was noted as a builder of temples and monuments, and a patron of the arts and sciences. This monarch was the Pharaoh who persecuted the children of Israel. Merenptah followed Ramses II., and is believed to be the Pharaoh of Exodus, as classified in Smith's 'Dictionary of the Bible,' which may be consulted in the library. [Mrs. Blossom made a note of it]. This king was defeated by the Israelites, which resulted in his overthrow, and brought his dynasty to an end."

At this point in the dynasties, the commander saw Mr. Boulong saunter up carelessly behind Felix, and put his hand on his shoulder while he took the trouble to gaze up at the rigging of the main topmast. The detective did not need to have a call sounded in his ears, and doubling himself up, he stole down the steps to the main deck, and no one appeared to notice him.

CHAPTER XIII

ABOUT THE DYNASTIES OF EGYPT

THE departure of Felix did not disturb the professor as a volley of questions did, and he proceeded without any pause in his remarks.

"The overthrow of the Pharaoh of the Exodus brought a new empire into existence, a very common event in the history of this ancient domain. Ramses III. was the king. Though he was successful in some of his military enterprises, he was unable to maintain the prowess of some of his ancestors. He appears to have been more devoted to the arts of peace, for the buildings he erected are the most magnificent of his age. His monument near Thebes is one of the finest now in existence. The rock-tombs of that city and the mausoleums of the kings were begun by his successors.

"The authorities I mention in speaking of Menes, the first king, differ by about 2,300 years in their dates; but in the reign of Ramses III. the variation is reduced to 88 years. Thebes is below the First Cataract, and perhaps we shall visit the site of it [the commander nodded assent]. When we are there we shall have the opportunity to fill up some of the blanks I have left in my notices of the kings, and the same will occur in many other places.

"After Ramses III. the priest-kings became the rulers of Egypt; but they were too weak to maintain their authority, and temporized with the chiefs of their domain. In the Twenty-third Dynasty came Sheshenk I. He was the Shishak mentioned in the Bible. He joined the forces of Jeroboam against Rehoboam, and besieged and captured Jerusalem. You will find the account of it in 2 Chronicles, chapter xii. [Mrs. Blossom made a note of it]. Then the successors of Sheshenk were defeated in Syria, and the Ethiopians invaded the country, conquered and obtained possession of Egypt. One of these kings sent an army to aid Hezekiah, but was defeated by the Assyrians, who held the country for a time, and divided it among twenty princes, who made themselves independent; but they were all driven out by Sardanapalus, the Assyrian monarch.

"His successors were not able enough to keep his conquests, and the beginning of the Twenty-sixth Dynasty was Psammetikh, the heir in the Ethiopian line. The second of that name went to the relief of Zedekiah, king of Judah, who was besieged in Jerusalem by Nebuchadnezzar, the greatest and most powerful of the kings of Babylon, who afterwards captured this city.

"Not long afterwards the king of Egypt was dethroned, and Ashmes II. took his place. The country was at peace then, and in a prosperous condition; but,

as we find it in more modern times, the sovereigns of
the nations were greedy for power, and were constantly at war with each other.   Cyrus the Great had
built up the Persian Empire, and became the most
powerful ruler in the East.   Cambyses, his son,
marched into Egypt to make a conquest of it, for it
was the only power that remained as a rival of Persia.
He defeated Psammetikh III., captured Memphis,
made a prisoner of the king, who was executed afterwards for getting up an insurrection.   This event introduced the Twenty-seventh Dynasty, the Persian.

"Cambyses ruled with moderation at first, and allowed the Egyptians to retain their own religion; but
after he had failed in some rash attempts at conquest,
he became ugly and vindictive.   Darius I. succeeded
to the throne of Persia.   He was a wise prince, and
did much to promote the prosperity of Egypt.   He
built canals and roads, established commercial routes,
and coined money, stamped rings and weights having
been in use before.   He made two attempts to conquer
Greece and failed in both.   He was followed by Xer-
xes I., who made another tremendous effort to subdue
Greece, as we learned when we were in that country.
He appointed his brother viceroy, or satrap, of Egypt.

Artaxerxes succeeded to the throne of Persia, and
was a brave prince; but intestine troubles which
finally led to the reduction of the realm had appeared,
and he was unable to stay its decadence.   This reign
began in 465 B.C., and during its existence a series of
revolts originated, with varying fortunes to the Egyp-

tians. At one time the native kings mounted the throne again ; but they lost and regained the kingdom by turns, till it was finally surrendered to Artaxerxes III., king of Persia, who ruled it through his satrap.

"Darius III. was the next king of Persia. He was defeated by Alexander the Great; and the latter marched to Pelusium, an ancient city on the Isthmus of Suez, where the Egyptians received him with acclamations of joy as their deliverer from the oppression of the Persians. This reign was from 332 to 323 B.C. Alexander permitted the Egyptian religion, and founded Alexandria, which afterwards became the centre of Greek letters, and of the commerce of the world. Then Egypt passed under Greek rule, and in 323 Ptolemy I. became king. He had to fight his way to the throne, causing the death of Alexander's son, who had assumed his title as the second of that name. On account of the institutions founded there, Alexandria became the chief seat of Greek literature, casting Athens into the shade.

"Two years before his death this king abdicated in favor of his son, Ptolemy II., called Philadelphus. In the reign of Ptolemy III. Egypt reached the zenith of its power and glory. The army of Egypt about this time was said to consist of 200,000 foot soldiers, 20,000 horse, 2,000 chariots, 400 elephants, and the navy of 1,500 ships of war, with 1,000 transports. Perhaps all this is true, and perhaps it is not, and we can't count up the material at this time; but probably most of the navy, called ships, were mere boats.

"Under Ptolemy IV. and his successors Egypt declined in power and prosperity. His successor came to the throne as a child five years old. In consequence of a revolt in Alexandria, and an attack of the king of Syria, his guardians were compelled to appeal to the Roman Senate for protection, and the result was that the country became practically a Roman province.

"The Ptolemys remained on the throne under the protection and influence of Rome. The thirteenth of them, called the flute-player, appointed his eldest children to succeed to the crown. They were Cleopatra VII. and Ptolemy XIV., and they were to marry, though brother and sister, in accordance with Egyptian custom, and Pompey, the Roman general, was appointed their guardian by the Senate. But the husband banished his sister-wife, though some say it was done by their immediate guardians.

"Just at this time, in 48 B.C., Pompey, the Roman guardian, was defeated in the decisive battle of Pharsalia by Julius Cæsar, and he fled to the dominions of his wards; but he was assassinated by the order of Ptolemy. Cæsar went to Egpyt in search of Pompey. He met Cleopatra, and was fascinated by her beauty. He earnestly espoused her cause, and defeated her recreant brother, placing her on the throne with a colleague in the person of a still younger brother.

"The next brother in the line was drowned in the Nile, and Ptolemy XV., at the age of eleven, was placed at the side of Cleopatra with nominal power. The beautiful but wicked queen soon poisoned him, and Cæsarion, her son, of whom the Roman dictator was the father, was appointed the co-regent with her. After the murder of Cæsar in the conspiracy of Brutus and Cassius, Marc Antony, who, you all remember, was the friend of the dead Cæsar, sought to avenge his death, summoned Cleopatra to appear before him and explain her leadings in the civil war that followed the assassination.

"The 'Serpent of the Nile,' as she has been called, was in doubt at first whether or not to obey, but decided to do so. She sailed up the river Cydnus to Tarsus, in Cilicia, a province of Asia Minor, to meet him in a magnificent galley, dressed like Venus rising from the sea, and surrounded by all the splendors of the Orient."

"I have seen the picture of that!" exclaimed Mrs. Blossom, unable longer to restrain herself.

"The picture has been circulated all over the world. She was twenty-eight years old, and in the zenith of her beauty, which she had derived from the Greeks. Antony was fascinated by her wit and loveliness. Without following out the romantic story in detail, the Roman general threw himself away for her, sacrificing his ambition and everything else. He lost his standing in Rome, and was declared an enemy of his country. Octavianus was sent to reduce him to subjection.

"Antony and Cleopatra were defeated in the naval battle of Actium; and Cleopatra fled with sixty ships, and made private terms with the victor. Indignant at her treachery, and informed that she had already killed herself, he fell upon his own sword, which was one of the ways of that age to commit suicide. Mortally wounded, he was told that the news conveyed to him was false; he caused himself to be carried into her presence, and died in her embrace. Octavianus made her a prisoner by stratagem ; but she could not melt his stern nature as she had others, and killed herself, by causing her chest to be bitten by an asp. I have finished the romance.

"The last event was in the year 30 B.C. For the next three centuries the Roman rule continued, though the country was invaded by Queen Zenobia of Palmyra, and she was acknowledged as the queen of Egypt ; but in a couple of years she was dethroned, and some doubt that she ever reigned over the land of the Nile. It was considered the most valuable of the provinces of Rome, for it was the granary from which the people of that empire were fed. During this period of three hundred years, the record was filled up with fruitless insurrections and savage persecutions of the Christians, whose religion had been introduced there, and had made rapid progress.

"In the year 306 (all the dates are now A.D.), Constantine the Great became the Roman emperor ; and after warring for some years with those who shared the throne with him, he overthrew Licinius, the last of them, in 323, and became sole emperor of the West, and of the East also. He selected Byzantium, or Constantinople, as his capital, and established the Christian religion, which put an end to the persecutions of its followers.

"For three centuries Egypt was a part of the Byzantine Empire. In 619 the Persians again invaded the country, Alexandria was taken by them, and they ruled about ten years; but they were driven out by Heraclius. Mohammed had no children, and his father-in-law, Abubekr, was made his successor. The third caliph was Othman, and his general, Khalid, called 'The Sword of God,' marched his armies into Persia, routed its armies in several battles, defeated a Roman army, and took possession of Jerusalem. At his death he was succeeded by Omar, another father-in-law of the Prophet; and he continued the war against all the enemies of his faith, and conquered Egypt in 638. For two centuries the country remained subject to the Arabian Caliphate, and then was ruled by one and another who had the power to capture the throne, till 1240.

"Saladin, or Salaheddin, who made himself Sultan of Egypt in 1169, created a body-guard called the Mamelukes. The word means slaves, and the men had been bought and trained as soldiers for the basis of an army to insure the security of the Sultan. These Mamelukes were all foreigners, brought from the dominions of the Turks around the Caspian and Black Seas, and they proved to be persons of talent.

"While the sons of the late Sultan were fighting

for the throne, the Mamelukes stepped in and put one
of their own number upon it, Melck es-Sâleḥ. He had
ability, and was disposed to play the ruler in earnest.
He carried his enterprise out of his dominion, and captured Damascus, Jerusalem, and other cities.

"You remember the Sainte Chapelle, in Paris,
which was the church of Louis IX., called Saint Louis.
He was engaged in the Crusades, and to prevent the
Egyptians from making further encroachments in the
Holy Land, he undertook a campaign against them.
He took Damietta, and then marched towards Cairo;
but he was captured with his army, and was released
only on the payment of a large ransom. But the
French did better in Egypt after that;" and the pro-
fessor smiled.

"The Mamelukes made Melik Sultan, because they
believed they could easily control him; but they
found they had caught a Tartar, for when his authority was established, he dismissed the Mamelukes from
his service. He recruited a new guard from the
Turks, and maintained his authority. But the original band had been largely increased by more men
from Circassia; and they succeeded in 1382 in upset-
ting the Turkish Mamelukes, and putting one of their
number on the throne again.

"Bebars, one of them, was a slave, and had risen
by his own ability to be the leader of the Mamelukes,
and then the Sultan. He ruled with justice and
moderation. He demolished what remained of the
Kingdom of Jerusalem. He brought the last of the

Caliphs to Cairo, acknowledged his authority, being a good Mussulman, and placed him on the throne as the nominal ruler. Now, ladies and gentlemen, will you give me a rest long enough to drink a glass of water?" And the commander sent for it.

CHAPTER XIV

SOME OF THE MODERN HISTORY OF EGYPT

"AFTER centuries of anarchy and confusion, as I have rehearsed the history to you," continued the professor, "the last Mameluke was dethroned by Selim I., Sultan of the Ottoman Empire, in 1517, and Egypt has ever since been a Pachalic of the Turks. The authority of the Osman rulers had even then begun to decline, and with it the powers of the governors of their dependencies. Several of the Mameluke rulers of Egypt were men of decided ability, and had broader views than many that preceded and followed them. The arts were cultivated to some extent, as may be seen by the mosques and tombs of these Sultans at Cairo, which rank among the finest specimens of Saracenic architecture.

"For a couple of hundred years Egypt was ruled by the Pachas appointed by the Sultans of the Osman family; but the Mamelukes were still in existence, forming the military power of the Pachalic, and twenty-four of them were Beys, who governed as many different divisions of the country. They merely paid tribute to the Pacha, and their consent was necessary to enable him to adopt any new measure.

They gradually regained a portion of their former power, and in 1771 they were bold enough to throw off the yoke of the Turks, and declared the independence of Egypt, as the colonists of America did four years later; but the result was quite different.

"The leader of the Mamelukes was Ali Bey, and he became Sultan. He had formerly been a slave; and taking advantage of the fact that the Turks were involved in a war with Russia, he established himself as the ruler. He conquered Syria and Arabia; but when he returned to his Sultanate, he was cast into prison by his own son-in-law, where he soon died, and was probably poisoned.

"After his death disorder and confusion reigned; a couple of the Mameluke Beys obtained the supremacy, and the Turkish authority was established again. The Beys were broken up into factions; but the invasion of Napoleon in 1798, made with the hope of destroying the English trade in the Mediterranean, united them for the defence of the country.

"The French captured Alexandria and Cairo, and eventually the whole of Egypt. The Mameluke cavalry, which had become famous, made a gallant resistance; but the skill and science of modern warfare were too much for them. In the battle of the Pyramids the Mamelukes were nearly destroyed. In 1801 the English took a hand in the business. The Turks had also declared war against England. In the Bay of Aboukir, about a dozen miles north-east of us, the British fleet under Lord Nelson very nearly annihilated the French squadron, only two ships of which escaped. In 1801 the French army surrendered to the English. But the French have since had a great deal of influence in Egypt.

"Through the interposition of the French government, who desired to counteract the influence of the English and the Mamelukes in Egypt, Mohammed Ali was called upon for this purpose. He was born in Roumelia, and was at this time in command as colonel of a regiment of one thousand Albanians in Egypt. Having produced a better condition of affairs by 1805, he was appointed Pacha, which is the same thing as Viceroy. He prevented the English from taking possession of the country in 1807. The Mamelukes stood in the path of progress, and Mohammed Ali dealt summarily with them, for he proved himself to be a very progressive ruler. In 1814 he treacherously caused the Beys and their followers, 470 in number, to be massacred.

" The resolute but merciless Pacha improved the agriculture of Egypt, introducing the cotton plant, restored the canals and embankments, appointed Frenchmen and other Europeans to various public offices, and sent young Egyptians to Paris to be educated. While the Greeks were struggling for their independence, he sent 20,000 soldiers to the assistance of the Turkish Sultan, and was rewarded by the gift of the island of Candia after the war.

"But the idea of entire independence took possession of his mind in 1831, and he made war on the

Porte, as the Ottoman government is sometimes called. His adopted son Ibrahim invaded Syria, conquered it and a considerable portion of Asia Minor, while his admiral Haleb destroyed the Turkish fleet, and then menaced Constantinople. Doubtless he would have succeeded in his purpose, if the war had not been terminated by the intervention of France and Russia, in order to prevent the subjugation of the Ottoman Empire.

"In 1839 England induced the enemies of Egypt to attack Mohammed Ali; but the 'Powers' arranged the difficulty, and the Pacha was compelled to yield a second time to the Sultan; but the hereditary sovereignty of Egypt was secured to him, Syria and Candia were given up, Mohammed was to reduce his army to 18,000 men, and pay the Sultan an annual tribute of £306,000.

"During the last years of his life Mohammed Ali was an imbecile, Ibrahim assumed the reins of government, and the Pacha died in 1849 at the age of eighty. Ibrahim died before his father, and Abbas Pacha succeeded to the Pachalic at the death of his grandfather. He is often described as brutal, vicious, and rapacious, especially by Europeans. Perhaps he inherited from his Arab mother a degree of ferocity, and with it the spirit of the Bedouins of the desert, for he had no fancy for the innovations of foreigners. He was a rigid disciplinarian among his officials, and the public safety was effectually secured under his government.

"He was succeeded by Said Pacha (pronounced sah-eed), the third son of Mohammed Ali. He was an enlightened prince, with a taste for European civilization, and Egypt made no little progress under his control. He completed the railroads from Cairo to Alexandria and to Suez, and supported Ferdinand de Lesseps in the construction of the Suez Canal. In the Crimean War he was compelled to send an army and a large sum of money to the Porte. He died in 1863, after a reign of nine years.

"His nephew, Ismâil Pacha, the second son of Ibrahim, born in 1830, was the next Pacha. He had been educated in France, and from the familiarity with European institutions thus obtained, he had a great preference for them. Unhappily, he was inclined to be an egotist, and given to practise cunning and duplicity. Mainly for his own interest he established manufactories, and constructed canals, railroads, bridges, and telegraphs, though, of course, the people had the benefit of them, if the profits did go into his own pocket. He appropriated to his own use about one-fifth of the arable land of his country. In 1866, by the payment of a large sum of money, of which the Porte was always in need, he obtained from it the concession that the succession should be based on the law of primogeniture, or, in other words, that the eldest son should succeed to his father in the government of the country, and also that he should be raised to the rank of Khedive, or Viceroy, having before been only a *wali*, or governor of a province.

"He also obtained many other concessions, which made him very nearly an independent monarch; but the annual tribute was largely increased as compensation for these favors. For about ten years past the Khedive, under these grants of power from the Sultan, has the right to make treaties with foreign nations, increase his army beyond the limit of 18,000, to coin money, and to borrow money. The latter has proved to be the cause of immense mischief to the country and the ruler.

"In 1878 the public debt had swelled to over £100,000, or about $500,000. The net debt of the United States this year is $841,526,164," continued the professor, reading from a paper in his hand, to which he had occasionally referred. "But the size of the debt is to be measured in comparison with the population and the revenues of the country. Egypt has about 7,000,000 inhabitants, and its revenues are about $50,000, as estimated for the present year, which falls short of the expenditures by $150,000. At this rate it will take a long time to pay its debt.

"In 1878 the finance minister had made loans so recklessly, and had become so powerful, that the Khedive deposed him, and caused him privately to be put to death. The vast debt of Egypt was due to foreigners, and the 'Powers' took the matter of payment into their own hands. They put such a pressure upon him that the Khedive was forced to pass over his personal and family estates to the State. The 'Powers' insisted upon a different management, and a new ministry was created, with an Englishman and a Frenchman having a supervisory control in certain branches.

"The Khedive encouraged a disposition to rebel on the part of certain disbanded officers, who demanded a change of the ministry, which was conceded. The 'Powers' lost their patience, and demanded the resignation of Ismâil, which was refused, and they called upon the Porte to remove him. This was done in 1879, and he was succeeded by Prince Tewfik, his eldest son, then twenty-seven years old (his name is pronounced Tev́-fik). The English and French supervisors in the interests of the debt were soon involved in trouble. Arabi Bey, the minister of war, took measures, without the consent of the Khedive, to reduce the foreign influence in the government.

"Egypt seemed disposed to resist any outside intervention in the affairs of the country by force, and the consuls were notified to this effect. The nominal ruler, as he appeared to be by this time, promised fairly; but affairs did not march to the satisfaction of the 'Powers,' and a British and a French fleet appeared before Alexandria. In June, 1882, a serious riot occurred in this city; and many Europeans were killed in spite of the promise of protection on the part of the authorities, and others fled to the ships for safety.

"In July the British fleet bombarded Alexandria; and the fortified camp of Arabi Bey, the recalcitrant minister, was stormed by a force under Sir Garnet

Wolseley. The plucky Egyptian and his associates were captured, and exiled to Ceylon. After this, English influence was dominant in Egypt, the French no longer taking an active part in the proceedings.

"In the fall of 1883 a very formidable rebellion broke out in the Nubian tribes of the Soudan under the lead of Mohammed Ahmed, generally called the Mahdi. He was a fanatic who claimed to inherit from the son-in-law of the Prophet, Ali, powers equal, and perhaps superior, to those of the founder of the Mohammedan religion. An Egyptian army of 10,000, under Hicks Pacha, was wiped out by his forces, and another of 3,500, under Baker Pacha, was totally defeated in 1884.

" In this strait the English government induced General Charles George Gordon, a wonderfully heroic and chivalrous soldier, as noble as he was humble, to proceed to the Soudan. He had achieved wonders in China, and as Gordon Pacha had reduced the tribes of the Soudan to subjection. A month later Gordon reached his destination at Khartum, which he proposed to save from the grasp of the Mahdi. He was besieged for five months, when an expedition was organized in England, where it was believed that one of the noblest, bravest, and most modest of men was in imminent peril. General Graham commanded this force, and he defeated Osman Digna, the Mahdi's lieutenant; but the chief still maintained his position in front of Khartum.

" Then a second expedition under Wolseley was

sent to the relief of Gordon. After many difficulties surmounted, and with considerable fighting on the way, this force reached the vicinity of the besieged town. It was too late. The place had been captured by the Mahdi two days before, and Gordon had fallen. His journal of the siege was found, and it was suspected that he perished through treachery. One of Gordon's lieutenants, Dr. Schnitzler, better known as Emin Pacha, was visited farther south by Stanley in 1888. His history is interesting; but he perished while still leading his wandering life.

" The English expedition withdrew from the Soudan after the loss of Khartum, leaving the Egyptians to fight their own battles with the turbulent tribes; but the Mahdi is dead, and Abdallah is his successor. The Soudan and its affairs are not very clearly understood at the present time. The Khedive Tewfik died less than a year ago; and in accordance with the new law of descent in the country, he was succeeded by his eldest son, Abbas, who is the present Khedive. He was born July 14, 1874, and is therefore only 18 years, 4 months, and 21 days old to-day," said the professor with a pleasant smile. " I give you his exact age so that the young gentlemen present can compare it with their own. He has one brother, seventeen years old, and two sisters, thirteen and eleven years old. I have finished my long story for the present, though as we proceed on our tour, there will be events to be given more in detail on the spot where they occurred;" and the professor bowed, and took his chair amid a hearty and prolonged round of applause.

"We are extremely obliged to you for the very interesting and instructive account you have given us of the ancient and the modern Egyptians," said the commander, and another volley of applause indorsed the statement.

Those who had questions to ask proposed them and they were answered. The only one of especial importance was in relation to the various marks which those who had the Baedeker in their hands asked.

"Where you find a diæresis over a *u* it is to be pronounced like the same letter in French, or the umlaut *ü* in German," replied the professor. "A circumflex over a vowel lengthens the sound as in French, as in *emîr*, pronounce it ay-meer; *shêkh*, shake, as in English; *tûlûl*, too-lool; *Abûkîr*, Ah-boo-keer."

The Conference closed at this time for the day.

CHAPTER XV

THE EXCURSION OF THE MAUD TO RAMLEH

HOWEVER long the history lesson of Professor Giroud may have seemed to Mr. Woolridge, though he was certainly greatly interested in the larger portion of it, hardly more than an hour had been consumed by it; and it was now only a quarter-past three. The commander was not willing to make these instructive lessons a burden to the party, and he had decided to continue them on the journeys ashore rather than have them all come in the beginning.

Before the Conference met, he had instructed Captain Scott to have the Maud ready for the company at half-past three. Second engineer Sentrick had been sent on board of the little steamer to assist Felipe, and four seamen to relieve the "Big Four," who were present, from duty. The pilot had remained on board the ship by request, and took the wheel. This man had listened to the remarks of the professor, and the officers and some of the seamen were always inclined to get within hearing of the lessons.

Louis, his mother, and Miss Blanche had taken seats on the forecastle, and the owner of the Guardian-Mother was again in the highest stage of felicity.

While he was not at all forward in his relations with the beautiful young lady, he was never so happy as when he was in her presence. She had given him a cordial welcome after the separation of a week on the voyage from Malaga to Alexandria, when both of them blushed, they knew not why, for they were as unconscious of what others realized as though they had been babies in their cradles. The other personages of the " Big Four " were apt to look askance at them when they were together ; but if they said anything, it was only in dark and remote hints.

The Maud got under way with the pilot at the wheel. He was a Maltese, of whom there were many in Egypt, who served in boats, as guides, and as dragomans on the Nile. Malta and Gozo are British, and these men speak English fluently. Agreeably to the direction of the commander, who had instructed him where he was to take the steamer, he stood across the harbor to the toe of what is as good a boot in shape as Italy itself.

" You are going right across the Harbor Bank, Mr. Pilot," suggested Captain Scott, who was at his side in the pilot-house.

" There is plenty of water for this boat, though there are some places with only nine feet on them," he replied with a smile. " You are the captain of this little craft, I believe."

"I am, and I should not like to have her take the ground, which she never did when I had the wheel."

" And she shall not while I have it, for I will not

take her into less than twelve feet of water; and we get more than that off the point ahead."

"What is this point we are coming to, Mr. Belgrave?" asked Miss Blanche.

"That is — I forget the name," replied Louis, with some confusion that he should not be able to answer a question put by her.

"Eunostos Point," said Scott, who was within hearing of them.

"Thanks; I can't remember all these Greek and Arabic words," replied Louis; but he had not studied the chart of the harbor for hours as the captain had.

"There is a palace, or something of that sort, on the point," added Miss Blanche.

"This promontory is called the Ras et-Tin," Louis explained, as he took his guide-book from his pocket. "You see I have put my armor on now," he added, holding up the book.

"Is there a tin mine there?" asked the fair girl, whereat the pilot laughed.

"Probably not, for the book says that the name means 'promontory of figs.' The palace was built by Mohammed Ali, and restored by Ismâil. The council chambers were destroyed by fire, and it is not interesting enough to pay for visiting it."

"I think I have been through about palaces enough, though some in Egypt may be novel and interesting," answered Miss Blanche.

The Maud continued on her course to the eastward,

and reached the heel of the boot, beyond which was the extensive fort of the Pharos, which protects the entrance to the eastern harbor. It seems to be called the New Port because it is the older of the two; but the French call it the "Port Oriental," and the other the "Port Occidental," meaning eastern and western, respectively. The eastern harbor is far smaller than the western.

"This place, now called Pharos, had a lighthouse on it in the time of Ptolemy which was five hundred and ninety feet high," said the pilot, who evidently desired to make himself useful.

"Whew!" exclaimed Scott. "Do you expect us to believe that?"

"Ask the French gentleman who preached to you this afternoon, for I believe he knows everything."

"I don't think he believes anything he don't know. Nearly six hundred feet high!" added Scott.

"I wasn't there to measure it," laughed the pilot; "but that's what they say, and you have it as cheap as I do. It was thought to be one of the seven wonders of the world by the ancients, and all lighthouses are called after it in French."

"The English authority puts it that it was said to be four hundred feet high, as though there was some doubt, even, as to this figure," interposed Captain Ringgold, who had come forward and heard part of the conversation. "There is no law that compels you to believe either of these stories, and you pay your money, etc. That is the place where it stood without much doubt, and it was formerly an island, connected with the land by a causeway now."

"That point on the other side of the eastern harbor is the Pharillon," the pilot interjected as the commander was looking about him.

"What in the world is that?" asked Scott.

"It is a place where the fishermen have a grate built in which they keep a fire at night to attract the fish," replied the captain of the ship. "It seems to have been built out so as to reach the deeper water. It is an extension of Point Lochias, and the entrance to the eastern harbor was between this and the Pharos. An attempt was made to open this port, called the New Port in ancient times; but it was so choked up with sand and mud that it was given up. It never was a good harbor, for there are many rocks at the bottom which sometimes extends too near the top."

"We can see the whole city from this place," said Louis.

"You can; and that is the reason why I asked the pilot to come here. The greater part of the city lies between the two harbors. Run down by the Governor's Palace, Pilot," continued the commander; and when the Maud had reached this point, he ordered him to stop her. "All the territory on which the arsenal and palace stand appears to have been an island. From the city to the island, Ptolemy I., or his son Philadelphus, built a causeway called the Hepstadium."

Scott and Morris both applied their hands to their jaws as though they had been broken.

"Not a very hard word if you divide into hepta, seven, and stadium, the eighth of a Roman mile, or about seven hundred feet, which was the length of the causeway. This great embankment has been enlarged to its present width by artificial filling, and by natural deposits brought in by the sea on both sides. You can see that the greater portion of the city is built on it."

The steamer went ahead again, headed down to the bight of the harbor. There are several shoals in this bay where the water was only six to nine feet deep; but the pilot skilfully avoided all of them, steering as nearly as the depth would permit for a tower on the shore.

"It is quite a pretty place on shore," said Mrs. Belgrave, pointing to a village of country houses, with pleasant gardens around them.

"Very pretty indeed," replied the commander; and Scott thought he knew why he was on the forecastle when most of the party were seated on the velvet cushions of the standing-room. "This is Ramleh, and it may be regarded as a sort of summer resort. On the hill is the summer palace of the Khedive. The rich people of Cairo and Alexandria have country residences here, where it must be cool in the hot weather. They have their Long Branch and Cape May here as well as those of New York and Philadelphia; and it is not a new idea here, for abreast of that tower you will find the ruins of Cleopatra's palace, and farther along those of the Ptolemys."

"But what is the tower?" asked the lady. "Is it an old windmill?"

"Hardly," laughed the commander. "It is called a Roman Tower, perhaps because it is believed by those who understand such matters that it was built by the Arabians. If anybody knows what it was erected for, I am not of the number, and I am unable to tell you anything about it, though I have inquired of those who ought to know."

"You have been here before, Captain Ringgold?"

"This is the fourth time I have been here; and the last time, near that Roman Tower, so called, stood another monument of the past, the famous obelisk known as Cleopatra's Needle. I do not find in any of my books the reason why it was so designated, and it may be that it received this name because it was located near her palace. It is a work of art covered with hieroglyphics which I did not stop to read. One of the last acts of the Khedive Ismail was to present this monument to the city of New York, where it was set up in Central Park, the expense being paid by William H. Vanderbilt."

"I have often seen it," added Mrs. Belgrave.

"The people of Alexandria, both native and foreign, were filled with indignation at this act; and they vented it vigorously as they saw it lifted from the place it had occupied for two thousand years by American machinery, and conveyed to the vessel which had been specially built to convey it to its destination. It was regarded as a piece of vandalism, and it nearly caused a popular outbreak. Tewfik, then Khedive, regarded the gift of his father as binding upon himself, and sympathy with him prevented a violent disturbance."

"Didn't we see another in London, Captain?" inquired the lady.

"And another in Paris?" added Miss Blanche; for all the party on the forecastle were listening to the commander.

"You are both right," replied Captain Ringgold. "The one in London is on the embankment, close by the Thames. It had lain for centuries by the side of Cleopatra's Needle. The one that adorns the Place de la Concord was presented to Louis Philippe, king of France, set up in 1836, after five years' labor in getting there, by Mohammed Ali. It is the Obelisk of Luxor, and you are likely to see the place where it came from. It was erected by Ramses II., or Sesostris. I believe there is another one in Rome."

"There are twelve more of them there," said Louis.

"Twelve of them!" exclaimed the captain. "Where did you find that out?"

"In Hare's 'Walks in Rome,' in the library."

"I am afraid we did not all do our duty faithfully in Rome if we failed to see them."

"I saw some of them; and I remember that I pointed out one of them to Miss Blanche."

"I was just going to say that I had seen one in

Rome, but I was not quite sure that it was there," added the fair maiden.

"I have seen so many things I cannot remember them," said Mrs. Belgrave.

"You will recall them when you get home, and enjoy them all the more when you have nothing else to think of," replied the commander. "The obelisk in London is only seventy feet high."

"But one I saw in Rome was a hundred and four feet high," added Louis. "I read about them in Hare, and most of them were brought over by Roman emperors, and I think the three you have mentioned are the only ones that have been moved from Egypt in modern times."

"Where shall I go now, Captain?" asked the pilot, who had been an attentive listener to all that had been said.

"I think there is nothing more in this section for us to see from the steamer, though we shall visit Ramleh by train at another time. You may go around to the other harbor, approaching the shore near Bab el-Arab, and following it as near as you can back to the ship," replied the commander.

There was nothing worthy of note on the narrow neck of land between the harbor and Lake Mareotis, though the captain pointed out the Arab gate, the workshops at El-Meeks, and the Maud reached the ship in time for dinner.

CHAPTER XVI

A RAINY DAY ON BOARD THE GUARDIAN-MOTHER

THE climate of Alexandria, and of the Delta generally near the coast, differs essentially from that of the rest of Egypt; for in winter it frequently rains, one authority says almost every day. When the tourist party "turned out" the next morning, which was Wednesday, December 6, as the calendar on the mainmast in the cabin indicated, Sparks and Sordy, the stewards, informed them that it was raining quite hard. They found it so themselves when some of them went on deck.

Louis went to the captain's cabin, and found him busy with his papers, for the business of the steamer was conducted in a very methodical manner. Felix McGavonty had been appointed captain's clerk at the beginning of the voyage, and had served as such since. It required very little of his time, and the place had been given to him so that he might hold a position on board, and to soften the wear against his pride of entire dependence. But his office was not a sinecure; for he had something to do every day, even when he was on board of the Maud, and sometimes he had all he wanted to do when not engaged with the party.

"You are at work early in the morning, Captain Ringgold," said Louis, after they had passed the morning greetings.

"I have been at work about an hour, for my clerk is absent," replied the commander.

"Then I will not disturb you," added Louis, as he walked to the door.

"I have about finished my work; I have made the entries on the daybook, and I will let Felix post them when he returns. Sit down, my boy, for I want to see you," interposed the captain.

"Didn't Felix come back last night?" asked Louis, somewhat astonished.   "I was tired and went to bed early.

"He has not come back yet; but I do not feel at all alarmed about him, for I have found that he has the ability to take care of himself as well as you can."

"But where is he?   I supposed he would only follow the Mussulman visitor to some hotel, and come back in the evening, if not earlier."

"I don't think Ibrahim was particularly well satisfied with his visit to the ship, and it may be that he has found it necessary to make some new combination," the commander suggested.   "If Felix were alone, I might have been troubled about him, for he speaks no language but his own, and might have got into difficulty. But he has John Donald with him, who appears to speak and write Arabic readily, though of course I am no judge of his ability, except as I have seen that he makes himself understood in speaking to Turks, Moors, or Arabs."

"I think that Don, as we all call him on board of the Maud, is a very honest man. He is a Scotchman, and he is very well educated, and is posted in history and geography. I have lent him books, and he spends his spare time in reading. More than all, I believe he is an upright and conscientious man."

"I am very glad to hear you speak so well of him, for I was thinking of giving him a better place during our stay in Egypt than that as second engineer of the Maud, for in that capacity he will have next to nothing to do," added the commander. "His knowledge of the language of this country will make him very useful to us, especially if we are compelled to keep the run of the movements of 'His Highness.'"

"I shall be glad when we get away from the Mediterranean Sea, for then we may hope to be entirely away from that villain," said Louis warmly.

"Forewarned, forearmed, and I do not feel much concerned about the machinations of the Moor," replied Captain Ringgold with a smile. "I don't know but that I rather enjoy the excitement of playing this game with him, as one who understands it delights in a game of chess."

"I did not take that view of the matter," added Louis, amused at this new phase.

"I do not feel at all alarmed for the safety of any of my passengers, and I have not at any time; if I did I should be inclined to alter the course of our voy-

age. If your mother and the Woolridges were aware
of the exact situation, they would compel me to abandon the route as originally planned. I have run
away three times from this Mohammedan humbug,
and I am not disposed to do it again. Our principal
business, aside from travel and sight-seeing, is to
be on the watch for the Pacha and his agents, and to
guard just as carefully our momentous secret, and keep
it confined to the four who have it in their keeping."

" We all understand that if the secret should come
out, the voyage would or might be broken up, and no
one in the ring would be willing to bring about such a
catastrophe," replied Louis. " But what do you suppose has become of Flix ? "

"Of course I can form no idea. I told him not to
follow Ibrahim to Cairo, and I am satisfied he would
not go there; that is all I can say about the matter," replied the commander as the breakfast bell
rang.

At the table Mrs. Blossom was very persistent in
her inquiries as to where Felix was; but the captain
warded off her questions, unwilling to permit Louis to
do so, fearful that he might tell too much. All the
commander would say was that he knew where the
absentee was, as he had sent him on an errand; and
he told no lies about it.

The party bemoaned their fate in being obliged to
remain on board on account of the rain, for all expected to go on shore and " do " Alexandria that day.
The captain told them that they had better make up

their minds to submit with good grace to their impris-
onment, for even if it cleared off before noon, they
would not be able to go on shore in the afternoon, for
they could not travel about the city with anything
like comfort.

"Why not?" inquired Mrs. Belgrave.

"Because the effect of a smart shower in the town
is about the same as an inundation of Nile mud, and
the streets are almost impassable in some parts of the
city. The place is a strange mixture of the Oriental
and Occidental. The native sections are not paved,
are mostly filled with huts and shanties, and on such
a day as this the streets are not passable for ladies."

"Is the whole city like that?"

"No; on the contrary, the European quarters are
paved, lighted with gas, and contain plenty of shops,
cafés, and three theatres; but the difficulty would be
in getting there. Our custom-house official says it
will soon clear off, and the sun will dry up the streets
before night. This afternoon we may be able to open
the Conference again on the upper deck."

The Conference was not just what they wanted
when they had expected to go on shore; but they
made the best of the situation, and in a short time
they were singing in the boudoir, and appeared to be
as happy as children when they have found a new
play in-doors if kept in by the weather. The commander was with them; but about eleven o'clock the
harmony was disturbed by the entrance of Felix, who
was well plastered with mud from head to foot.

"Where in the world have you been, Felix McGavonty?" almost shouted Mrs. Blossom, as the wanderer halted at the door.

"Ye're quite right, Grandma, for I haven't been out of the wurruld at all at all; but in the wurruld, I have been over a dale of it for a schmall b'y of eighteen," replied Felix; and the good woman wanted him to call her mother, but he sometimes compromised by calling her grandma, which she did not like at all.

"That don't answer my question," protested the lady. "I asked you where in the world you had been?"

"And I tould ye's I hadn't been out uv ut. I didn't fale quoite aisy in me moind whoile the professor was talkin' to us, and I joost thought I'd mahke a bit up a thrip over to Cilicia, and have a bit uv a schwim up the Cyndicus to Tarsus, where St. Paul, lahng loif to 'im! was born and lived for a whoile, though the professor didn't tell us about that. I troid could I foind anything of Cleopathra sailin' up the river wid that foine barge, which must have been nairly aiqual to the eight-oar barge of the owner of the Gairjin-Mudther; but sorra one bit of it cud Oi foind."

"You are fooling me, Felix, for Cleopatra died from the bite of a p'ison snake two thousand years ago. But I am glad you went to see the early home of St. Paul, and I hope you will be more like him than you are now," replied the excellent woman, who

discovered the hitch in the chronology, but had no
idea that Tarsus was on another continent. "I hope
the commander will take us all to the birthplace of
St. Paul."

The fiction of Felix had set the party to laughing
in a mild way, but the reply of Mrs. Blossom, so very
innocent, rendered their mirth uncontrollable.

"I don't see what under the canopy you are all
laughing at," added the worthy lady, as she looked
from one to another of the baker's dozen.

"I only came to the door to show myself, so that
you could see just how much Nile mud is lying loose
about the streets of Alexandria," continued Felix,
dropping his brogue when he realized that the diversion had saved him from any further questions on
the part of the devoted woman. "If you will excuse
me, I will put myself into a more presentable condition," and he hastily retreated from the door; and
what he had done in showing himself was only his
way of reporting to the commander that he had
arrived.

"What under the sun were you all laughing at
just now, Mrs. Belgrave?" asked the companion of
that lady, as soon as Felix disappeared. "What ter-
rible blunder have I made now? Didn't I know that
Cleopatra was dead and gone long before I was
born?"

"You were quite right so far as Cleopatra was concerned; but Felix was jesting with you when he said
he had been to Tarsus, and all the rest of the com-

pany understood it, though you swallowed it like a sugar-coated pill.   Of course no one but you supposed he had been to Tarsus; for Cilicia is on the other side of the Mediterranean Sea, five hundred miles from Alexandria at least," the owner's mother explained.

"Why didn't you nudge me, Maud, and tell me that I was making a fool of myself? I begin to think I don't know enough to travel with this party," replied Mrs. Blossom.

"If you should talk less, the party might take you for the wisest of women," suggested her friend.

"A body can't hold her tongue all the time, and I wasn't brought up that way. I am almost sorry I came on this trip," added the mortified lady.

"You talk as well as anybody when you confine yourself to subjects that you understand; but you speak of matters on which I think it is prudent to be silent.   All on board respect you and have the highest regard for you."

"But Felix loves to tease me," suggested the motherly widow of Ezra Blossom.

"And you love to tease him, Sarah," added Mrs. Belgrave with a smile.   "Why can't you fall in with his humor, and not insist upon hugging him, and trying to make him call you mother?"

"And he called me grandma to-day!" exclaimed the troubled lady.   "He isn't a bit like Louis."

"We can't all be alike, and if Louis did not like to have me treat him like a mother I should not do so.

Felix is as good a boy as ever lived, and it is about time for both of us to cease treating him and Felix like little boys, for they are eighteen years old, and boys of that age do not like that sort of endearments."

The singing proceeded; but the commander very soon excused himself on the plea that he had business in his cabin; and no one presumed to question him. He found Felix and Don on the main deck, not far from the boudoir, where they were waiting for him, the engineer with a huge bundle under his arm.

" I am glad to see you on board again, Felix," said the commander, giving his hand to the amateur detective. " You both look as though you had been through a war with the Nile mud."

" That is just what we have been through; and my feet are wet to the bones, as Louis puts it in French," replied Felix, as he looked over his garments.

"Have you been to Cairo?" inquired the captain with a smile.

"No, sir; you told me not to go there."

" Where have you been? "

" To Ramleh."

" That is not far off; and I thought, as you did not come back last night, that you might have gone to Rosetta."

"Not till this morning; but the Abdel Kadixie, or whatever his name may be, led us a long chase, and finally brought up at Ramleh. I stopped in the city to buy a suit of Oriental togs for Don John, as you ordered me to do."

"Then he may go and put them on; and you may change your wet clothes for dry ones, and then report in my cabin with Louis and Scott," said the commander, as he started for his private apartment.

CHAPTER XVII

THE TRANSLATION OF THE ARABIC LETTER

WHEN he came out of the boudoir, Captain Ringgold found that the sun was shining brightly, and the black clouds were rolling away where they would be dried up in the airs of the Libyan desert. The party were so anxious to go on shore after their confinement of over a week on board the ship, that he changed his mind, and decided to gratify them in the afternoon. He called Felix back, and authorized him to announce his intention to the party when he summoned Scott and Louis to his cabin.

Felix changed his dress and went to the boudoir, where he contrived to call the ones wanted without attracting the attention of Morris, who was not wanted. His announcement was very favorably received by the party, and the one whose presence was not desired happened to be busy playing dominoes with his mother.

"What's up, Flix?" asked Scott, when they reached the main deck.

"You must tell Félipe to have the Maud ready for this afternoon, and then come to the captain's cabin," replied Felix, as he led the way to the room indicated; and Scott appeared there a few minutes later.

"As you are aware, our detective has been at work since yesterday afternoon, and I have called you to hear his report," said the commander, as he settled himself in his easy-chair.

"I am all ready to report, though what I have t - tell is of no great importance, and I can finish my yarn in ten minutes or less," replied Felix. "We dogged Ibrahim through various streets, into three hotels, and watched him in about half a dozen *cafés* for six hours."

"I wish to inquire in the beginning if you have allowed the Moor to see and identify you?" asked the captain.

"We looked out for that, for I thought it possible that he might recognize me, though he had hardly seen Don John, if at all, for he was in the fireroom of the Maud when we saw the most of him in the skirmish with the Samothraki. I sent Don into the *cafés* to look him over and see what he was driving at. He showed himself to the Moor, but he made no sign of recognition."

"Go on," said the commander.

"Don said Ibrahim looked as though he was study-ing up something all the time, and hardly took any notice of what was going on around him," continued Felix. "About nine o'clock in the evening he left the last *café*, and we followed him to the railroad station, which is just outside of the fortifications."

" What station was it ? "

" *Gare de Ramlé* was on the sign.   That was French, but I knew it was the Ramleh station.   Don bought the tickets, and we went to Ramleh, taking care to keep out of sight of Ibrahim.   We followed him to a building on which was the sign ' *Pension Beau Séjour*,' if you know what that means, but I took it for a hotel, and we went in."

" It means a boarding-house, and you were not far out of the way."

" We waited outside for a while before we went in; and I saw Mr. Ibrahim go up-stairs with a candle in his hands, and I concluded that he was going to bed. The woman in charge spoke English, but she looked at us rather suspiciously; but I had not been in the mud then, and I believed that I looked respectable, and I took the trouble to show her that I had plenty of money in a careless way, and she was as polite as a basket of chips then."

" Very polite, no doubt," said the captain with a smile.

" I bought a couple of cigars for Don, for he smokes and I don't; and while he was puffing at them, I took a seat by the landlady, and proceeded to pump her to the best of my ability, and found out all I wanted to know.   I won't take the time to tell how I worked it, but I was a polite as two baskets of chips, and she told me all she knew.   Mr. Ibrahim was a merchant from Rosetta, very rich, and had to leave early the next morning for his home.   I informed her that we were going to Rosetta, and asked her to call me in season for the train."

"Was there a train from there to Rosetta ? " asked Captain Ringgold.

"Yes, sir, but not from the station where we had come in."

"Then it has been built since I was here."

"I saw the road on the map in my book, and it runs along by the seashore nearly all the way," added Louis.

"We took a double-bedded room, and went to Rosetta early in the morning, dodging Ibrahim all the time. When we got there we saw him take a boat and go off to a small steamer which we identified as the Fatimé. Don asked some questions about her, and we were perfectly satisfied it was she. It rained hard in Rosetta, and the mud here is nothing to what it is there. I suppose the merchant from Rosetta went on board to take counsel of his employer; at any rate, the Fatimé is not more than twenty-five miles from Alexandria," said Felix in conclusion.

"You have brought important information, Felix, and you have done your work well," added the captain.

"I have made up my account, and I will return the balance of the money you gave me, sir," continued the detective, as he handed a paper to the commander, and produced his portemonnaie.

"The account is all right, and you may retain the money, for I may have occasion to call on you again for similar services," replied the captain as he took a letter from his pocket. "But I expect you to keep an account of your expenditures on such duty and report to me."

"Every farthing shall be accounted for. But we did not find out what this heathen was driving at when he came on board of the ship."

"And you don't even know who or what he is aside from what seems to be proved, that he is an agent of the Pacha," suggested Scott, who had not taken part in any of the proceedings in relation to the Mohammedan visitor.

"But we do know who and what he is," replied the commander with a smile; and he called upon Louis to repeat his description of the scene in the boudoir the day before, whereat the listener was very much amused.

"But that is not telling who or what the fellow was that could not speak French till he was afraid he was going to be shot," said Scott.

"Do you remember a certain Moor who was kept a prisoner on board the ship?" asked the commander.

"I ought to remember him, for I lassoed him in the water when he was trying to escape in the harbor of Hermopolis," replied Scott.

"Ibrahim Abdelkhalik, as he calls himself now, is the same person," the captain announced.

"Captain Mazagan!" exclaimed Scott, jumping out of his chair. "I don't believe it!"

"Perhaps you would not believe it if he should

come into this room this minute," said the commander. "I could hardly admit to myself it was he when the boys had identified him."

"Who identified him, I should like to know? I saw this visitor alongside the Maud, and he did not look any more like Captain Mazagan than he did like me," returned Scott somewhat excited.

Both Louis and Felix explained in what manner and by what marks they had identified him, but the captain of the Maud seemed to be still sceptical.

"I have no doubt on this point," said the commander as he opened the letter he had taken from his pocket, which proved to be the one in Arabic. "Now ask John Donald to come to my cabin, Felix."

While the detective was absent Scott expressed again his doubts in regard to the identity of Ibrahim and Captain Mazagan. But he admitted that he had seen him only as he saw a score of other Mussulmans about the ship, and had taken no particular notice of him, while the others had carefully studied his form and features in the belief that he was the Moorish captain.

"He may have been about the same height, but his face as I recall it was quite different," said he.

"Of course he was fixed up for this visit by a change of dress, and he had done all he could to alter his face and expression," added Louis.

"I have been in Paris several times, and have spent many months there," interposed the commander. "Without my experience in that city I should have found it more difficult to believe that our visitor was Mazagan.   The detectives there have a marvellous skill in disguising themselves.   I mean those in the employ of the police department, and not merely those who figure in private service, and are represented on the pages of the French detective stories of Gaboriau and Boisgobey."

"I have read some of those books," said Scott.

"So have I, though I do not regard them as very profitable reading," continued the captain.   "A friend of mine had occasion to employ one in the public service after his room had been robbed in a house where I was also lodged.   I saw the official at the first interview my friend had with him, and he looked like a tall and rather spare man.   He believed he knew who the thief was from the character of the work he had done, and the manner in which he had entered the room.   Without going into the details, which were more interesting than any story I had read, I saw the detective a second time, when it became a rather difficult affair to satisfy my friend and myself that he was the person employed.   His complexion was entirely changed, he wore a full black beard instead of a grizzled mustache only, and he was a large man with a corporation.   The same night he brought to our rooms the watch, money, and valuable jewellery of my American friend, though he took them away with him after they had been identified, for use at the trial of the robber whom he had arrested, and who was afterwards convicted."

"You ought to tell that story to Felix, Captain Ringgold, for he enjoys such stories," said Scott.

"Not at present," replied the commander as the amateur detective entered the cabin followed by Don.

The change in the appearance of the engineer was almost as great as that which Mazagan had wrought in himself. He had washed himself thoroughly, trimmed his beard, and put on his new clothes. The costume was completely Turkish, while the one he had worn on his excursion with the Milesian was of a mongrel character. The color was a bluish gray, and he looked like a Mohammedan gentleman, though there was no finery of any kind about him. The Arabic letter was handed to him, and he was asked if he could read it.

"Without the least trouble, though I don't think it was written by an Egyptian," replied Don, explaining some peculiarities about it.

"I don't care who wrote it; I only wish to know what it is all about," added the commander.

"I will write out a translation of it," suggested the engineer.

"Do so; and take a seat at my desk," said the captain, as he rose from his chair, giving it to Don, and providing him with paper and pens.

The letter was evidently not a scholarly production, for the engineer translated it very readily, and it was not supposed that he was skilled in the language of the Koran. In ten minutes he had finished his work, and handed the letter and the translation to the captain.

"I am very much obliged to you, John Donald," added the commander.

"And I am very much obliged to you for this suit of clothes. I should not have bought such a rig out of my own money, sir," replied Don.

"I have given it to you because I wish to employ you while the ship remains here as an interpreter, and if you do not object, you will go with the party to Cairo and up the river; and I shall give you extra wages for this service."

"Thank you, Captain; I will do the best I can wherever you put me;" and he left the room.

The commander seated himself in his chair again, holding the letter in Arabic and the translation in his hand. The three young men were very impatient to know the contents of the epistle, and they thought the captain was very slow in his movements. After he had glanced at the Arabic, he read the English version, as follows : —

"ILLUSTRIOUS CITIZEN OF THE GREAT REPUBLIC, —

"Your reputation and that of the magnificent young nabob who voyages over the world with you has gone before you, even as the dawn precedes the rising of the sun, and its brilliancy has penetrated the gloom of my sombre palace, where I lie helpless on my couch, unable to see any one except my doctor and nurse, or I should open wide the doors of my palace to receive you and the illustrious members of your company as my guests for as long a period as it would be your pleasure to honor me and my domain with your illustrious presence in Cairo.

"Sick and disabled as he is, your humble supplicant is richer than His Highness the Khedive, and as the radiance of your illustrious fame penetrates the shadows hanging around my couch, I am moved by the desire to serve you, and render happy your visit to Egypt. By the favor of Allah I am possessed of a steamer on the Nile at Boulak, large enough to be the dwelling place of your illustrious party for three months, which I humbly tender without price for the use of your illustrious party for as long a time as you will honor me by using it.

"This letter will introduce to you my servant, Ibrahim Abdelkhalik, who will be the bearer of your reply to my darkened chamber, and he will also be your dragóman for the journey. Allah be with you.

ABDALLAH."

CHAPTER XVIII

AN EXCURSION ABOUT ALEXANDRIA

"Bully for Abdallah!" exclaimed Felix, who had perhaps been more interested in the translation of the letter than any other of the number present, as the commander finished the reading of the epistle, and cast both papers rather contemptuously on his desk.

"This is thinner than water," added the reader. "I am inclined to believe that the inventive powers of Captain Mazagan have given out."

"But if he had been smart enough to send another person with the letter instead of bringing it himself, the result would have been different," suggested Felix.

"I don't think it would," replied the captain.

"If we had not discovered the Fatimé in the offing, you might not have suspected any mischief," argued the detective.

"But I should not have accepted the offer of an unknown Egyptian to furnish us with a steamer for a trip up the Nile," protested the commander. "Probably if the letter had had a more scholarly translator than the second engineer of the Maud, the missive would have sounded a little more Oriental, and some of the repetitions would have been saved; but we have the substance of it, and it indicates a shallow trick on the part of Mazagan, and we should have been simpletons to be taken in by it."

"I suppose Mazagan has gone on board of the Fatimé to report the failure of his plot to the Pacha," said Felix.

"I doubt if the Pacha is on board of her," replied the commander. "I hardly believe he would be cruising about the Mediterranean for months on such a mission as that in which he has been engaged. More likely he has given Mazagan the use of his steam-yacht to do the business for him, for he must have affairs at home which require his attention. But there is the gong for lunch, and we will drop the subject for the present."

At two o'clock the Maud was ready, and the party went on board of her. Don excited considerable attention in his new costume; and Captain Ringgold introduced him as the interpreter, for they all knew him as one of the engineers of the little steamer. But French was quite as useful as Arabic in the better parts of Alexandria.

"You must land at the custom-house," said the official on board. "You must give up your passports, and they will be returned to you at your consul's office, or sent to Cairo."

The commander had provided for this formality by announcing at lunch that the passports would be needed. They had been provided for the entire party before they left New York, bound in a blank book

with a morocco cover, with plenty of leaves for the
visé. In addition each book contained the photograph
of the bearer, pasted on the inside of the cover. The
pilot was still on board of the ship, and the fasts were
cast off. A few minutes brought the little steamer to
the walled enclosure in front of the custom-house.
The tourists landed and entered the building, and
their first business was in the passport office. These
documents were given up; but the polite official said
they were not necessary, as the port physician and
the officer on board the ship had fully explained that
the steamer was a yacht, and those on board of her
were a pleasure party.

No luggage was brought on shore, and there was
therefore none to examine, the officials politely declin-
ing to look into the satchels of the ladies. The
examination of the baggage of those who land is generally quite minute, tobacco, cigars, diamonds, and
weapons, firearms especially, being the articles particularly sought for. Taking Don with him, the commander left his charge in the waiting-room, and went
out to look for a suitable vehicle for the party. For-
tunately he found a wagonette large enough for the
whole of them, which seemed to be in waiting with a
swarm of other vehicles for the arrival of a large
passenger steamer seen in the offing.

As soon as the party came out of the building, led
by the captain and Mrs. Belgrave, they were assailed
by a noisy crowd of drivers and donkey boys, who
were even more persistent than New York hackmen

of an earlier date than the present, for the latter have greatly improved in manners, and perhaps in morals.

" *Mush durak!* " shouted Louis at the boys, as he conducted Miss Blanche toward the wagonette. " *Imshi!* "

" Do you speak the language of these people, Mr. Belgrave ? " asked the fair maiden, astonished to hear him address the crowd.

" Only a few words which I picked out of the guide-book."

When the commander had seated his lady, the driver pointed to a place at his side, and Louis handed the young lady up to it, and placed himself at her side. The rest of the company seated themselves according to their own preferences, and were ready for a start, when a well-dressed man in European costume touched his cap to Louis, and asked if a *commissionaire*, or guide, was wanted. The owner referred him to the commander.

" You speak English very well," replied he to the man's question.

" I am a Maltese," answered the guide. " My name is Paul Comino; " and he passed a card to the inquirer.

" What is the price per day for your services ? "

" Seven francs."

" Half a day ? "

" Five francs; " and he did not seem to be able to divide seven into two more equal parts, which is generally the case with these persons in other cities.

He was engaged without requiring a better division of the fee, and took his place on the steps of the carriage, which was arranged like an omnibus. The captain told him they wished to visit the principal sights of the city, and left it to him to arrange the order of his going. He instructed the driver, who proceeded along the new quay, at the head of the harbor.

"The names of these streets are all printed in French!" exclaimed Mrs. Blossom, as she looked over the map in the hands of Mrs. Belgrave, to which those who had them had all opened. "I can't read a word of them."

"I shall be happy to translate for you, Madam," said the professor. "This is Custom-House Street;" and he continued to announce the names of streets and buildings given in French, till the carriage stopped at an opening in the fortifications, inside of which they had been riding for some distance.

They passed through, it and soon came to a vast Arabian cemetery, with its curious tombstones; but as they had visited several of them more imposing in Constantinople, they were not much interested in it. A little later the driver stopped near a pillar in the field, and the party alighted at the request of the guide.

"This is Pompey's Column," added the professor, translating from the map.

"Is that what they call it here?" asked the captain.

"It is; and it is put down in French as '*Colonne Pompée.*'"

The tourists walked to the monument, and the guide told all he knew about it. It was the only important relic of antiquity left in the city. It stands on a hill covered with rubbish and ruins, and is a single shaft of red granite from Assouan, up the Nile, 67 feet high, but the column is increased to 104 by the pedestal. It is nine feet in diameter at the bottom, and a little short of eight at the top. It is supposed that there was originally a statue on the cap.

"I suppose that is the monument of General Pompey, who was murdered here when he escaped from some fight in Rome," said Mrs. Blossom; and Mrs. Belgrave immediately nudged her, intimating that she had better say nothing.

"Not at all, madam," replied the professor. "It was erected by the Roman prefect Pompeius, in honor of the Emperor Diocletian, called 'the unconquered and the defender of the city of Alexandria,' as stated in the inscription."

"I don't quite like the name, for in my school days it was called Pompey's Pillar," said the commander. "There was a piece in the reader I used, the old 'American First Class Book,' the best work of that kind that ever was compiled, about it, and an interesting account of the frolic of a party of British sailors who visited it. They took it into their heads to climb to the top of it. They flew a kite over it, lodging the string on the cap, by which they hauled up a larger line, and by this in turn a rope large enough to bear the weight of their bodies. They all mounted to the top, and drank a bowl of punch there. That is all I can remember about it."

"In the Mohammedan cemetery above us stood the Serapeum," said the guide, as he pointed to the spot, when he found a chance to speak. "It contained the Alexandrian Library, which was burned."

"What's the Serapeum?" asked Uncle Moses, though he was well versed in classic lore.

"It was a building said to have four hundred columns around it," replied the professor, as the guide did not answer. "The great library was founded by Ptolemy I., and increased by his successors. It is said to have consisted of 400,000 volumes in the time of the next Ptolemy, and afterwards increased to nearly or quite a million; but the figures are not reliable. These were not such books as we have now, but were large manuscripts and parchments and rolls. In the time of Julius Cæsar it was destroyed by fire; but it was afterwards largely replaced, and a mob of fanatics nearly destroyed it again.

"It was in 641 that the Caliph Omar captured Alexandria, and the work of destroying the library had begun centuries before; but he completed the destruction. Perhaps the story told of him is true, for it coincides with Mohammedan ideas. He declared that, if the books were in accordance with the Koran, they were not needed; if they were not, they ought to be burned, and he gave the order to commit

them to the flames. An ancient but foolish story
says that the Arabians found books enough to heat
the baths of the city for six months. You cannot
believe all you read or hear."

At the request of the captain the vehicle descended
to the canal, which, after Sultan Mahmoud of Turkey,
is called the Mahmudiyeh Canal. From the vehicle
the party could see Lake Mareotis beyond it.

"That lake was filled in former times from the
Nile by means of canals like the one before us. The
water irrigated the land around it, where vineyards
were cultivated, from the fruit of which an excellent
white wine was produced, celebrated in the classics
by Horace and Virgil. Some wine-presses hewn in
the rocks are still to be found. This lake formed an
inland harbor in early days, which brought a great
commerce to the city, as did also the other harbor.

"This lake lies eight feet below the sea-level, and
much of the fertile region around it was also lower
than the salt water. The water in Mareotis had begun to subside when the English, besieging Alexandria, cut a canal through from the main harbor, and
the salt water flowed into it, inundating and destroying about one hundred and fifty villages. Mohammed
Ali did all he could to repair the damage, by bringing
fresh water to this locality. That for domestic and
other uses is brought by this canal, filtered and distributed from a point outside the Rosetta gate."

"Place Mohammed Ali," said the guide to the
driver.

The carriage passed through the Pompey's Column gate, and entered the city within the fortifications. Turning to the left the party reached Ibrahim Street, which was followed; and the last part of it began to look like a European city. At the end of it they came to the square, in the centre of which is an equestrian statue of him for whom the locality is named. The figure is sixteen feet high, standing on a pedestal twenty feet above the ground. The place also contains two fountains, and is beautified with trees and plants.

"What is the population of this city, guide?" asked the captain.

"It is 200,000, one quarter of whom are Europeans; it used to have half a million," replied the man.

The wagonette was then driven through some of the principal streets in the most densely populated part of the place, on the isthmus between the two harbors, as far as the governor's palace. The party found enough that was new and strange to keep them interested. The excursion terminated with a ride out at the Rosetta gate, by the Christian and the Jewish cemeteries, to the shore of the eastern harbor. They looked with little interest upon the ruins of the palaces, with nothing like a building remaining, and then crossed the city to the landing-place, where the Maud was waiting for them.

At dinner the commander announced that they would proceed to Cairo the next day.

CHAPTER XIX

ANOTHER AGENT OF THE MOORISH ENEMY

THE commander thought the party had seen enough
of Alexandria, for there is not much there to interest
an American, unless he is an antiquarian, and wishes
to study the ancient history of the place.   Our tourists
had seen about all the specimens of the ruins, which
were mostly detached blocks of stone.   Pompey's
Pillar was really almost the only monument of the
past, and the guide-books do not recommend a stay of
more than a single day in the place.

"Captain Ringgold, what little I have had to do
with the money of Egypt has perplexed me not a
little," said Mr. Woolridge.   "I have plenty of circular notes, besides a letter of credit; but I have no
idea of the value here of an English pound, or a
French twenty franc piece, and I have a supply of
both these coins in gold."

"Both are current in Alexandria and Cairo; but
for small amounts you will have to use the Egyptian currency, especially the copper," replied the
captain.

"I could not make head nor tail to the money when
I looked it over in the books," added Louis, who sat

opposite to the New York magnate. "The 'States-
man's Year-Book' gives one thing and Baedeker
another."

"Doubtless you will find the latter the more intelligible," replied the commander. "The value of the
Egyptian unit varies at different times and in different
places. This unit is the piastre."

"But I bought another Baedeker to-day," said
Louis, taking the book from his pocket. "This is
Upper Egypt, and I happened to open to something
about the money, but I have not had time to read it,"
and he passed the book to Captain Ringgold.

"I see," said he, after he had looked in the book
where the owner had opened it for him. "The government of the Khedive has recently issued new gold
and silver coins, and these are now the only legal
currency all over Egypt; and this quite agrees with
the Year-Book. The unit in use still is the piastre.
The Egyptian pound contains one hundred piastres,
or one thousand millième. According to the United
States standard," and the speaker consulted his
standard diary, "the Egyptian pound is worth $4.943
of our money. A piastre is therefore 4.94 cents,
or five cents, as nearly as you can make it, and a
millième is one-tenth as much, or half a cent."

"That makes it plain enough," added Louis.

"But how much is a piastre?" inquired Mr. Woolridge.

"The hundredth of a pound, or five cents of our
money," replied the commander. "The gold coins

are the pound and half-pound; the silver coins are of the value of one-fifth, one-tenth, and one-twentieth of a pound; and all these pieces have Arabic names which none of us could possibly remember. There are also, I find, three nickel coins, half a piastre, or two and a half cents, two millième, or one cent, and one millième, or half a cent. You will know these three last by their size, I think."

"I understand the whole thing perfectly now, Captain, and I am much obliged to you for your lucid explanation," said the New York magnate, who seemed to be delighted that he had solved the mystery.

"But there is more of it, which will be useful to you up the Nile," continued the commander. "Copper coins are still in circulation up the river, of the value each of half and a quarter of a millième."

"That is coming down to a pretty fine point if a millième is only half a cent," laughed the New Yorker. "By the way, Mr. Belgrave, what does millième mean?"

"A thousandth, sir," replied Louis. "The thousandth of an Egyptian pound."

"The half-millième piece is also called the two-para coin, and the quarter the para. The latter is one-eighth of a cent, and the former a quarter of a cent of our money. These names come out of the old system, and the copper is used only by tourists for bakshish."

"But wouldn't an American be ashamed to give

even to a heathen a perquisite of the eighth of a cent?" laughed Mr. Woolridge.

"Our countrymen are generally altogether too prodigal in their 'tips,' and these infinitesimal coins will give them a needed lesson."

"The coat fits, and I put it on," added the magnate.

"Up the Nile you will be beset before and behind and in swarms by the people, and you will have to carry some pounds in weight of these small copper coins for them; and you may be even compelled to use the toe of your boot in getting rid of them," said the captain, rising from the table. "I will meet you on the upper deck to arrange for the trip up to Cairo."

The commander took a thick red book from a case, and went on deck, where Mr. Boulong saluted him, and said another Mohammedan wished to see him, and was on the forecastle of the Maud. He preferred to meet him there, and went over the side, calling Felix and Louis to follow him.

The new visitor was dressed in full Turkish costume, precisely as Ibrahim had been. He was not so tall as Mazagan, and his full trousers seemed to be too long for him. He was as polite and deferential as his predecessor had been.

"Good-morning, sir," the captain began. "I am exceedingly busy this forenoon, and have little time to spare."

"I don't speak ze English," replied the stranger.

"Here, John Donald! Speak to this person in Arabic," called the commander to the second engineer, who was seated on the rail. "See what he wants."

Don obeyed the order; but the visitor did not speak Arabic.

"I am French," he added in that language.

"See what he wants, Mr. Belgrave."

"What is your business with Captain Ringgold, who is very much occupied at the present time?" asked Louis.

"I have a steamer at Bûlâk, and I learn that your party wish to go up the Nile. I can furnish you with the steamer and everything required for the excursion," replied the stranger.

"Then you have gone into the steamboat business, Monsieur Ulbach," said Louis.

"That is not my name," replied the man; but he was startled by the remark, and was very much confused.

"Excuse me, but we have met before. Your trousers are too long for you, and I believe they are the same as those worn by Mazagan when he visited the ship on the same errand that brings you here," said Louis.

"You seem to have recovered from the wound I gave you in Zante, Mr. Ulbach, and to have escaped from your prison," interposed Felix, who had been the first to identify the French commissionaire they had seen in Athens. "You spoke English when we met last, though it was a beggarly English."

"TUMBLE 'IM INTO HIS BOAT, DONALD!" Page 179.

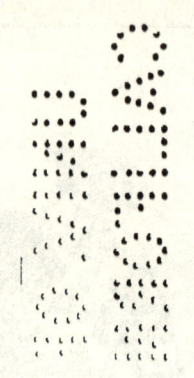

"This is the detective employed by the Pacha, and his agents here seem to be ready for business again, Captain Ringgold," added Louis.

"You can return to your steamer at Rosetta, tell Mazagan we have our eyes open, and that he had better sail for Mogadore at once. Tumble him into his boat, Donald!" replied the commander, as he started on his return to the ship.

Don took him by the collar and threw him over the rail into the boat by which he had come, and Louis and Felix followed the captain. The affair seemed almost like an every-day incident, and no one was at all disturbed by it. The commander hastened to the upper deck where the party had already assembled, and seated themselves in the armchairs. He had brought the red book with him, which appeared to be "Bradshaw," containing the railroad time-tables for the whole of Europe, as well as for Algiers and Egypt.

"The railroad information in Baedeker is not quite up to date, and it does not give the time of starting. The time taken for the trip to Cairo has been reduced to three and a half hours, distance a hundred and thirty-one miles. We are too late for the morning train, which leaves at nine," the captain began, referring to his book. "The next is a slow train, which takes about eight hours, and we must leave by the express train which goes at quarter-past four, and makes the journey in three hours and twenty minutes, arriving at seven thirty-five."

"That is very fair time for this country," added Mr. Woolridge.

"I am going on shore this forenoon to engage a steamer if I can for a trip up the Nile. It will not be a very large one, and the less baggage we have the better. I do not presume to dictate what the ladies shall wear, but I will say that they will be subjected to considerable heat in the middle of the day, though not above 80°, while the temperature will fall somewhat in the evening, and at sunrise will drop as low as 50°, or even lower. You must be prepared for these changes, for I should be sorry to have to work Dr. Hawkes too hard on the excursion."

"I have looked up the maladies of the Nile, and I think your direction will cover the ground. I will see that proper medicines are at hand," said the doctor.

"Chloe the stewardess has been up the Nile with a party, and she can tell you better than I can what you will need. For the gentlemen, ordinary suits will be enough, with a dress suit, for not a little visiting is done on the river between parties in steamers and dahabeahs; and we may have to present ourselves before some distinguished person, native or foreign. What the masculines need and have not got we will provide at Cairo. Now you will need all your time for packing, and I will go on shore," the commander concluded.

He. landed, and went to the Place de l'Église, the office of Messrs. Henry Gaze & Son, where he engaged the steamer Karnac, of nineteen berths. Of them also he procured the tickets for the railroad journey, and a conductor would be sent on board in the afternoon to take the entire charge of the party. This was more than he expected to obtain, though the company had travelled in Europe on the tickets of this tourist agency.

At three o'clock in the afternoon the Maud conveyed the party and their baggage to the shore by the custom-house. The trunks had to be examined, though rather as a matter of form. Most of the males, and four seamen the captain had decided to take with him, had each a revolver in his pocket, which might have occasioned some trouble, but their persons were not searched. The conductor declared that the sailors were not necessary; but the commander, keeping his own counsel, insisted on taking them. He knew not what trap the Pacha's agents might spring on him, and he deemed it advisable to have a body-guard with him; and he believed that with ten available fighting men he should be ready for any emergency.

The seamen were dressed in their best uniform, and each had his kit, so that they excited quite as much attention as the members of the party. In leaving the custom-house they found the usual throng of donkey-boys, carriage-runners, and a multitude of others. The conductor had provided two wagonettes, but it seemed to be almost impossible to reach them so persistent were the crowd each with his own specialty.

"Clear a path for us, Knott," said Captain Ring-gold to the leading man of the seamen.

"Heave ahead, my hearties!" shouted he, as he led the way through the rabble; and when they were obstinate, the sailors tossed them aside without ceremony.

Even the more respectable of the throng, the hotel men and those wishing to be employed as dragomans, were not spared. The men saw the party seated in the vehicles, and then hung on them where they could find places.

The party reached the station, not far from Rosetta Street, where they had been before. The cars were the same as in England and France, in compartments. Only first and second class passengers were taken on the express trains. The fare was a hundred and seventeen piastres, first-class, and seventy-eight second, not quite six and four dollars. The sailors lent a hand in putting the baggage, which had come by a wagon, into the station. The conductor attended to it, and in due time the train started The sailors went second-class, but the best places in the first-class compartment had been engaged for the party; and they all set themselves to the business of looking out at the windows to survey the strange, but not very interesting scenery. The conductor announced all the objects of note, and told all that was worth knowing about the various localities.

CHAPTER XX

On one side of the train could be seen Lake Aboukir, and on the other Lake Mareotis, which the tourists had viewed before from the shore of the canal. It was some distance from the railroad, but the road was washed by it during the inundation. The sails of the freight boats on the canal were in sight, and the travellers were much interested in observing the long strings of loaded camels moving on the embankment which confined the water to its bed. They had all seen camels before at Algiers, but they were still a novelty.

"This is Damanhur," said the conductor as the train made its first stop. "It is thirty-eight and a half miles from Alexandria, and the train has made not quite thirty-one miles an hour, which is very well for Egypt. Napoleon marched his army by this route in July, and his men suffered severely from the heat and drought. You can see the minarets of the town."

The two compartments occupied by the tourists had a connecting door, and when the conductor had any-thing to say he stood between the two, so he could be heard in both. As the train advanced the country was more highly cultivated, more trees were in sight, and they looked with interest on the tamarisks, a flowering evergreen. Cotton was cultivated here. When the train stopped at a station on the Rosetta branch of the Nile, the passengers got out to stretch their limbs after two hours of confinement, and some visited the restaurant, where they found that their French money was available.

From this point the views from the windows became even more novel and interesting, for the train follows the Rosetta branch all the rest of the way to Cairo. Water-wheels for the purpose of irrigation were turned by what are here called buffaloes, donkeys, and more rarely by camels and by steam. The canals, built as in Holland, are flanked by dikes to protect the land from undesired inundation; and these are the roads of the region, in use by processions of camels, donkeys, and people on foot.

Tanta, within an hour and a half of Cairo, contains about sixty thousand population, with many fine looking buildings, such as mosques and an extensive palace of the Khedive, and is noted for its three annual fairs. It pays to stop there if one has time enough. The mosque of the most popular saint in Egypt is here. He was born in the twelfth century at Fez, and is said to have been a person of great strength, which causes him to be invoked when great power is needed to save a sufferer. His tomb or catafalque, covered with embroidered red velvet, is magnificent, though the temple that contains it is not yet finished.

It is said that two hundred thousand people visit the fair held in honor of the saint, and that a million head of cattle are sold during its session. Pilgrims, beggars, showmen, dervishes, and farmers mingle. It is made a gay occasion at times. As the train approached its destination, views of the mountains which flank the Nile and a glance at a pyramid were obtained. Villas and gardens became more numerous, and the train stopped on time at the Cairo station.

The crowd about the station were not quite so stormy as at Alexandria, and the conductor handed the party over to the commissionaire of Shepheard's Hotel; the sailors assisted in carrying the baggage because the movements of the Egyptians and Arabs were too slow to suit their ideas; and the tourists were conveyed to the hotel in omnibuses. Captain Ringgold had written and obtained accommodations for one week as soon as he arrived at Alexandria, for the hotels are liable to be full at Cairo.

It was Friday when the travellers arrived, and this is the Mohammedan Sunday. The "Big Four" were anxious to take a walk, and see what they could of the Oriental city, and they were in the street before the rest of the party had left their rooms. Of course Don, in his new clothes, accompanied the excursionists, and was ready to go with the young men; but Mr. Hornbrook, the Gaze conductor, volunteered to go with them, and they accepted his services.

As they went out of the hotel they found it was located on the west side of a large square, handsomely laid out, with a pond in the middle of it. There were a theatre and a restaurant within the grounds, which were filled with Orientals and Europeans.

"This is the Place Ezbekiyeh," said the guide. "It was named for Ezbec, a general of Kait Bey, the last of the independent Mameluke Sultans, as they called them then, of Egypt. He was at war with Turkey, and Ezbec beat the Turks and captured the son-in-law of the Sultan of Turkey and his principal general. They built a mosque in his honor here, which does not exist now, but this square bears his name."

"That is all very well, Mr. Hornbrook; but I don't think we have time to listen to any long yarns, for it is almost dinner-time for our party, and we only want to take a look at the streets," said Louis. "We are going up the Nile, and we shall have a Conference every day to talk about Egyptian things."

"What time do you dine?" asked the guide.

"Our party has a special dinner at half-past seven."

"Then you have not much time. Will you take donkeys, gentlemen?"

The four jumped at the idea, and Mr. Hornbrook was instructed to procure them. He shouted "hammar," and about two dozen juvenile Egyptians and Arabs presented themselves, each leading a diminutive donkey. Others in the hands of full-grown men also appeared, and all of them were as vociferous as though it had been the Egyptian Fourth of July, if there is any such day in the calendar.

" Take the boys and not the men, for they are more honest and better behaved," interposed the conductor, when the Americans began to look over the steeds, which were not much bigger than good-sized dogs.

They mounted the tiny beasts, and it seemed to the riders more like an immense frolic than sober sight-seeing, which was the business of the tourists. The rest of the donkey-drivers sought employment else-where; but the streets were full, and the five drivers ran ahead to clear the way, shouting with all their might as though they had a monopoly of the thorough-fares of the ancient city.

The guide told the boys to go into the Muski, one of the busiest streets of the place. It was thronged with people of all nations, but the young Egyptians made an opening for the procession. The crowd gazed at them, even the Europeans, to whom they were no novelty, and evidently believed they were on a jolly lark. But the sights in the street soon began to at-tract the attention of the four, and they opened upon the guide, who rode the fifth donkey, with a volley of questions. A man with a box of coins in his hands was rattling them as if to attract custom.

" What is the matter with that fellow ? " asked Scott.

" He is a money-changer, and that is the way he makes his business known. But you had better not change your coins with him ; for there are plenty of counterfeit piastres, and he will cheat you out of your eye-teeth if you don't know the pieces well."

" There are plenty of carriages here, Mr. Hornbrook, which I did not expect to see."

" Plenty of them, but they are not convenient in going about the narrow streets of Cairo. The donkeys are better, and the boys will make a path for you through the crowd. Some of the carriages employ a boy when needed for this purpose."

" What is the price for a carriage here ? "

" There is a tariff of prices, but these drivers evade it when they can. The fare is about the same as it is in Paris : a franc to a franc and a half for a short drive, and two to three francs for half an hour, and twenty francs for a whole day."

" Why do you say francs instead of piastres ? "

" Because business with Europeans is about all done at the stores and hotels in francs, and strangers talk in francs," replied the conductor, laughing.

" A piastre is five cents, we found out this forenoon on board of the ship, and I suppose there are about four of them in a franc," suggested Louis.

" Very nearly ; four piastres and two millième make a franc."

" What are they doing in there ? " demanded Scott, stopping his donkey in front of a shop with an open front. " Is that fellow with a knife in his hand going to cut up the one in front of him ? "

" That is an Arabian barber's shop, and the man with the knife, which is a sort of razor, is shaving the head of the other," replied the conductor, laughing heartily. " But they will cut your hair, and charge you about two and a half francs for the job, which is robbery."

"The women here are dressed just as they were in Constantinople, and veil their faces the same," said Felix, as they started again.

"They are Mohammedans here, and they follow the fashions of that sect, which seems to be no fashion at all, for they don't change the style of their garments. A young man may wear his grandfather's clothes without being out of fashion," added Louis.

"There is a Turkish beauty," said Felix, indicating a woman, veiled as closely as the others, who was so fat she could hardly waddle, though a portion of her rotundity was no doubt owing to the flowing robes she wore.

"To be stout is one of the points of beauty with Mohammedans," said Morris.

"Some of these buildings are really very fine," said Louis, as they halted when several camels obstructed the street. "I see that about all the houses have the bay window in the second story, as they do in Constantinople."

"You have come too late to see the Dancing and the Howling Dervishes to-day, for this is Sunday," said the guide.

"I don't want to see any more of them, for I had enough of that sort of thing in Constantinople. But it is quarter-past seven, and it is time to go back to the hotel," said Louis, as he turned his donkey; and the drivers faced about and ran ahead again in the opposite direction. "Now how much have we to pay ?" he asked as they dismounted at the hotel.

"One piastre for such a short ride, and a bit of backshish is usually given to the boy," replied the conductor.

"Five cents!" exclaimed Louis. "That is ridiculous;" and he gave each of them a double piastre, a silver coin, of which he had obtained a supply.

The boys seemed to regard this sum as princely, bowed with all their might, and began to jabber about something which no one could understand except the guide.

"They want you to engage them for your next excursion," interpreted the conductor; but Louis declined, and they entered the hotel.

It seemed to have been already noised about that one of the four boys in the yacht uniform of the Maud was a millionaire, and the guests were evidently trying to ascertain which he was. The manager, Herr Gross, informed Louis that the dinner was ready, calling him by name; and the mystery was solved.

The dinner was a most excellent one, and it was disposed of with a complimentary zest after the long afternoon and long journey. The commander announced at the close of the meal that he had requested the professor to give the party something of the history of Cairo in preparation for the sightseeing in which they were to engage.

"I promise not to be long in doing so," said the

A STREET SCENE IN CAIRO.   Page 190.

learned gentleman, as he rose from his chair, with an apologetic tone and manner. "Egypt, you will remember, was subdued by Cambyses, the son of Cyrus, king of Persia, five hundred and twenty-five years before the Christian era. The Babylonians are said to have founded Old Cairo, at the most southern point of the town, and this was the headquarters of one of the three Roman legions stationed here during the sway of Rome; A.D. 638 the place was taken by the Caliph Omar. The victor started for Alexandria, and some discord crept into his camp, threatening an insurrection. Then he concluded that the city by the sea was too far from the centre of his newly acquired domain to be the capital. He had left his tent standing near Old Cairo, and he returned to it; and here he began to build a city. I have not time to follow the history in detail till, in 1517, Selim I., Sultan of Turkey, gained a victory here, and entered Cairo. But Tuman Bey, the last of the Mameluke Sultans, gained possession of the city very soon. In turn he was driven out, captured, and executed the next day.

"Since that time the city has been merely a provincial capital. Napoleon remained here with his army for several months. When he went on his Syrian expedition he left General Kleber in command; and he was assassinated in 1800. The French could not hold their own here, and were compelled to surrender. In 1805 the Pacha caused the massacre of the Mamelukes, the last scene of that kind in Egypt. The

English name of the city, as well as the French, Caire, comes from the Arabian word Kahira, or Masr el-Kahira. That is all I have time to say now," the professor concluded, and the party left the room.

CHAPTER XXI

SOMETHING ABOUT CAIRO AND CAMELS

THE commander suggested that the professor had made his account of Cairo very brief, and there was much more that might be profitably said of it, though so far as the historical portion was concerned, none of the party were antiquarians or archæologists, and only the salient incidents were digestible. When the company had assembled in the private parlor provided for them, as no one cared to go out in the evening, the conversation turned very naturally to the subject uppermost in all minds.

The conductor was a gentleman, and he had been invited to dine with the tourists, and had come with them to the parlor. He was a very well informed man, and his occupation had required him to be thoroughly instructed in regard to the history, manners, and customs of Egypt; and he also conducted parties through Syria, Asia Minor, and Turkey in Europe. In fact, he was a walking guide-book to the Orient in all its phases. But the commander was not disposed to have the party listen to a set discourse from him, and proceeded to draw him out by questions.

" What is the population of Cairo, Mr. Hornbrook ? " asked Captain Ringgold, as he noted on a card suggestions for other questions.

" It would be impossible to tell exactly the population of Masr el-Kahira, as the Egyptians call it, though they generally use only Masr, which means 'the victorious,' for every nation has its vanity," replied Mr. Hornbrook with a smile; "and judging by some Americans I have met here, America is not without it. That reminds me of a story I heard one of them tell."

" Let us hear it," puffed Uncle Moses, who had eaten a very hearty meal.

" Probably it is a 'chestnut' with you."

" Tell the story," added Dr. Hawkes.

" An American with more than his share of the national vanity was looking at Vesuvius in a state of eruption, and a Neapolitan was speaking of the volcano as one of the wonders of Italy. 'It's a pretty smart volcano,' replied the American; 'but we've got a cataract over in our country that would put that fire out in less than two minutes.' "

The anecdote received the tribute of a hearty laugh, for things American were highly appreciated at just that time by the party.

" You have larger cities in America than Cairo," continued the conductor.

" We don't know whether or not we have till you tell us the population of the capital of Egypt," said the commander.

"As I was saying, it would be impossible to tell exactly what it is. One of your census-takers would find it difficult to make his way into many Mohammedan residences; for strangers are not admitted to an interview with the lady of the house, and those in charge do not always tell all they know about the domestic arrangements. Some think such a visit would relate to taxes, and they are shy about answering. But the population of Cairo is estimated at 400,000; and I don't believe it would fall below that if an accurate census could be taken."

"Then we have seven cities that are larger, three of them having over a million inhabitants each," added the captain.

"America is a great country," replied the conductor.

"I think you must be an Englishman," suggested the commander.

"No, sir; I am a German, though I have changed my name from Hornbach to Hornbrook, because people in England, where I lived many years, would not give the Hanoverian German pronunciation to the word, and called me Hornback, which seemed too much like a scarabæus."

"Who's he?" asked Scott.

"If you have studied any hieroglyphics, you have often seen a beetle among the figures, which represents the sacred scarabæus of the Egyptians. Ptah is the greatest of the gods of this ancient country, and is pictured as a beetle, because this god is the organizing and motive power of the universe."

"What has that to do with a beetle?" inquired Scott.

"The beetle here, and some elsewhere, puts its eggs in a ball of mud which it rolls along the ground, increasing its size till it is as big as the bug itself, and when it reaches a soft place it buries it. This work is done by the insect with its hind legs, backing and kicking at the ball all the time. The warmth of the soil hatches the egg, and the beetle is born, organized, and put in motion. From this peculiar operation the creation of the world and all that therein is has been symbolized by the beetle, or scarabæus, which is the learned name for it. The Arabian name is khepera, which you will please to remember," said Mr. Hornbrook, with a suggestive smile.

"Very good, sir; and you had a very good reason for translating the last part of your name into English in England," added Captain Ringgold. "I suppose you have all noticed that Egypt is in the same latitude as the northern part of Florida and the southern part of Louisiana."

"I had not noticed it," said Mrs. Blossom.

"Hold your tongue, Sarah!" whispered Mrs. Belgrave in her ear.

"Then you had better consult your atlas. The longitude is about the same as Asia Minor and the western part of Russia," continued the commander. "I suppose Cairo has a mayor and aldermen like other cities," he added facetiously.

"Hardly; but it has a governor, for it is the residence of the Khedive and his ministers.   It is the largest city in Africa, or in the Arabian countries of the world.   Of the 400,000 population of the city, something like 21,000 are Europeans," replied Mr. Hornbrook.

"As many as that?   Which country has the most here?" asked the captain.

"Italy; and there are 7,000 Italians here.   The Greeks come next with 4,200, and there are 4,000 French people here, while the English have 1,600. The police of the city consists of three hundred men under a proper officer.   They are a very efficient body, and some of them are Europeans, mainly Italians; and you may go to the worst places you can find in Cairo without danger."

"How do carriages, of which I see there are a plenty, get about in these narrow and crowded streets?" asked Dr. Hawkes.

"They don't get about much except in the wider streets," replied the conductor.   "When they attempt it they have runners to clear a path for them.   The best way to go about here is with the donkeys, of which you will always find a great number about the Ezbekiyeh, which is the court end of the town!   They are better than we see in Europe."

"But they are very small," said Louis, glancing at Uncle Moses and the doctor, who were nudging each other and jarring their ponderous bodies with half-suppressed chuckles.

"Very well put, Mr. Belgrave," laughed Dr. Hawkes.

"Do you think the donkeys would fit my case, Mr. Scarabæus ? "

"You don't weigh over three hundred, and some of them will carry that," answered the guide, amused at the name applied to him, but taking it in good part. "There is some difference in the size of them."

"As there is in the size of men. Perhaps I shall experiment with a good-sized donkey; but I weigh only about two hundred and a quarter."

"I will agree to find a donkey that will carry both you and the gentleman who sits next to you."

"I am afraid the 'last needle would break the camel's back,'" chuckled Uncle Moses.

"You are a good-sized needle Uncle Moses," suggested Louis.

"That's a hint, my boy. What is the reason the twins cannot be provided with camels for their steeds," added the squire, as he was sometimes called.

"I doubt if you would like your steed," said Mr. Hornbrook. "There may be lots of poetry in a camel to you Occidentals; but when you come down to the hard pan of fact on the back of one of them, you will think you are riding in a tip-cart over a corduroy road — I have been in America."

"In Brazil or Peru, I suppose you mean," said the commander gravely.

"I mean the States."

"That is better, and we can understand you. I was about to say before, when I suggested that you

must be an Englishman because you called our country 'America,' that Patagonia and Terra del Fuego
were included in that grand division of the world,
and I think it is necessary to be a little more definite.
However, 'the States' will do very well, for not even
the Dominion of Canada can be included in this statement.   In England most people mean the United
States when they speak of America.   You were
speaking of camels, Mr. Hornbrook."

"I stand corrected, Captain Ringgold.   There are
two kinds of camels, that with one hump, and the one
with two.   We call the first a dromedary, though that
word is not used here.   He is called a *hegin* in Egypt,
and one that carries freight across the desert is the
gemel.   We have only the former here.   Those to be
ridden have to be properly trained for this use, and
even then one has to get accustomed to the gait of
the animal before he can stand much of it.   The
camel saddle is a wooden frame, from which projects
in front and behind two sticks called crutches.   A
leather cushion is placed on the frame, and the comfort of the rider is increased by the skilful placing on
the frame and crutches of a number of rugs."

"Do we straddle the beast?" asked Uncle Moses.
"My legs are short."

"You do not.   You put your leg over the forward
crutch, just as a lady does on a side-saddle.   Then
the heel of the right foot rest on the instep of the
left.   You have to get used to it, and you soon learn
to better your position.   A sort of howdah may be

used on the back of a camel, as on elephants in India."

"We shall try the howdah on the elephant in India," said Scott.

"For a beginner it is not easy to mount a camel at best; and the animal has a trick of rising while you are getting on, which the driver prevents by putting his foot on the fore legs."

"Do you ride him lying down?" asked Mrs. Blossom, who was promptly checked by her friend.

"I supposed you all knew that the camel is made to kneel when he takes on a burden, either human or goods," continued the conductor, laughing; and probably every one did know except the inquirer, whose reading had been chiefly confined to the Bible, sermons, and the newspaper. "The first movement of 'the ship of the desert' is rather violent in rising, as though it required a struggle, and the intending rider must hold on with might and main at the crutches, or he will certainly be upset."

"I have lost some of my desire to ride a dromedary, though Napoleon did it before me," chuckled the doctor.

"The camel, to speak nautically, gets up stern first, and when he elevates the after part of his body on his hind legs, the rider must lean forward to counteract the motion, and back when he straightens his fore legs."

"Do you mount on the starboard or the port side?" asked Scott gravely.

"On the port, just as you do a horse."

"Then keep your weather eye open tight," added the captain of the Maud.

"Yes, if you don't wish to be thrown overboard. When you get used to it, the walking motion is pleasant, and some even prefer a camel to a horse, though I am not one of that number. But if you crack on more sail, and make the beast trot or gallop, you will wish you were somewhere else."

"This is the first hotel we have visited in Egypt, and I have not yet arranged with the manager about prices," said the commander. "What are the rates here?"

"This and the New Hotel are the best in Cairo, and the prices are high. At the Hotel d'Orient and d'Angleterre, they are more moderate; and the fare is good enough for ordinary tourists," replied Mr. Hornbrook. "As in America — I beg pardon, in the United States — the charge is generally by the day, from three to five dollars in your money, for all items except wines."

"We don't use any," added the captain.

"The hotels in the East, as a rule, are not on what you call the European plan in the States. There is no extra for attendance as in London and Paris; but it is the custom to tip your waiter with two or three francs a week, and his assistant, a native, with a franc and a half. The porter will take two francs a week without scowling, and all of them will accept as much more as you please to give them without feeling insulted. You call your waiter by clapping your hands; and if this does not satisfy you, and you feel that you ought to say something to a native, just call out '*Ya weled*,' 'Come here, waiter.'"

"I think that will do for this evening, though we might talk about camels all night and be interested," said the commander, rising from his chair.

CHAPTER XXII

A DONKEY AND CARRIAGE RIDE IN CAIRO

Before breakfast the "Big Four" were on their feet, and renewed their wanderings in the streets of Cairo. They had been about Mogadore, Algiers, and Constantinople, and the character of the sights was not new to them, though there was much still that was new and strange to them. The middling and the poorer classes of the people were out at this early hour. Their first walk was around the Esbekiyeh, which is a parallelogram with the four corners cut off, less than a quarter of a mile in length, very handsomely laid out with walks, trees, and flowers.

"This isn't bad," said Scott. "Did you bring your guide-book with you, Louis?"

"I did not; but I have a map of this locality near the hotel in my head," replied Louis. "That is the Opera House on the right, and the square in front of it takes its name."

"Twig that woman carrying a baby!" added the captain of the Maud. "She takes it on her shoulders pigback, with the infant leaning over her head. There is another toting the youngster on her hips."

"The babies don't wear any more clothes than they did in Santiago de Cuba, where it was fun to see the boys and girls trying to handle them," added Felix.

"Everybody in the streets seems to have something to say," said Morris; "for about all the men we can see are yelling. I suppose they have something to sell. There is a fellow with a bag of something on his back."

"He is a *sakka*," replied Louis gravely.

"He looks exactly like one, even to the end of his nose," added Felix, who had not the remotest idea of the meaning of the word.

"You remember how they transport wine in Spain?" continued Louis.

"Oh, yes; they pour it right on the back of a donkey, and take it all over the country."

"Correct so far as the donkey is concerned, Flix; but they first put the wine into bags" —

"And what better is that than pouring it on the back of the donkey?" interrupted the Milesian. "Do you mean to tell me here in this great city of Cairo that a meal-bag will hold wine?"

"I did not say a meal-bag, for the sacks in Spain were goat-skins; and that is just the kind that fellow yonder has on his back. They sew them up so tight in Spain and here that they will hold water."

"So will your story, now you have explained what you mean. But what's the use of a water-carrier here like that, when they have water from the Nile all over the city. I see that some of the houses have brass pipes in front of them, where the passers-by can take a drink."

"But you don't see any bar-rooms, for the Mohammedans don't drink whiskey or wine."

"But I saw twenty *cafés* in our tramp last evening."

"They drink coffee and smoke the chibouk, or water-pipe, just as we saw them doing in Gallipoli when we visited one. They sell beer at ten cents a glass; but I fancy their trade in this article is mostly with foreigners."

"There is a woman with a fruit and vegetable stand," said Morris, when they had reached the opposite end of the square. "She looks as though she had a fish-net hanging down from the end of her nose."

"That is a kind of veil, tied around the back of her head, which conceals all her face below the eyes. She has oranges, lemons, lupins, lentils, and such things."

"You might as well talk Arabic, darling, as to speak of lupins and lentils," added Felix.

"You have read your Bible enough to know that Esau sold his birthright, and the consideration was in part this very vegetable you see on that table: 'Then Jacob gave Esau bread and pottage of lentiles.'"

"Mrs. Blossom ought to be here to hear you quote Scripture, Louis. How do you happen to know anything about these things any more than I do?"

"Because I read them up last night after I went to my room; and I looked up lentils on board of the ship," replied the young millionaire. "Lentils belong to the pea family, and are largely used for food in

Egypt and Syria, as well as in some countries in Europe, where they will grow. Pottage is a sort of porridge made of lentils here as it is of various grains elsewhere. In a word, lentils are a sort of bean; and the climate is too moist to raise them at home. Lupins are found with us cultivated as a pretty flower. Here and in Italy the seed is used for food, though they are rather bitter."

"You must tell grandma about this," laughed Felix.

"You should not tease the good lady, for she is one of the best women in the world, though not a graduate of Vassar College. There is the Exchange and the two hotels the conductor spoke about last night; and everything of any consequence seems to be on the Ezbekiyeh," said Louis, as they continued on their way back to the hotel.

Breakfast was disposed of, and the question of the business of the day came up. The conductor was asked what he had to propose. He replied that if he had to show them Cairo in one week, it was necessary to be industrious.

"But we are not antiquarians, unless the doctor and Uncle Moses have a touch of the malady; and we don't wish to dig into every hole and corner. We wish to get a general view of the city, and a closer view of its specialties. We have all been in several Oriental cities, and everything here is not entirely new to us," replied Captain Ringgold.

"Then I think you will need about four carriages,

"HE LIFTED THEM CLEAR OFF THE GROUND."   Page 207.

and we will ride about in such parts of the place as
we can get along with the vehicles, and take in the
other places on foot or on donkeys," replied Mr. Hornbrook.

"Then you will go with us, Mr. Belgrave?" asked
Miss Blanche, who sat next to Louis. "You seem to
know all about everything, and understand whatever
you see."

"I shall be most happy to be with your family,"
replied Louis.

"But we don't want any carriages," interposed
Scott. "The donkeys are what we depend upon for
our locomotion."

The conductor's plan was adopted in part, and three
carriages were ordered. In the first were the commander, Mrs. Belgrave (of course), and Mrs. Blossom.
In the second were the doctor, the lawyer, and the
professor. The last contained the Woolridges and
Louis. Then Mr. Hornbrook shouted "Hammar!"
and a dozen donkeys instantly appeared.

"We want four of them, for Don John will go with
us to manage the gibberish," said Scott.

The conductor selected the animals very carefully,
taking those in charge of boys for the reason he had
given before. The commander, who was looking on,
was greatly amused at the little beasts; and before the
boys mounted, he stepped between a couple of them,
and, stooping down, passed one of his arms around
each of them. Then he lifted them clear off the
ground, and walked off to the carriages with a donkey

under each arm. But he brought them back again, to the great comfort of the boys in charge of them.

This scene called out a tremendous flood of applause on the part of the party and the spectators in front of the hotel. Not every man could have achieved this feat; but the captain was a very powerful individual. The four sailors belonging to the ship were standing near; they roared with laughter, and then broke out in three cheers, in which the boys and some of the bystanders joined. The commander wore a grave face all the time, though he had sacrificed his dignity in a degree for the amusement of the party.

The conductor mounted the box with the driver of the first carriage, in order to direct him. The procession had hardly started before the four donkeys galloped up abreast of them, the riders shouting like madmen, and the boys following at a dead run, yelling at their beasts to keep up the pace. The ladies waved their handkerchiefs at them, and the gentlemen their hats, the commander joining the others. Everybody seemed determined to have a "good time," and gravity was at a discount. The people of all nations stopped to gaze at the spectacle, and saluted the frolicsome party.

The carriage turned in at a street south of the Opera House, the conductor pointing out the French Theatre, the police-office, adding that the place where criminals were executed was in the eastern section of the city, and that they were turning into the Boulevard Abdul Aziz.

"As was," replied Captain Ringgold. "I was in Constantinople while he was Sultan of Turkey; and he abdicated a few years later, and came to a bad end. It was believed that he was murdered or committed suicide. I saw the gentleman one day, and thought he was quite a good-looking man."

"I suppose you have noticed the houses of the magnates of Cairo," said Mr. Hornbrook, whose seat in front permitted him to converse with the occupants of the carriage. "They are all surrounded by high walls, so that only the tops of the houses can be seen from the streets. But the buildings are not so high as you make them in New York and Chicago. Now we are coming to the palace of the Khedive, or, rather, to one of them, for he has several, though this is the principal one, called the Palais Abidin."

"What sort of a man is the young Khedive?" asked the commander.

"People who ought to know more about him than I do say he is affected by what you call 'the big head' in the States. You may meet him about the streets or elsewhere. If you do, you must take off your hat, and bow quite low, for he takes offence, they say, when he is not saluted in the most deferential manner. The domestic arrangements of a Mohammedan family, especially the harem, require these high walls; and, besides, they are very exclusive. You have seen all you can of it. The palace of Ali Pacha, his brother, is next to that of the Khedive, but with a street between them.

" Now we will turn into the Boulevard Sheik Rihan.
On the right is the palace of Bey Mabdul, who is the
public officer in charge of the mosques; and it is
walled in like the others. I could point out the residences of more of the grandees; but it would be the
same old story; you would learn nothing but the
name."

" Don't trouble yourself to do it, for there is nothing in a name in Arabic to us," added Captain Ringgold.

" This is the city canal," said Mr. Hornbrook, when
they came to a bridge. " The old water-works which
supplied the citadel are at the south end of this canal,
where it takes its water from the arm of the Nile between the island of Roda and the main shore. The
new water-works are in a northern suburb of the city.
They include two towers with iron basins, into which
the water is pumped by two engines. Part of the supply is passed through immense filters, and the city is
furnished with the quantity needed through two sets
of pipes, one distributing filtered water for domestic
use, forcing it to a height of eighty feet, and the other
with unfiltered, for sprinkling streets and similar uses,
and it is forced up only thirty feet. Now we come to
the Boulevard Mohammed Ali, one of the principal
avenues of the city."

After a ride of a quarter of a mile more the carriages came to the Place Sultan Hasan; and in this
square the carriages stopped in front of a mosque.
The donkey-riders rode up to the carriages, and re-

ported that they had seen everything there was to be seen, which was not much.   Don knew something about the city, and he translated what the donkey-boys said about palaces and other sights.   The party got out of the vehicles, and the equestrians dismounted.

"This is the Gami Sultan Hasan," said Mr. Hornbrook, when the tourists had gathered around him.

"What's a Gami?" asked Mrs. Belgrave.

"It is a name given to the mosques, and this was erected in honor of the ruler whose name it bears. He was dethroned and assassinated in 1361."

"Let him rest, then, if he has been dead as long as that" interposed the captain, "for the accounts of these Sultans were about all of a color."

"As you please, Mr. Commander," laughed the conductor." "This is the 'superb mosque,' for it is considered the finest existing monument of Arabian architecture.   The lofty building, you observe, has six windows, one above the other, but not along the whole front.   This is the only mosque I shall ask you to enter, unless you wish to see the interior of others; and we will now go in."

The main entrance was on the boulevard by which they had come, though the Sultan had a separate door. In the vestibule they were admonished to take off their shoes, though the ladies compromised by putting over their boots the slippers which were to be had for a consideration.

CHAPTER XXIII

THE CITADEL AND THE TOMBS OF THE KHALIFS

THE straw slippers which an attendant brought looked too small for the gentlemen, and they had begun to take their boots off when another attendant brought some of larger size, and replacing their footwear, they put them on outside. They had been obliged to comply with this requirement before, and it was no new thing to them. The fee for their use was one piastre each, paid on leaving the sacred building, for though the Orientals call the Christians "infidel dogs," they have unbounded confidence in their integrity and honor.

After taking several turns, the party reached the inner court, which is 114 feet long by 105 in width. The interior of the mosque is in the shape of a cross, with pointed dome above. Of course the cruciform shape of the interior has not the same significance as in a church, for the symbol of the Mohammedans is the crescent. The first thing that attracted the attention of the visitors, after they had taken a general view of the proportions of the principal apartment, was two fountains, now in a state of decay, though they still contained much of their original beauty. The one in the centre was much larger than the other.

"What's the use of two of them in the same room?" asked Uncle Moses.

"The one in the middle," replied Mr. Hornbrook, "was for the Egyptians, and the smaller one for the Turks, for in earlier days they kept entirely apart from each other. The two small arms of the cross on each side of us are open for the prayers of the faithful, though the one on the north side of us is really the grand entrance, whose lofty arch and magnificent proportions you observed in the boulevard.

"Now we will pass into the sanctuary," continued the conductor, leading the way. "That arrangement with stairs in front of it is the *mambar*, or pulpit, from which Sultan Hasan sometimes addressed the people."

"One who wants to know all about a mosque, as described in Badaeker, ought to understand Arabic." said Louis. "I have studied the book faithfully, but the technical names of various parts are printed in that language, often with no explanation. The book is evidently prepared by learned men, but they fly too far over the heads of some of us. What is called by one name here goes by another in another place."

"But I am not using any Arabic words without telling what they mean, and I am not responsible for the book," replied the conductor.

"I have no fault to find with you, sir," added the objector, exhibiting the plan of the building in his guide-book. "The place we are about to enter by the door on the right of the *mambar*, which is the pulpit, I judge from this diagram leads to the *maksura*, 'an interesting and majestic structure, which has recently been restored,' and must be very interesting from the looks of the word. But the book says it contains the tomb of Sultan Hasan, and we get an idea what the word means."

"This dome is 180 feet high, and certainly that is majestic," added the conductor.

The party looked over the tomb, and then retired from the mausoleum, or *maksura*. Mr. Hornbrook then told them that the corner on the south contained the rooms of the schools, and the minaret rose from that part of the building, near which was the Sultan's door.

"I haven't got at the *kibla* yet; but there it is, according to the plan, between the two doors which lead to the tomb," said Louis, pointing to the centre of the head of the mosque. "It looks like the place for the president; but as they don't have such an official here, I conclude it is the seat of the Sultan or the grand high priest."

"But you are abusing Badaeker without reason," interposed Professor Giroud. "All these Arabic terms relating to a mosque are explained in the introductory chapters; and this is not the place for the president or the Sultan. The *kibla* is the prayer-niche, facing Mecca. On page 184 you will find all these terms explained."

"Then I beg Badaeker's pardon," replied Louis.

"One easily forgets the names of things in Arabic, and I suppose I did so, for I have looked over all this part of the book."

"I think we must be moving," interposed the conductor, looking at his watch ; and the party followed him.

The use of the slippers was paid for, and they passed out of the building. With what mosques they had seen before, they thought they did not care to visit any more of them.

"I see that old fish story is told about Sultan Hasan, that he ordered the hands of the architect of this mosque to be chopped off to prevent him from building another which might equal or surpass this one," said Louis.

"That's a ' chestnut,' " said Scott.

The party entered the carriages and mounted the donkeys. A little later they came to an open place beyond the mosque, with two more *"Gami"* on the left.

" This is Rumeleh Place on the right, with a fountain in the centre of the circle," said Mr. Hornbrook to those in the carriage.

" Is it a circular square, or a square circle, for they call these places squares, plazas, and the like ? " asked Felix, who had brought his donkey alongside the vehicle.

"You pays your money, etc. Here are two more mosques," replied the guide. "One of them is the Gami Abderrahman, and the other " —

" Have mercy upon us, Mr. Hornbrook!" exclaimed the commander. " These names mean nothing to us. When we are on board of our steamer sailing up the Nile, we shall study up something about the religion of these people; and Arabic words convey no idea to us."

"As you please, Mr. Commander. We are now approaching the Citadel, which is on the hill before us. *Andak!* " said the conductor to the driver, which meant " Stop! " " Here is a narrow and crooked road leading to the fortification, through which the donkeys may pass, but not the carriages. This lane is the scene of the massacre of the Mamelukes by the order of Mohammed Ali. He invited them to a banquet in the Citadel; and when they had entered this passage the gate was closed behind them. Then his Albanian soldiers began firing upon them, and killed all but Amin Bey, who escaped by leaping his horse through a hole in the wall. The horse was killed, but the rider saved his own life; and he was the only one of four hundred and seventy that escaped."

" What in the world did the Viceroy do that for ? " asked Morris.

" Because the Mamelukes wanted to have everything their own way. They expected to rule him while he governed the country, but they made a bad mistake in their man; and that was the last of Mameluke influence in Egypt. Young gentlemen, you can go through this lane on your donkeys if you like. We will meet you near the mosque."

Of course the boys preferred the way indicated, and the donkey-drivers forced the diminutive beasts into a gallop. The carriages ascended by a broad thorough-fare, and soon reached the place indicated in the Cita-del, where they all stopped. The boys soon appeared, and Felix declared they had seen no ghosts of Mame-lukes, though he should have his doubts about going through the lane at midnight.

"This stronghold was built of stone brought from the smaller pyramids, which you are still to visit, in 1166, by Salaheddin " —

"Call him as Scott did in the 'Tales of the Cru-sades,' " interposed Captain Ringgold.

"Saladin, then, if you please. The Arabians say the site was selected because meat kept twice as long here as in the city without spoiling; but you can believe that or not, just as you like."

"I think we may believe that the air up here was pure and clean ; and that is the moral of the yarn," added the commander.

"But it is not a good military position; for the Mokattam Hills on the south command it, and Mo-hammed Ali, when he took possession, compelled the Pacha in command to surrender the Citadel, by plant-ing a battery on one of those heights. In front of you is the Gami Mohammed Ali, called the 'Alabaster Mosque,' which can be seen all over Cairo. Architects don't laud it to the skies, but some think it is a very handsome building. The minarets are especially tall and elegant, and the alabaster on the outside, not all of it blocks, but veneering, gives the structure a very imposing look," said Mr. Hornbrook, as he led the party, who had descended from the carriages and donkeys, towards the mosque.

"We won't go in !" protested the commander.

"Fear not," laughed the conductor. "I shall take you only to the platform of the mosque, for it commands the best view. I had a couple of gentlemen up here the other day who declared that this was the finest view to be obtained in the whole wide world ; and it is now in order for you all to go into ecstasies over it," he added, when he had reached the esplanade. "I don't do so any more."

"It is certainly a magnificent view," replied the commander.

"It is perfectly lovely !" exclaimed Mrs. Belgrave.

"Domes, gardens, and minarets without number!" ejaculated the doctor. "We must come up here again, for I am inclined to agree with the gentlemen who considered it the finest view in the world."

"Worth the voyage to Egypt !" chuckled Uncle Moses.

"Quite a smart outlook," said Scott, rather languidly, as though he did not intend to be carried away by anything Oriental. "It is the minarets and things which make it odd to us. If you could plant one or two of those twenty-story buildings they have just put up in New York City, it would make these Islamites open their eyes."

"But would not add to the magnificence of the view," added Louis.

"There is a palace of the Khedive here, which is quite European," said the guide, "and there are two others within the fortifications."

"I suppose the Viceroy and his family want a safe place when there is any trouble in the city," suggested Uncle Moses.

The party walked around the mosque to the rear, and then descended to the ground.

"This is Joseph's well, two hundred and eighty feet deep. It is square, as you see, and was cut through the limestone to supply the garrison with water, though it is decidedly bad, which was brought to the top by an apparatus worked by oxen half-way down the hole. This is said to be the well into which Joseph was cast, in the Bible."

"Joseph's brethren did not cast him into a well, but into a pit," protested Mrs. Blossom.

"This hole would pass for a pit," replied Mr. Hornbrook. "Saladin's name was Yusuf, which is Joseph in English, and probably the well was named after him."

"Not for Joseph," added Scott.

"Besides, I thought that pit was in the Land of Canaan," persisted the good lady. "Joseph in that well! I don't believe a word of it."

"I don't think any of the rest of us believe it," added the captain.

As the party were in the vicinity of them, they next proceeded to the tombs of the Khalifs. They are on tolerably level ground at the foot of Windmill

Hill, over the lower part of which the road led, and the procession halted on a considerable elevation, which commanded a fine view of the structures on the lower ground. They were mostly partially dilapidated, though the domes and minarets were still to be seen.

"It looks like an Oriental city on a small scale," said Louis. "There are at least a dozen domes and half as many minarets to be seen rising above the old walls and other rubbish."

"Most of these tombs are very large, as you can see. Formerly there were funds provided for keeping them in good condition, and each had officers appointed to take care of them; they and their families resided on the ground. These revenues were confiscated nearly a hundred years ago, and the tomb-mosques have gone to decay," said the conductor. "Some of the descendants of the persons who had charge of them have taken up their abode here, and you will probably have a call upon you for bakshish."

The procession proceeded again; and when they alighted at the tomb of Kait Bey, the most imposing of them all except perhaps that of Sultan Barkuk, the natives appeared. The commander requested the party not to give them a millième, for the more one gives, the greater the demand. The beggars came upon the tourists with outstretched hands. The captain caught the foremost of them by his rags, and pitched him a rod, shouting to them "Imshi!" (begone!) Scott upset a couple of them at the same time, and Mr. Hornbrook laughed till his sides ached.

The lofty dome and the graceful minarets of the tomb-mosque of Kait Bey are very generally regarded as the finest remains on the ground, and they were looked upon with wonder and admiration by all the visitors. They were so enchanted by the beautiful structure that the conductor had to hurry them away.

"The tomb-mosque of the Sultan Barkuk was hardly less magnificent. It has two wonderfully fine domes, and as many exquisitely ornamented minarets. It was difficult for the Americans to imagine that such an imposing and beautiful building had been constructed to commemorate even a dead Sultan."

"The tombs of the Mamelukes, meaning the Sultans of this line, are not far from here; but we have not time to visit them before luncheon," said Mr. Hornbrook. "Next to nothing is known in regard to them; and though there are stately ruins among them, they do not compare with what you have just seen. We will return to the hotel now."

"I think we can omit the Mamelukes, as we have had the best specimens of the whole thing," added the commander. "We should like something a little different for this afternoon from buildings of any kind."

Mr. Hornbrook promised to govern himself by this direction, and the carriages and donkeys returned to the hotel.

CHAPTER XXIV

A VISIT TO BÛLÂK AND ITS MUSEUM

By the time the party had assembled for lunch Mr. Hornbrook had arranged the programme for the afternoon, and he was inclined to hurry the tourists in order to make the time for the excursion the longer.

"You have taken a very rapid survey of the city to the east and north," said he, as he took his seat at the table. "This afternoon we will go to the western part of the city. We crossed the Ismailiyeh Canal when we came from the railroad station, which is on the other side of it. We will go to the westward now, and make a visit to Bûlâk."

"Can we go on the donkeys again?" asked Morris.

"We will let them rest this afternoon so far as we are concerned, for I have ordered the wagonette for this occasion, so that you can all ride together," replied the conductor. "But you will have all the donkeys you want, and camels too, those who prefer the ship of the desert, before we go up the Nile. The vehicle is already at the door."

Not a great deal of time was spent at the lunch, and very little was said, though the table was always enlivened with pleasant conversation at other times.

They left the hotel, and found the usual animated scene in front of the hotel. The donkey-boys were there in full force, including those who had served the boys in the forenoon; and they were greatly disappointed to learn that their services would not be required, for they had been paid very liberally by Louis.

The wagonette crossed the canal, and the party soon found themselves in the midst of more Oriental surroundings than they had observed before, for Bûlâk is the port of Cairo. The streets were narrow, and a couple of young Egyptians volunteered to serve as outrunners, and clear the way. It was also the market for the merchants; and the shore was lined with freight boats from all the sections of the Nile, from Darfur, Dongola, Kordofan, Khartum, and other parts of the south, as well as from various places in the Delta. Here the merchants of Cairo come, generally in the morning.

"You see here more camels than you have in the city," said the conductor, as the driver stopped his horses in a nook in the street.

"What have we stopped here for? I don't see anything worth looking at," inquired Morris.

"There comes a caravan, and our driver thinks we had better keep out of the way of it," replied Mr. Hornbrook, as the head of the camel procession came abreast of the vehicle, and he spoke to one of the men. "This one comes from Darfur, though it is not nearly as large as some that come in; but it has traversed the desert, and in one place they get no fresh water for twelve days."

"And they don't have any ice to cool the water they carry in the goat-skins," added Louis.

"Ice would not last long in the desert. These camels, you notice, are not like those you have seen about the streets of Cairo. They are Bactrians, with two humps, and they carry big loads."

"They are ugly-looking beasts," added Mrs. Woolridge.

"They excite our respect because they are so useful, and can go so long without 'taking a drink,'" replied the conductor. "But, unlike a lapdog, they do not call out the affections. A great many valuable articles of merchandise are brought here, and from this market go all over the world. Gums, senna leaves, ivory, and ostrich feathers are brought here."

"I don't see any ostrich feathers," said Miss Blanche, as the wagonette moved on.

"They are very carefully tied up in bundles, with pepper sprinkled on them to keep the moths out. They come from Kordofan, where the natives bring up ostriches as you do chickens in the States," replied Mr. Hornbrook, directing the driver to stop at a certain point. "We shall see some here."

He called a man, and presently some specimens were brought out for the inspection of the ladies; but they have to be washed and prepared before they are offered for sale in Paris, London, and New York.

"How much do they cost?" asked Louis.

"They are sold by the pound, and you can see that
it takes a great many of them to make this weight;
and the very best of them bring as much as a hundred and fifty dollars of your money," replied the
conductor. "Let them see the best feather you have,
Muley."

He brought out one which had been dressed for
use, and the ladies were in raptures, it was so
beautiful.

"That is perfectly lovely!" exclaimed Miss
Blanche.

"That one is worth twenty-five francs," said the
dealer in broken-down English.

"Will he sell it for that? and is the price he names
reasonable?" inquired Louis.

"It is cheap for it," answered Mr. Hornbrook;
and somewhat to the surprise of the rest of the party
the young millionaire produced his purse and purchased the feather.

"Will you allow me to present it to you?" asked
Louis, as he tendered it to the fair maiden.

"How very kind you are, Mr. Belgrave!" she exclaimed, looking at her mother; and as no objection
was made by Mrs. Woolridge, she consented to receive
it, and the merchant prepared it for transportation.

Scott nudged Felix as they observed the blushes
of both parties to the gift; but nothing in the way of
comments was made by any one. The carriage proceeded on its way, the conductor describing what was
to be seen.

"Below at the *Embabeh* are the dehabeahs used by some travellers up the Nile; but you will have abundant opportunity to see many of them in a few days. There is an arsenal at the north end of Bûlâk where arms are kept, with a machine-shop for their manufacture attached to it; and on the island is a government printing-office, chiefly for the issue of scientific works of all kinds, as well as a paper mill, an iron foundry, and other public institutions."

The party rode about the island for a while longer, and made a short trip to the château and garden of Gezireh, for admission to which Mr. Hornbrook was provided with tickets, as he had been to the mosques and Citadel. It contains suites of apartments for the Khedive, which he seldom occupies himself, though it was used for the entertainment of the invited guests at the opening of the Suez Canal. The rooms were of course elegant; but the party were by this time accustomed to regal apartments, and they were not greatly interested. The garden, with its fountains, kiosk, grotto, and its tropical plants, pleased them more.

Returning to the wagon, they were driven nearly to the southern end of the island, and a stop was made in front of a large building, the Bûlâk Museum, on the bank of the Nile, where it was placed for convenience in landing heavy statues and other relics. They were first conducted to the garden, where the tomb of Mariette was the prominent object. Professor Giroud was greatly impressed when he came to the resting-place of one of the great Egyptologists of his native country.

"Mariette was born at Boulogne in France in 1821. He was liberally educated, and was a teacher in his earlier years. He made the acquaintance of a companion of Champollion, the discoverer of the Rosetta Stone, which afforded a clew to the hieroglyphics, and he turned his attention to the wonders of this country," said the professor. "He was appointed keeper of monuments, and made very important discoveries. This museum was founded by him, and he was its director till his death, eleven years ago. He was the author of one of the systems of chronology I mentioned to you on board of the ship."

"The professor has told you what this place is, and who was its distinguished director, and the position has been filled for the last six years by Monsieur Grébaut," said the conductor. "Through the influence of Mariette a law was passed which forbids the exportation of antiquities of any kind; and this museum was established for their preservation. You will not, therefore, be able to put a mummy or a pyramid in your pocket when you leave.

"But this location was found to be unsuitable several years ago for the institution, and arrangements were made for its removal to the vice-regal palace of Gizeh, on the other side of the west arm of the Nile. This is an immense edifice, containing five hundred apartments, built by Khedive Ismâil for his harem at a cost of a hundred and twenty million francs.

The contents of the museum are now in process of removal. Thirty-one rooms are now completed, and filled with antiquities. You can, therefore, visit only a portion of the institution to-day ; and I advise you to reserve the part on the other side of the river till your return from the tour up the Nile, for you will then be in better condition to understand what you will see there.

"What is left here forms an immense collection, numbering thousands of objects of interest; and if you intend to examine them in detail, you must take a week or a month for the purpose."

"We have seen plenty of these things in other museums, and I don't think we shall care to weigh or measure many of them," added the commander. "Just show us the most noted of the curiosities, and that will answer our purpose. If the doctor or any of the party wish to see more of them, it is easy for them to make another visit."

The objects were all numbered, and catalogues were procured, so that all could know what they were looking at for example : " 409. Limestone coffin of a woman, Ankh ; 160. Coffin in green basalt of a woman named Betaita, both of the Ptolemaic period."

"It is a good thing to have the names of the occupants of these coffins," chuckled Uncle Moses ; "but I don't think we shall find those of any of our deceased relations among them."

"'Tombstone of Entef (Eleventh Dynasty),'" read the doctor, as he pointed to the object. "How long ago was that, Professor ? "

"Over five thousand years, according to Mariette."

"That was some time ago," added Uncle Moses. "Osiris, Orus, Apis, Isis, all seem to be here."

"'Jewels of Queen Somebody, mother of Somebody, found with the mummy of Queen Somebody at Thebes (Eighteenth Dynasty),'" read Mrs. Belgrave, as Mr. Hornbrook indicated a special object, substituting "Somebody" for the proper names she could not pronounce. "How long ago was that, Professor Giroud?"

"Just 3,595 years ago," replied the learned gentleman, consulting his guide-book.

"That is longer ago than I can remember, and I never heard the name of Queen Somebody before, or the other queen either," laughed the lady, as she proceeded to read the list of the jewels. "'Bracelet for the upper arm, adorned with turquoise; a vulture with wings of lapis lazuli, cornelian, and paste in a gold setting; dagger formed of four female heads in gold, with the blade damascened with the same metal.

"'Axe with a handle of cedar-wood encased in gold and inlaid with the name and titles of Aahmes in precious stones; pliable chain of gold, thirty-six inches long, to which is attached a scarabæus with wings inlaid with lapis lazuli,' and so on to the end of the chapter."

"I should think Khedive Ismâil might have paid the debts of his government by confiscating the gold and precious stones in this Museum," suggested Uncle Moses.

"So might England pay off a portion of her national debt by selling off the crown jewels, or the articles in the British Museum," replied the captain. "But that would not do in either country."

"Here is the wooden statue from Sakkara, railed in to keep Yankees from chipping it off," laughed Mr. Hornbrook.

"Or Germans either," added Captain Ringgold.

"All right, Mr. Commander. This figure is called the Shekh-el-Beled, which means a village chief, because it resembles one of these well-fed officials," continued the guide.

"But the man that statue was made for did not weigh as much as Brother Avoirdupois," remarked Dr. Hawkes.

"Or Brother Adipose Tissue," added Uncle Moses.

"This statue, dating back to the early days, say six thousand years ago, proves that the ancient Egyptians knew" —

"Call it four thousand, according to Mariette."

"But it shows that they knew how to sculp in that day," said Felix, who had been giving no little attention for him to the figure. "It is a capital piece of sculptuary."

"Here is the statue of Hathor, the goddess of the infernal regions; but as none of you expect to visit her domain, we will pass on," added the conductor. "Here are models of boats, in which you nautical gentlemen may feel an interest. Some of the craft were used for transporting mummies. Here are the playthings of children, including wooden dolls. Here is a ball, and there are pictures and other objects which prove that the subjects of the Pharaohs played games of ball, though there is nothing to show that they played base-ball. Sometimes one fellow stradlled on the back of another, and played catch and catch with one similarly mounted. Others had a game with sand-bags. Checkers were used then, and bull-fights were known, though not like those in Spain."

"I see scarabæi without number," said the professor.

"No end of them," replied Mr. Hornbrook. "They are found in mummies from which the heart had been removed, and the bug is an emblem of that organ. But it is getting late, and it would take us a week to go through the Museum at the rate you have used some of the time."

The party loaded themselves into the wagonette, and when they reached Shepheard's they were tired and hungry enough to spend the evening in-doors, though the boys said they should take another ride on the donkeys.

CHAPTER XXV

AN OVERTURE FROM THE CHIEF CONSPIRATOR

THE following day was Sunday. Most of the party were glad to have a day of rest, and the ladies were quite worn out by the exertion of the visit to the Bûlâk Museum. Only a fraction of what they examined could be given on these pages, and they saw but a fraction of what there was to be seen, even without the portion removed to Gizeh.

"I am going to protest," said Mrs. Belgrave, when they were seated at the breakfast-table.

"To the government of Egypt?" inquired Captain Ringgold, quite surprised that this lady, who was one of the pleasantest and most amiable in the world, should have any fault to find with anybody or anything.

"No; to the commander of this expedition," replied the mother of the owner of the Guardian-Mother.

"Indeed! And what have I done?"

"You have permitted us to be hustled about this country as though we had but a month more to live, and all Egypt must be explored before the final hour," added the lady languidly.

"Then I must protest to Mr. Hornbrook," answered the commander, turning his gaze to that gentleman.

"I was just going to ask you whether you would go to the pyramids of Gîzeh, to Shubra Village, or the petrified forest, to-day?" said the conductor, with a cheerful laugh on his face.

"But this is Sunday," protested Mrs. Belgrave.

"So were yesterday and the day before, for we have three Sundays in succession here; and very few take any notice of any of them," replied Mr. Hornbrook. "As a general rule my parties improve Sunday in the same manner that they do other days."

"This is the Christian Sabbath, and for one I propose to observe it, wherever I may be."

"So do I for another!" exclaimed Mrs. Blossom, as though she was ready to be a martyr.

"Would you like to go to church?" asked the conductor in a rather cynical tone.

"Can we go to church here? I don't mean to a mosque."

"Certainly you can. The American Mission has services just around the corner, and the English Church is close by," added the conductor.

"I wish to go to the Catholic Church," added the professor with a smile.

"The French Catholic Church is near the Muski; turn to the right at the next street before you come to the City Canal, and it will take you to it," the guide explained.

"I am not particular that it should be French, for in our services the same language is used all over the world, and I should be as much at home in a church in Italy as I should be in one in France," added Professor Giroud.

Mrs. Belgrave preferred to go to the American Mission, and Mrs. Blossom, Captain Ringgold, Uncle Moses, Louis, and Felix went with her. The Woolridges were Episcopalians, and they all went to the English Church. Scott went with the professor, partly for the walk through the Muski, and Dr. Hawkes wished to write some letters. Mr. Hornbrook conducted the larger party to the Route de Bûlâk, around the corner, but would not attend the service, and acted as though he thought that such was wasting time. As the Americans entered, they were somewhat surprised to see the four American sailors from the ship in the church.

There was no service in the afternoon, and after luncheon Louis and Felix went out to walk in the Ezbekiyeh garden. They seated themselves where the crowd of strollers was the thickest, to observe the people of all nations as they passed. This afforded them abundant occupation for some time; for there was hardly anything more interesting to them than to watch the faces and study the costumes of the Orientals.

"Hold up, my darling!" suddenly exclaimed Felix, grasping the arm of his companion.

"What's the matter now, Flix?" asked Louis; but

he was sure that the Milesian had seen something strange or startling.

"Don't you see that couple on the other side of the pond ? " demanded Felix with energy.

"I see twenty couples at least," replied Louis, looking in the direction indicated.

If his eyes were not quite so sharp as those of the amateur detective, he immediately discovered the two persons who had attracted the attention of his companion. One of them was dressed in full Oriental costume, while the other wore a European dress, and looked like a French dandy. He had no difficulty in recognizing both of them. They seemed to be in earnest conversation, and both of them bestowed an occasional glance at the two young men, who were seated alone on a bench long enough for half a dozen.

"Do you make them out now, Louis ? " asked Felix.

"I do; I should know them with half an eye," replied the young millionaire. "But don't make any demonstration, or use any exclamations ; keep perfectly cool."

"It is not easy to be an iceberg in this hot country, when you see the villains who have been hounding us for the last six months; and the wonder is that you and Miss Blanche are not prisoners in a castle in Mogadore," replied Felix.

"I don't think either of us have been within a thousand miles of any such fate," replied Louis with a cheerful smile. "They are not going to lay hands upon us here, with five hundred people within knock-down distance of us. Be as cool as Captain Ringgold always is. I wish he were here at this moment."

"If he were here, those pirates would soon be some-where else. But I am as cool as you are, darling," returned Felix with a smile, and perhaps not as good an opinion of his detective skill as usual. "If you think I am afraid of them, Louis, you are as much mistaken as a chicken in a duck-pond. I was a little startled when I saw them, as you would have been if you had seen them first. They are coming over this way," he added, as he put his hand into the hip-pocket where he carried his revolver.

"I saw Knott and Stoody just now," said Louis, looking about him.

"And there are Lanark and Ball on the other side of the pond," added Felix, both of them alluding to the four sailors who had come up with the party, each with a revolver about him, and all of them old man-of-war's-men who had been in actual service. "I wonder if Captain Ringgold instructed them to keep a lookout for you."

"I don't believe he did anything of the kind, for that would have been a point towards giving away the secret," replied Louis. "The kidnappers are coming over this way; but let them come. Don't say anything more about them."

Felix thought his "darling" was not exactly recog-nizing him in his capacity of a detective, whose special office just then was to protect him, for he was rather taking the lead in the preparations for whatever might ensue from the *rencontre* with the enemy. But he had always followed his friend in everything else, and he was content to take charge of him as a mother does of her baby, whether the subject of his care was conscious of his protection or not.

The Moor and the Frenchman did not act as though they had a mission to carry out, for they sauntered along very carelessly, the latter with a light cane in his hand which he was twirling as though life had no object for him.   Without seeming to care where they went, they wandered around the little sheet of water, keeping in the pathway between the benches and the shore.   The young men looked as though they were utterly unconscious of the proximity of the enemy, and gazed about at the people around them.

Both parties were superlatively indifferent, and on the stage they would have been commended for good acting.   As the pirates or brigands, for both of them had served in these *rôles*, approached the bench where the young men were seated, the Oriental gave a well-acted start, and came to a full stop, fixing his gaze upon Louis.   The Frenchman went through a similar bit of pantomime, and fixed his eyes upon Felix.

It was evident that the performance, whatever it was to be, had actually begun.   Louis took no apparent notice of them, though he could not help seeing that the comedy or tragedy was about to develop itself.   He was entirely satisfied that the villains did not mean to assassinate him, for this would have ruined the hopes of the Grand Mogul. At the same time, he kept his hand on his revolver, imprudent as it would have been to exhibit it.

From the point where he halted, the chief conspirator, his face beaming with the pleasantest of smiles, walked directly up to Louis, and extended his hand to him as though they had been friends for years. The Frenchman went through the same ceremony with Felix, who politely intimated that the Evil One might shake his own paw, and kept his right hand on his weapon. Louis, without reasoning why he was so, was more courteous, accepted the hand of the piratical Moor, perhaps because he was curious to know what particular form the present overture was to take.

"I am very happy to meet you, Mr. Belgrave," said he; and he was artful enough to make his manner correspond with his words.

"I have no doubt of it, for you have always been glad to meet me in order to carry out the purpose for which you are employed by His Highness, the Pacha Ali-Noury," replied Louis.

"I am glad we understand each other so well," continued Captain Mazagan, otherwise Ibrahim Abdelkhalik, who had been the bearer of the letter to the commander on board of the Guardian-Mother. "For a time it puzzled my friend the Pacha and myself to understand how you happened to be ready for us every time we met, and why no notice was taken of the letter of His Highness, Abdallah, delivered on board of your steamer."

"Then you understand the matter now?" queried Louis.

"Perfectly; as soon as it occurred to me that an American was close by the Pacha and myself while we were talking in the cabinet at Gallipoli, it all became plain."

"Then you were very imprudent to talk over your wicked plans almost in the presence of a stranger," suggested the young nabob.

"We were speaking French, and did not dream that any one in the *café* in Gallipoli could understand a word we said. But I have since learned that the young millionaire with a million and a half could speak French as perfectly as he can English," added the Moor.

"You flatter me, though I will not deny that I can get along with the language, as you did in the boudoir of our ship."

"You are too cunning for us, Mr. Belgrave, and I have become weary of trying to do what the Pacha employed me to accomplish."

"Where is His Highness now?" asked Louis bluntly.

"At home in Mogadore, where he was called by his government; and I believe he is in command of the Morrocan army by this time."

"But his steam-yacht is at Rosetta," added one of the intended victims of the conspiracy.

"How well you are informed!"

"We know all about your movements. But **do**

you expect me to believe the Pacha has returned to
Morocco ? "

Instead of answering the question, Captain Mazagan took a letter from his pocket and handed it
to Louis. It was postmarked at Mogadore in French
and in English. He was requested to open and read
it, as it was written in French ; and this evidence
satisfied him that the conspirator had spoken the
truth.

"I am in command of the Fatimé, with orders to
convey any passengers I may have to Mogadore,
where I shall be paid in full for my services," added
the conspirator. "In Egypt you have foiled me
completely."

"Then I trust you will return to Morocco and report
accordingly," suggested Louis.

"But I cannot afford to do that," protested Captain
Mazagan. "I left my steamer four months ago to
enter the service of the Pacha, and he was to pay me
two hundred thousand francs if I succeeded, and half
that if I failed," said the captain.

"Then you had better sail for Mogadore, and accept
the price of your failure," added Louis.

"Not at all ; I have been looking for you, for
Captain Ringgold is an unreasonable and bull-headed
man, and it seemed useless to talk with him, in order
to make what you Americans call a compromise."

"And that is your business with me ?"

"Precisely ; and I think we shall be able to come to
an arrangement."

"I think not."

"I don't ask you to pay me the full amount the Pacha promised me; only the half I was to get if unsuccessful. His Highness will pay me the other half."

"You are a bigger villain even than I supposed, for you are as ready to plunder your friend as your enemy!" exclaimed Louis. "But here comes Captain Ringgold, and you had better make your offer to him."

But instead of doing this, as Louis knew he would not, Captain Mazagan abruptly rose from his seat and disappeared in the crowd, followed by Monsieur Ulbach.

CHAPTER XXVI

THE PROCESSION FOR THE PYRAMIDS

CAPTAIN RINGGOLD had come out to walk in the
Ezbekiyeh with the "Cupids," as the conductor, behind their backs, called Dr. Hawks and Uncle Moses.
He promptly recognized the Moor and the Frenchman,
seated on the bench with Louis and Felix. He was
greatly astonished; but he could say nothing in the
presence of his two companions, who supposed the
two strangers were guests at the hotel, or some chance
acquaintances the young men had made.

In the evening Louis found an opportunity to speak
to the commander in regard to the interview with the
enemy, and he related minutely how it had happened,
confining himself to the facts, without comment upon
them.

"When you came in sight with the 'Cupids,' I
advised Captain Mazagan to speak to you in regard
to his proposition; but instead of doing so he and his
assistant took to their heels and disappeared in the
crowd," Louis concluded.

"You could have given him my answer as well as I
could myself, for you knew what it would have been,"
replied the captain.

"I did not give him a particle of encouragement, and I told him he was a bigger villain than I had supposed even, for he was as ready to plunder his friend as his enemy," added Louis.

"You told him the truth; but I think, if I had not interrupted the interview, that he would have tried to convince you that it would be wise and prudent for you to use your influence to have his proposition accepted," continued the commander. "I am not your guardian or trustee; but so far as I am concerned, I would give up the voyage and return to New York, before I would yield a point, or suffer you to be blackmailed by these villains. Even if there were no principle in the matter, to pay a dollar for immunity from the persecutions of such reprobates is to open a channel for thousands to flow out in the same direction. Perhaps your mother and Uncle Moses, whom this business directly concerns rather than myself, might be induced to pay the money in order to prevent the voyage from being broken up; and it would be immoral and wicked to do so, to say nothing of merely worldly policy."

"You may be very sure that no word of mine will induce my mother or my trustee to do anything of the kind; and I should protest against it," replied Louis vigorously.

"But I think this proposition means something; for it looks as though the conspirators had reached the end of their rope, and are ready to resort to even more desperate measures in case of a refusal, and we must be all the more guarded in regard to traps and tricks," continued Captain Ringgold. "You are inclined to walk with Miss Blanche, and she is as much inclined to these promenades as you are; and under ordinary circumstances there is not the least objection to them. On the trip up the Nile, the steamers lie up at night, and in the evening parties usually stroll about on the shore. You must not wander about with the young lady away from the rest of the party. As I did in the Archipelago, I shall use extraordinary precautions, even without knowing here in what direction to look for an enemy. Be wise, Louis, and don't be too proud to be extremely cautious."

Louis determined to profit by the advice for the safety of the fair maiden; but he felt abundantly able to protect himself even from such desperate foes as Captain Mazagan. The interview terminated, and Louis slept as well that night as usual. The next day the tourists were to visit the pyramids of Gizeh. As the steamer was all ready for her passengers for the voyage up the river, the commander had decided to leave what remained to be seen of Cairo until the return from the First Cataract, which was as far as he proposed to go.

It was emphatically a miscellaneous procession that was drawn up in front of Shepheard's Hotel on Monday morning for the trip to the desert. The weather was mild and pleasant, neither too hot, nor too cool. The wagonette was at the head, ready for its passengers. Four camels stood ready to receive such riders as had the temerity to mount them. Two Arabian horses, saddled, one for a lady, and about a dozen donkeys with their boy drivers, completed the procession.

Mr. Hornbrook was on the ground, impatient at the delay of a couple of ladies who had not yet appeared, for he was a very faithful conductor, and made it a point to expedite all business in which he was professionally engaged, as he termed it. He was standing by the wagonette, which was a Gaze institution; and though he was always very polite and kind, he was evidently vexed at the delay.

" Where are the other two ladies, Mrs. Woolridge ? " he asked.

" Mrs. Belgrave and Blanche have had some difficulty in preparing themselves with suitable dresses for this occasion; but a couple of ladies who are going to the Holy Land will lend them riding-habits, and they will be down in a moment," replied Mrs. Woolridge.

" Great bodies move slowly, but the Cupids are here," added the conductor, " and the others ought to be here."

" Whom do you call the Cupids, Mr. Scarabæus ? " inquired Dr. Hawkes, who had just come up behind him.

" I beg your pardon, Doctor," stammered the guide

" But who are the Cupids ? " persisted the surgeon

" It is a name I had very innocently applied to you and the other stout gentleman."

" Cupids ! " exclaimed the doctor, doubling himself

up as much as his aldermanic organ would permit, and laughing with something more than a chuckle. "Brother Avoirdupois!" he shouted to Uncle Moses, who was studying the structure of one of the camels, "Brother Cupid!"

"Brother what this time?"

"Brother Cupid; our gentlemanly conductor calls you and me 'Cupids!'" exclaimed Dr. Hawkes, doubling himself up and roaring with laughter again; and he was immediately joined by Uncle Moses in a similar cachinnatory display. "Have you found any pin-feathers on your shoulders?"

"We shall need the wings of eagles," replied the lawyer, chuckling so that he could hardly speak. "You must have thrown a dart that pierced the bosom of Captain Ringgold, Brother Cupid."

The commander actually blushed, but Mrs. Belgrave was not present to observe the telltale crimson.

"I noticed that you were very busy studying the build of one of those camels," added the doctor.

"That belongs to my department," interposed Mr. Woolridge. "The camel is a very interesting beast, though he is not so handsome as the horse. He is a big creature, noted for his humps; some have one, and the Bactrians, such as we saw Saturday, have two, and can carry half a ton on the back. These here are often called dromedaries; but some of the writers say they are a different breed. The two-humpers jog along about two miles and a half an hour, take in a bucket of water at a drink, and can stand it for three days without taking another drink; but you should water your camels every day, Dr. Hawkes."

"I will try to do so," laughed the doctor, "when I am within ten miles of an oasis with a spring in it."

"The dromedary is good for ten miles an hour, and can make a hundred miles in a day, if there is a ten-hour law here. Camels don't eat meat any more than the professor does on Friday, and gets along on very little vegetable food. A thousand or more Bactrians may journey across the desert in one string; but it doesn't take another thousand to carry hay and grain for them, for they feed on the meanest kind of vegetables, including dry sticks when greens are scarce.

"They call him 'the ship of the desert;' yet he don't beat to windward in a sirocco, but sticks his nose into the sand and weathers the gale. He is something like the greenhorn who, when a gale came on, and he was ordered aloft, proposed to turn in and call it half a day. He might be called the reindeer of the desert, for he does as much for the Arabs as that animal does for the Laplanders. His flesh is eaten, his milk is made into butter and cheese, his hair is woven into shawls, his skin is tanned, and he furnishes the fuel for cooking, and the fat from the hump furnishes the oil for the lamps. I have got rid of one of my animals, and here come the missing la lies."

The auditors, including not a few that did not belong to the party, applauded vigorously, even to Mr. Hornbrook, vexed as he was at the delay. The two ladies appeared in the borrowed dresses of the Syrian party, and they seemed to have been made for them. Captain Ringgold gallantly assisted Mrs. Belgrave to mount the white Arabian steed that was waiting for her. He had life and spirit, though he was as gentle as a lamb. The commander mounted the other horse, and galloped off with the lady, both proving that they were at home in the saddle.

One of the camels was brought up, and Uncle Moses was the first to "go aloft" "on the ship of the desert," as he termed it. The doctor had "stumped" him to ride on a camel to the Pyramids, which he agreed to do if Brother Adipose Tissue would do the same. It was a mutual challenge, and perhaps neither of them enjoyed the prospect of such a ride, but their pride closed every avenue of retreat. Mr. Hornbrook and the camel driver superintended the operation of mounting, and it produced no end of laughter among the observers. All the guests in the hotel had turned out to see the performance, and it must go on.

"Look out for yourself, Uncle Moses, for that ship will soon get a heavy sea," said the commander as he and Mrs. Belgrave rode up to the scene. "Hold on hard at the life-lines."

The unwieldy animal had dropped his calloused knees on the ground, and the cushioned and be-rugged saddle frame was ready to be occupied. The stout gentleman grasped the two crutches as directed, and put his left knee on the cushion. The next movement

was a difficult one for a man of his obesity, for it
consisted in swinging his right leg over the hind-
quarters of the camel, and dropping it into the space
inside of the forward crutch. It produced a great
deal of laughing among the bystanders, but he accomplished it bravely, though with a mighty effort.

"Hold on with all your might at the crutches, Mr.
Cupid!" said the guide.

The camel raised his stern end, and it looked as
though Uncle Moses would be pitched over the head
of the beast; but he saved himself by lying down on
his forward crutch. Then he leaned back as far as
his heavy frame would permit, as the "ship came
up on an even keel," as Scott stated. Then followed
a volley of tumultuous applause, in which the boys
and the four sailors did the greater part. The hero
of this exploit raised his hat, and acknowledged the
salute that greeted his success, as the second camel
was brought up for Dr. Hawkes.

"You are shaking in your shoes, Brother Cupid!"
shouted the lawyer, happy that he had passed the
ordeal. "There is room in the wagonette for you
though, and you can let one of the Jack tars go
through the sacrificial performance for you."

"Never!" responded the doctor. "I will ride this
camel to Gîzeh, or leave my adipose in the desert for
the vultures!"

He went through the performance very well till he
came to the swinging of the right leg over the forward crutch; but either because the beast started a

little, or because he loosed his hold, he rolled off the
saddle like a lump of lead. The sailors sprang to
his assistance, and " put him on his pins," as Seaman
Knott phrased it.

" That's all owing to the quarter of an ounce which
my weight exceeds that of my Brother Avoirdupois
Cupid," returned the surgeon, who did not appear to
be injured at all. " If I had been as light a body as
he is, I could have done it as well as he did ; " and he
hustled and puffed around to the other side of the
camel, and grasped the crutches again.

" I hope you are not hurt, Brother Cupid," said
Uncle Moses seriously.

" Not the least bit in the world ; my adiposis saved
me. The victory is not yet to the light body," he
replied.

This time he declined to follow the orthodox directions of the conductor, and did not attempt to swing
his leg over the rear crutch ; but, holding on with both
hands at the front crutch, he sprang into the saddle as
he would have seated himself on a high table. His
success was roundly cheered, and he made a humorous
speech to the crowd.

" This is worth more than seeing Egypt," said
Scott.

" But these dignified gentlemen will not perform
for us every day in the week," replied Felix.

Miss Blanche had taken a fancy to ride a camel,
and after Mrs. Woolridge had tried in vain to have
her substitute a horse or a donkey she had consented.

"LOUIS ASSISTED HER TO HER SEAT." Page 251.

But the camel driver had a different programme for a lady, and Louis assisted her to her seat just as he would have done if the steed had been a horse, though he was obliged to lift her much higher; but she was safely mounted, and the crowd cheered again. Louis made easy work of getting into his seat.

The boys and the sailors mounted the dozen donkeys, and the conductor started the procession. The party took the whole thing as a frolic, the introductory scenes leading in that direction. Scott was especially hilarious, and the young men and the seamen yelled forth their delight. The crowd cheered, and it was certainly a lively occasion. First came the commander and Mrs. Belgrave, then the four camels, then the wagonette, and the boys and sailors brought up the rear, all being in high glee.

CHAPTER XXVII

A LECTURE FROM THE BACK OF A CAMEL

THE procession contained no little variety, and it was novel enough to attract the attention of the natives as it passed through the streets. The occupants of the houses could see without being seen, and the tourists knew not how many persons observed them as they were passing. Some of the younger people about the hotel had mounted donkeys, drawn by the hilarity of this portion of the procession, though they went no farther than the bridge.

"How do you like riding on a camel, Miss Blanche?" asked Louis, after they had gone a short distance and the mirth of the donkey brigade had begun to subside.

"I think it is real fun so far," replied the fair maiden with a silvery laugh. "But the motion is very strange, and I should think it would tire one out in a little while."

"I am told that when one gets used to it the motion seems easy enough; the camel takes long strides, and that produces a different feeling from the gait of a horse. Perhaps you are a little nervous; but you can't fall off if you try to do so."

"I shall not try, and I feel safe enough. But how will it be when we move faster ? "

"I don't think we shall go any faster. Your father gave us a very interesting talk about the camel while we were waiting, and he said the dromedary could travel ten miles an hour; that is much faster than we usually ride a horse, and I should suppose the motion at that speed must be tremendous compared with that of a walk. But I don't think we are likely to go any faster than now."

"How far is it to the Pyramids, Mr. Belgrave ? "

"I believe it is about ten miles."

"Then it will take us four hours to get there," said the young lady with a look of dismay.

"If you get tired of the camel before we come to the Pyramids, the wagonette is large enough to hold all the party, and you can change at any time," suggested Louis.

"But I should not like to back out, for mother would laugh at me."

When they came to the bridge over the Nile it was not a new thing to them, for they had crossed it to Bûlâk, as the island, about three miles in length, is called. The bridge, built by French engineers, crosses this island, and is a little more than two-thirds of a mile in length.

"I took a donkey early Saturday morning and came over here with Don," said Louis. "This bridge was crowded then with peasants, who were paying the duties on the provisions they were taking to market."

" Duties ? " queried the lady.

"You remember the *octroi* in Paris, by which a tax is levied and paid on all market wares taken into the city, and it is about the same in most of the large cities of Europe. Something has to be paid on every leg of mutton and bottle of wine that passes the gates."

After crossing the bridge over the western branch of the river, they came to several palaces, surrounded by the usual high walls, and with beautiful gardens. Then a canal was followed for a short distance, with the railroad to Upper Egypt on the other side; the procession then turned into a road shaded with trees, which looked very inviting.

" The Pyramids ! " exclaimed Louis, as an opening presented them to their view.

" They don't look so big as I thought they would," added Blanche.

"They are still five or six miles from us. I believe we are to have an oration from Uncle Moses in relation to them when we get there, and then we shall know all about them. Does the motion of the camel trouble you much now, Miss Blanche ? " asked Louis.

" Hardly at all, for I have got used to it, and I don't believe it will tire me any more than riding in that wagonette would," she replied.

"The road is bad nearer the Pyramids, and your father and mother and the professor will get well shaken up, while the ship of the desert will make good weather of it. We shall be tormented by the

Arabs as we approach our destination. The rascals carry sand to the road in order to make their assistance necessary to carriages containing visitors."

"Where do you find out so much about all these things, Mr. Belgrave?" asked the young lady with a smile of approbation.

"I have been reading up, as I always do, if I have time, in regard to the places we are to visit," replied Louis. "Captain Ringgold occasionally reminds me that this trip around the world is not simply a pleasure excursion, and that with me it takes the place of a college course. How do you get along on your desert steed, Uncle Moses?" he called to his trustee, who rode in front of him with the surgeon.

"Excellently well," returned the lawyer. "My brother Cupid feels just now as though his wings were fully grown, and he were flying."

"We like it so well that we are tempted to buy a couple of dromedaries and make a trip across the Great Desert to the Atlantic coast," added the doctor. "It is not a bad way to travel."

"Halt!" shouted the commander, as he drew up his steed at the side of the road, and the procession obeyed the order. "Are you quite ready, Uncle Moses?"

"As ready as I ever shall be," replied the legal gentleman, as the captain rode up to him.

The riders of camels, horses, and donkeys were then assembled around the wagonette.

"This is a shady place; and, as we shall soon be

vexed by the wild Arabs, I have concluded that it is best for us to hear the gentleman to whom this subject was assigned in this place, where the Pyramids are in plain sight, rather than after we get into the desert," said the commander.

"You can all see this chain of hills in front of us," added the conductor, who had been consulted in regard to the halt. "This chain of elevations is the boundary line between the cultivated lands of Egypt and the Libyan Desert, which is a part of Sahara, extending very nearly across the continent. That is all from me."

"I have the honor to present you to Judge Scarburn," added the captain.

"Judge of a good dinner, and we get plenty of them on board of the Guardian-Mother," said the lawyer. And he did not take the trouble to admit that he had sat on the bench for a term, though those from Von Blonk Park knew it very well. "I had occasion to speak seven hours once in a case I was trying; and if I should do justice to my present subject, I should want all of that time."

"Don't!" exclaimed some irreverent person whose voice was not identified, though it was supposed to be Mr. Hornbrook.

"I won't! I solemnly promise not to use up more than one-fourteenth of that time, though I should lose my case, as I probably shall. Stepping outside of what is mixed about the history of these big monuments of the ancient world," continued the speaker, striking into his subject, "the biggest pyramid you see before you was built by Cheops about three thousand years before the birth of Christ. This is the figure of Lepsius, though the professor's late friend Mariette makes it twelve hundred more. The next in size is that of Chephren (commonly called Cephrenes), a brother of Cheops, and the smallest that of Mycerinus. All of them were erected in the same century; and it is not possible to give the day of the month on which any one of them was begun or finished. Pyramids continued to be built down to 2300 B.C.; and you will see some comparatively insignificant ones in other parts of Egypt.

"Sitting on the back of a camel is not exactly a desirable position for the delivery of a lecture," continued the speaker, as he took a paper from his pocket.

"You can dismount and stand in the wagonette," suggested the commander.

"No, I thank you; I should have to mount again, and the experience of my Brother Cupid is an impressive warning to me."

"You weigh a quarter of an ounce less than I do, and you could do it safely," added the doctor.

"Herodotus, who travelled in Egypt, says it took a hundred thousand men three months in the year for ten years upon each of the jobs of quarrying the stone, carting them to the river, and ferrying them across it, for the stone was taken from the east side of the Nile. They did not have newspapers five hundred

years before Christ, or I should suppose he got his
fact from a sensational sheet.   And this work was not
done on the pyramid, but only on the road from the
Nile to this place.   Then it took Cheops twenty years
to build the pyramid itself; and the stories are decidedly mixed just now, but when we go around the
world next time they may get settled.

" The ancient Egyptians believed that in order to
save the soul the body must be preserved, for they
accepted the immortality of the spirit.   Now, Cheops
dug down deep, and cut his tomb out of the solid
rock, and then planted the pyramid on the top of it,
in order safely to keep his remains from returning to
their original dust.   More than this, he had to put his
body out of the reach of the inundation, and selected
this high ground in the desert.   What Cheops did for
his own body Chephren and others did for theirs.   It
was not kings alone who looked out for the immortality of their bodies, but the ' bloated aristocrats' of
the time used up some of the coupons on their bonds
in hewing out tombs from the solid rock in dry
places.

" But kings and magnates have been euchred in the
flight of time, for enterprising seekers for truth have
opened these tombs, even when under a pyramid, and
mummies, fixed up to last forever, are to be found in
all the museums of the world; and one of them without a mummy is not of much account in these times.
Our beloved commander saw a room full of them in
the University of Kazan in Russia.   The Persians

first began to open these tombs; and from their time to ours, natives and foreigners have continued to do the same, sometimes in search of hidden knowledge, and sometimes in search of buried treasure," and the speaker appeared to have finished.

"But who was Belzoni, Uncle Moses?" asked Scott.

"It would take me the whole seven hours to tell you what little I know about pyramids, and those who have opened them; and if I gave their names, there are no reporters present, and they would not get into the papers in Cairo, and so it would do no good," replied the speaker. "Belzoni was the son of a poor barber, and was born in Italy in 1778. He travelled a great deal, and brought up in Egypt, where he came at the invitation of Mohammed Ali as an engineer to irrigate the land around Cairo. He did this job to the satisfaction of his employer, though the water plan was abandoned by the Viceroy. Then he turned his attention to the antiquities of Egypt, and became a great tomb-opener, as well as a distinguished expert in his chosen specialty. He sent mummies and other relics of Egyptian history to the British Museum, where they were the lions of the day, for they were then a new thing. Horace Smith wrote a famous poem addressed to a mummy, which still lives in the literature, not only of England, but of our own country."

"You have used up but twenty minutes of the time you claimed, and I shall invite a young orator we have with us, whose recitations from Byron delighted us in

Greece, to fill up the other ten minutes. Mr. Morris
Woolridge, ladies and gentlemen," interposed the
commander.

Morris dismounted from his donkey, and took a
stand in the wagonette.

"About half a dozen stanzas will fill the time,"
added the captain, and the young gentleman began:

"And thou hast walked about (how strange a story),
    In Thebes's streets three thousand years ago,
When the Memnonium was in all its glory,
    And Time had not begun to overthrow
Those temples, palaces, and piles stupendous
Of which the very ruins are tremendous!

Speak! for thou long enough hath acted dummy;
    Thou hast a tongue, come, let us hear its tune;
Thou'rt standing on thy legs above ground, mummy!
    Revisiting the glimpses of the moon,
Not like thin ghosts of disembodied creatures,
But with thy bones and flesh, and limbs and features.

Tell us, for doubtless thou canst recollect,
    To whom should we assign the Sphinx's fame?
Was Cheops or Cephrenes architect
    Of either pyramid that bears his name?
Is Pompey's Pillar really a misnomer?
Had Thebes a hundred gates as sung by Homer?

Statue of flesh — immortal of the dead!
    Imperishable type of evanescence!
Posthumous man, who quit'st thy narrow bed,
    And standest undecayed within our presence,
Thou wilt hear nothing till the judgment morning,
When the great trump shall thrill thee with its warning.

Why should this worthless tegument endure,
  If its undying guest be lost forever ?
Oh let us keep the soul embalmed and pure
  In living virtue, that, when both must sever,
Although corruption may our frame consume,
The immortal spirit in the skies may bloom!"

The young orator was greeted with hearty applause, as he descended from his rostrum, and remounted his donkey.

"The last verse was the best of the whole," Mrs. Blossom ventured to declare, and perhaps some of the party agreed with her; for it corresponded with the spirit of the present age.

The procession was reformed as before, except that the sailors and the donkey-riders were placed on each flank, the line of march was taken up again, and in half an hour they encountered the troop of wild Arabs.

CHAPTER XXVIII

ASCENT OF THE PYRAMID OF CHEOPS

THE caravan had hardly emerged from the shaded road over the fertile land that borders the Nile before a group of houses was seen; and from this locality hardly less than fifty Arabs emerged, and rushed upon the party as though they intended to annihilate them. They were hungry for *bakshîsh,* and that was all that ailed them.

"Don't give them a millième!" shouted Mr. Hornbrook from the wagonette. "If you give them a penny they want a pound. Don't take any notice of them!"

Early warning had been given to the members of the company of the probable assault of these vagabonds, and the sailors and the boys had armed themselves with sticks at the halt. The commander had placed two of the sailors and two of the boys, Don taking the place of Louis, on each side of the vehicle. But the assailants all appeared on one side, and they united as the beggars approached.

"If you use those sticks, don't hit them over the head," said he to this improvised guard. "Keep right on, and don't mind them unless they attempt to break through your line."

They came with open palms and hands extended, crying out for *bakshish*. The captain's order was obeyed to the letter, and the guardsmen hardly bestowed a glance upon the vagabonds. The leader of the procession continued to converse with the lady at his side; for she was somewhat nervous as the Arabs began to gather on the flank of the caravan, for they looked as though they were capable of committing acts of violence.

"Don't be in the slightest degree alarmed, Mrs. Belgrave. There is no possible danger," said Captain Ringgold to her in the most assuring tones. "You have read about the Arabs of the desert, and perhaps have admired some of their traits of character, as you have about the noble Indians of our Western territories; but our savages are a higher class of men than these vagabond sons of the desert, who have but one object in life, and that is *bakshish*. We could scatter the whole of them in two minutes if we were so disposed; but we do not care to make trouble."

The beggars were not satisfied to follow on the outside of the cavalcade. Those who were mounted on the camels or the horses, and those who were seated in the wagonette, looked more hopeful in the matter of "tips" than the boys and the sailors. They wanted to get at them, and perhaps expected a shower of coppers if they could get near them.

Suddenly they massed themselves, and made an

attempt to crowd through the guard at the side of the only vehicle in the procession. They seemed to be bothered by the manner in which the visitors had come, for parties usually appeared in carriages, and with no outriders to block their way.

"Close up!" shouted Knott, as soon as he saw what the vagabonds had in mind.

"*Mush auzak! Imshi! Imshi! Ruh! Ruh!*" yelled Don, who was the only one of the company dressed in Turkish regimentals. He simply intimated that they were not wanted, and ordered them to begone. They paid no attention to his speeches, but made a rush to get nearer to the wagonette.

The donkey-boys knew a few words of English, and the jolly tars, who thought the whole affair was fun, made them force their donkeys upon the assailants. Then the sticks came into play, and the Arabs were drummed on their backs and limbs till, like Cain, their punishment became more than they could bear, and they fell back. They seemed to be rather stupefied by the reception given to them. They looked aggrieved, persecuted, as though they had been deprived of the divine right to extort bakshish from innocent travellers, and they wanted to be ugly about it.

If they were not satisfied with the situation, they submitted to it when the guard fell back, and brought up the rear of the caravan. They doggedly followed, as though they had not lost all hope of reaching the pockets of the tourists. Farther along the head of the column encountered the shiekh, who had some authority in connection with the visits of strangers to the Pyramids. A fee was paid for the whole company, and half a dozen of the Arabs were employed to assist those who wished to climb the sides of Cheops.

In places the desert wind drove the sand upon the road, and made it difficult to travel for the wagonette, and the Arabs had assisted the breeze, in order to render their help necessary; but the sailors kept them at a distance, and the vehicle was not stopped, for it was drawn by four horses and had a light load. The Pyramids of Gîzeh are on an elevated plain, not quite a mile in length and three-quarters of a mile in breadth, which is gradually ascended, though in some places it is a headlong steep. When the sand deepened and the rise began, the vehicle was left behind; but the horses, camels, and donkeys were compelled to bear their burdens up to the base of Cheops.

The sailors gave up their steeds to the party in the wagonette, piloting the ladies, and holding them on in their places; for they could only sit as on a bench in the absence of side-saddles. The tars were glad to walk, for it was even greater enjoyment to them to take charge of the ladies than to ride. The horses from the wagonette were taken to a stable provided for their use.

"The deserted building on the other side of the road was intended for a hotel," said the conductor.

"I should say that it was a good place for a hotel," added the commander.

"It would be very convenient, and I think it would be well patronized. But these dirty Arabs would not tolerate it; for it seemed to be an infringement upon their right to rob travellers, and they made it a failure," replied Mr. Hornbrook.

"If I were in the government of Egypt I should proceed to civilize them at once. They make travelling here a nuisance," said the captain, "and I would find some means to abate it. It has been said in our country that the best Indian is a dead Indian. I don't subscribe to the sentiment by a good deal, but I should judge that it might be truer of these vagrant Arabs than of our aborigines."

The caravan without the vehicle resumed its march up the hill, and continued on the way upon the crest of an elevation, with the sandy desert on each side, till they reached the plateau at the base of the Great Pyramid. The time had come to dismount from the animals. The half-dozen Arabs were officious to assist, but did not omit to extend their open palms. The conductor, who carried a pound or so of coppers, was told to give them something to keep them good-natured. They took the horses in charge as the riders dismounted, and rode them back to the stable.

The donkey-boys were as lively as ever, though they had walked and run a dozen miles. They led their little brutes back to the abandoned hotel, where provision for feeding them had been made by order of the commander. Then came the interesting exploit of getting off the camels. Louis had jumped down before his camel could kneel, and then handed down Miss Blanche.   Uncle Moses came to the ground without accident, but Dr. Hawkes went down by the route over the animal's head; he was unharmed, for the sand was soft, and his bones were heavily cushioned with adipose tissue.

" All on account of that extra quarter of an ounce," puffed the obese gentleman, as Don picked him up, and brushed off the portions of the desert that clung to his clothes.

" You will wish to return to Cairo in the wagonette, Doctor," laughed Uncle Moses, with a triumphant expression on his fat face.   " You and I will have to play leap-frog, or something of that sort, to limber up that clumsy frame of yours, Brother Cupid; then you may become as supple as I am."

" All right, Brother Avoirdupois ; and we will begin now.   Put yourself in position, and I will take the first leap over your distended proportions," replied the surgeon, swinging his arms in preparation for the spring.

" But I might be crushed under your preponderating weight of a quarter of an ounce; judging by the way you dismount from a camel, I should be sure to be reduced to the thinness of a slap-jack.   Excuse me, Brother Cupid, and give me the first leap over you."

" I see you wish to back out from your own challenge, and you are at liberty to retire the proposition," added Dr. Hawkes, as he gazed up at the summit of Cheops.

"Now, ladies and gentlemen, we are prepared for your first exclamation of ecstatic admiration and astonishment!" shouted the commander, letting himself down from his usual dignity. "You have been looking at pictures of these things since you were little children, no bigger than the two Cupids of the company, and now you are in the presence of three of them, to say nothing of the baby pyramids, of which there are no less than half a dozen in sight. And there stands the Sphinx, the representative of Napoleon's idea, contained in his inspiring words to his soldiers at the Battle of the Pyramids, 'Forty centuries look down upon you!'"

"Has the crathur got eyes in the bachk of his head?" asked Felix. "Sure the bayst is loohkin' the odther way, kaypin an oye on thim blackghards uv Arabs we met forinst the village."

"Don't you try to look the Sphinx out of countenance when you get on the other side of him, Flix," added the captain, who was in a more playful mood than usual.

"Oi kin say acrost his face from here, and Oi think he is purty well looked out of countenance now, for his nose is gone, and his upper lip hasn't room enough left for a mustache. Faix, he's purty much out of a countenance already."

"Shall we take a walk now among these sights, Mr. Hornbrook?" asked the commander, as the conductor joined them.

"Not yet; this building near the corner of the

pyramid is the Viceroy's kiosque, and I have just engaged the lower floor for your use. The lunch I
brought out will be ready in a few minutes, and we
will take it there."

It was about noon, and the ride had prepared the
party for this refreshment. It was soon disposed of,
and the tourists devoted themselves to an examination
of the Pyramids and other objects of interest on the
ground.

" The Great Pyramid, as this one is called *par
excellence,* is four hundred and eighty-three feet high,
and the base of it takes in twelve and a half acres,"
said the conductor, when the party had gathered again
at the corner of the monument. " Though it does not
look so at a distance, you can see that it appears like
a triangular staircase. I suppose some of you wish to
ascend to the top of it."

" I do!" shouted the boys as one.

" The blocks of stone of which the exterior is built
are three feet high, and make the steps somewhat
high for young gentlemen like you."

" What's three feet ? " said Scott contemptuously.

" It is easy enough for men and boys ; if any of the
ladies wish to go up, I can get a stool at the kiosque,
with which the step may be reduced one half."

Only Miss Blanche wished to make the ascent, and
the stool was procured. Louis and two Arabs he engaged, for they were still about fishing for backshish,
attended her ; before she was out of hearing she cried
out that it was " nice." The stool made it easy work

for her; but Louis was too proud to use it, and sprang up every one of the steps in season to take his charge by the hand, and assist her in the second step. They went to the top, and took a survey of the surrounding country. Then they waved their handkerchiefs and shouted, all six of them, for Don was with them.

The descent was not so easy for Miss Blanche; for it made her dizzy to look out into vacant space in front of her, and Louis's agreeable labors were doubled. They reached the ground in safety, and the boys did not think it was much of an achievement to climb a pyramid.

"Now, Brother Cupid, it is time for you and me to go up, as no one has been killed so far," said Uncle Moses to the other twin.

"Only one thing deters me: I should lose the supreme delight of seeing your gymnastics as you made the ascent if I went up with you, and I prefer to stand on the ground and see you do it," replied the doctor. "Perhaps you had better get one of the smaller Arabs to take you in his arms and carry you up."

"Anything for an excuse, Doctor Cupid," added Uncle Moses, as the party started to obtain a nearer view of the Sphinx; and in a few minutes they were looking the figure in the face.

"And is that what you call the Sphinnix?" exclaimed Felix. "Faix, he looks joost loike a mahn I knew in Von Blonk Park, after he got his nose smashed in a bit of a foight. The top of the mahning to ye's, Musther Sphinnix. Do you fayle as well as ye's do now after stahnin' there foor or foive t'ousand yayres ? "

"This figure formerly had the head of a man and the body of a lion," said the conductor; "the length of the body was one hundred and forty feet, and the top of the head is sixty-six feet high. The face is thirty feet from chin to forehead, and thirteen feet wide."

"That is a queer shaped head," added the doctor.

"The ear is four and a half feet high, and the mouth seven and a half wide."

"He was the fellow for a good dinner," said Scott, "with a mouth seven feet long."

Everything in the vicinity was visited, including the interior of the Great Pyramid; but it would take another book to tell all they saw. They were very much interested in the rock-tombs, the second and third pyramids, as well as in what the commander called "the baby pyramids."

The party walked down to the place where the animals had been brought up, and the proceedings of the arrival were reversed. The doctor succeeded in mounting his camel without tumbling off this time, and cheers greeted his triumph. The tourists were very tired, and even the ride was a rest for them. They reached the hotel in season for dinner, and they voted that they had had a "grand time."

CHAPTER XXIX

WANDERINGS IN THE STREETS OF CAIRO

THOUGH it was not quite possible to keep the "Big Four" quiet for any great length of time, most of our tourists were tired enough after their trip to Gizeh to rest on the following day. A considerable package of letters, which had come during their absence, assisted them in remaining at the hotel half of the day in order to reply to them. But Scott, Felix, and Don John had no letters; and they wandered about the "Streets of Cairo," of which the American people have had some specimens at the Columbian Exposition, during the forenoon.

There were still a couple of days of the week assigned to the capital of Egypt; and there were a number of "odds and ends" yet to be picked up, though the party on the return from "Up and Down the Nile" could take as much time as they pleased for sight-seeing if there should be anything to detain them.

After the letters were written, and the lunch had been disposed of, a ride was taken to the Nilometer, on the Island of Roda. It is a square well, sixteen feet across, with a column of eight sides rising from the middle of it, covered with ancient measures and inscriptions. This pillar is thirty feet high. Of course the water of the river flows freely into this pit, and its exact height is indicated by the gauge.

Its lowest point is twenty-eight feet above the average level of the Mediterranean Sea. When the water of the Nile is lowest it covers seven ells, or about twelve and a half feet of the measure on the column; and when the height mounts to about twenty-eight feet, the proper official proclaims the *Wefa*, which means the abundance or the superfluity of the Nile. Then the cutting through of the dam, which allows the water to flow over the waiting fields of the country, takes place.

This is a religious festival, which inscriptions indicate was celebrated fourteen centuries before the birth of Christ. The Nilometer was built A.D. 809. The rate of taxation in ancient times was regulated by the height of the inundation. The river must rise about twenty-eight feet, or sixteen cubits, in order to insure good crops; and a famous statue of "Father Nile," in the Vatican, is surrounded by sixteen genii, representing this number of cubits.

Even to the present time the degree of the rising of the water governs the taxation of the country; and it is still for the interest of the government to obtain as favorable reports as possible from the Nilometer, in order to prevent the people from grumbling at their tax-bills. The sworn official in charge of the Nilometer has to be watched by the police, to make sure that he does not falsify the record.

Later in the afternoon the party proceeded to the village of Shubra, two miles and a half from the city. Carriages had been taken for this excursion, though the young men preferred the donkeys. A broad, straight avenue leads to this locality, shaded by *lebbec* trees, which is the favorite shade of this region. Hundreds of thousands of these trees have been planted here, and they have produced a great change in the appearance of the landscape. In former times no effort was made to extend the culture of trees, and timber was exceedingly scarce.

The *lebbec* is doubly valued; first, for the extent of the shade it affords, and second, for the excellence of the wood it produces. In forty years it attains the height of eighty feet, the trunk having an immense diameter, and the branches projecting a long distance over the roads by which they are set out, forming a beautiful arcade over them.

It was therefore a delightful drive over Shubra Avenue, and it has become the Central Park of Cairo. All the fashionable people of the city, Mohammedans, Jews, and Christians, turn out in their elegant equipages, especially on their own Sunday, and promenade this favorite resort. The party had ridden through the Bois de Boulogne in Paris at the fashionable hour, and they liked this better, for it presented a greater variety in the Oriental costumes and manners of the people and the turn-outs.

From the harems of the magnates came the veiled ladies; and as the tourists had observed in Algiers and Constantinople, the better-looking they were, the less opaque were the *yashmaks*. The party were seated in open carriages, so that they had abundant opportunity to see all the gay equipages, and to observe their occupants, as well as to see some of the beautiful villas built near the avenue.

"The carriage of the Khedive is coming!" exclaimed Mr. Hornbrook impressively from the driver's seat. "Salute him very politely."

"Of course we shall treat him like a gentleman, whether he is one or not," replied the commander.

The conductor leaped to the ground to convey the intelligence to the other carriages, and to the donkey-riders in the rear. His Highness came in a very elegant carriage, and rode in state, suitably attended. He was not yet out of his teens, and as Uncle Moses remarked, he did not look as though he "would set the river afire." Hats and caps were removed, and all, including the ladies, bowed to the young gentleman. He was more polite than the Sultan of Turkey was when the writer saluted him, for he nodded slightly. But he fixed a staring gaze upon the lovely face of Miss Blanche, and her father hoped they would not have to run away from another Pacha of higher degree than Ali-Noury.

The boys were particularly careful to "make their manners," though the Viceroy took no notice of them. They looked him over very thoroughly, and found it very difficult to believe he was the ruler of a country containing seven million inhabitants.

"He left his manners in the bog," said Felix. "If I meet him again I will be as stiff as he was."

"Don't do that, Flix; you ought not to hurt his feelings," added Scott.

"Somebody told me he never rode out on this avenue except on his own or our Sunday," added Morris.

"He had better stayed in the house to-day," growled Felix.

"*Plus qu'on est élevé, plus qu'on doit être poli*," added Louis. (The more elevated one's position is, the more polite he ought to be.)

"My sentiments exactly; but if you had said it in Chinese I should have understood it just as well," replied Felix; and Louis translated it.

A garden château had been erected by one of the viceroys at Shubra, which was very beautiful both in its natural and artificial ornamentation, and the conductor insisted that his charge should examine it. They did so, and were glad they had complied with the request. For a franc apiece the gardener showed them over the grounds, and presented each person with a bouquet. The return to the city was quite as interesting as the coming had been.

"Day after to-morrow we embark on the steamer for up the Nile," said the commander, at the end of the dinner. "I warned you before to have all your washing done before we start. We shall be gone at least three weeks, and there are no washerwomen on board or by the way."

The next day the party made an excursion to see the Virgin Tree and the Petrified Forest. The former is a sycamore in a garden, and looked as though it had been blasted by all the lightnings since the Christian era, though its branches are still alive. It gets its reputation from the story that Mary and her Son rested under its shade during the flight into Egypt; and when Mr. Hornbrook told the circumstance, Mrs. Blossom straightway went into ecstasies, without inquiring into the truth of the statement.

"I don't know whether or not the story is true, and I leave every one to judge for himself," said Mr. Hornbrook. "But, madam, there is a more wonderful event alleged to have occurred here than the Virgin simply reposing with her Son under this tree; and you can believe as much of it as you please. The fugitive mother was persecuted even here, and she fled for safety into the hollow of this tree, where she found an opening large enough to receive her and her sacred charge. Perhaps that was not very strange; but the tax upon your credulity is the statement that a friendly spider immediately wove his web at the opening of the hiding-place, so that it entirely concealed the occupants of the hollow from the scrutiny of all pursuers. The Copts believe this story."

"Were the cops looking for the Virgin?" asked Felix demurely.

"That slang is wasted on Mr. Hornbrook, for he does not understand it," interposed Louis, who did

not like to have even a marvellous story with sacred
bearings treated with levity.

"I learned that cops were policemen when I was in
America — in the States, I mean," replied the conductor, with a glance at the commander.

The boys thought the Petrified Forest would do very
well for scientific people, but there was no "fun" in
it for them. The surgeon had considerable to say by
the trunks of the old trees, half buried in the sand,
but the young people were listless listeners. This
region has been examined in the search for coal-
mines; but none of any consequence have been found.

In the afternoon some of the tourists went to see the
Viceregal Library, which is thrown open to foreigners
as well as natives. It contains 25,000 volumes, chiefly
Arabic and Turkish works, and the party did not stay
to read any of them. The treasures of the institution
are the copies of the Koran, the Mohammedan Bible.
They were collected from the mosques of Cairo, so as
to insure their preservation, for they are of priceless
value to the "true believers." The oldest is in Cufic
characters, and this was the name of a certain Arabian
alphabet. This book is believed to have been written
many hundred years ago, and is in a very dilapidated
condition, having been once injured in a fire.

There are about twenty other copies of the Koran
in the library, all of them of a later date. One of
them is written in gilded letters, and this and several
others are several hundred years old. Some of them
are in Persian characters, and other Eastern languages

are represented.   There are also many other volumes
in Oriental languages, which are eagerly consulted by
scholars from all over the world.

While some of the tourists were examining these
musty relics of ages gone by, the boys were roaming
about the streets.   Those who were given to "tinker-
ing" stumbled upon some carpenters at work in a
shop.   They had hardly any tools, no bench, vice, or
other apparatus to hold the work.   They kept a board
in place by the weight of their bodies, assisted by their
toes and their teeth, and the observers could not help
laughing at the primitive manner in which they oper-
ated.   For a rule they used a piece of string; for a
gimlet or auger they had a spike fixed in a circular
piece of wood, which they turned with a string attached to the two ends of a stick, after the manner of
a fiddle-drill.   It was all decidedly "funny," as Scott
called it.

A *kuttab*, as Felix insisted in calling it after Don
had given him the word, which means a school, afforded them no little amusement.   The scholars were
repeating the Koran, which is the principal study,
swaying their bodies back and forward, occasionally
"cutting up" a little like schoolboys all over the
world.   Then the master scolded and punished them
with blows.

In one place they found a cook, who travelled about
with a portable range, and cooks and sells pottage,
meat-puddings, fish, and other items in his bill of fare.
His customers do not require a table, but seat them-

selves cross-legged in the street and devour their food. They went into a *café* from which the sound of music issued, called for coffee, and listened to the band, whose instruments were a sort of guitar, a queer fiddle, and a cross between a flute and a clarinet. But the music was vastly better than the coffee, served in a miniature cup, without cream, one-half of its contents being mud.

"A squad of these dogs waked me last night, and made the night hideous," said Louis, as they came to a canine group on their way to the hotel.

"The same lot vexed my spirit, and I had a mind to get up and shoot some of them," added Felix.

"That would not do; for though the Mohammedans regard a dog as a specially unclean beast, they are very tender of all animals, and, as in Turkey, they will not allow them to be killed. They are all masterless curs, for no one will own them; and they have to live on the garbage thrown into the street."

"They are nothing but 'yaller dogs,'" added Scott.

"The dog row we had last night was probably to expel some intruder dogs who had invaded the territory of others, for each colony of them has its own precincts. You can't make friends with them, even though you feed them, as I did in the City of the Sultan."

At dinner the voyagers compared notes of what had been seen, and then went to their rooms to prepare for the embarkation the next morning.

CHAPTER XXX

A MISSING YOUNG MILLIONAIRE

THERE are two usual methods of making the trip up the Nile. Two lines of steamers ascend the river as far as Assouan, a distance of five hundred and eighty-three miles, making the journey and return in about three weeks, enabling the tourist to see most of the wonderful monuments, tombs, and temples in Egypt.

The price of passage is about two hundred dollars; but this sum includes board, not only on the steamer, but for a three or four days' stay at Luxor, the donkeys for excursions on shore, small boats when needed, and, in fact, everything required, except wine and other personal extras, and the tax of the government on all travellers who visit the antiquities of the country, which is one hundred piastres, or about five dollars. *Bakshîsh* to the guides employed is paid by the companies; but the tourists will find abundant opportunity to open his bag of coppers, or even to make use of his nickels, if he is so disposed.

The Gaze steamers make fifteen-day excursions to Assouan, and return as far as Luxor, where they are provided with three days' entertainment at the company's hotel; then they are taken by steamer to Girgeh, thence by the railroad to Cairo, for a hundred and twelve dollars. All necessary expenses are included, except the government tax, though the traveller is his own master so far as bakshish is concerned; and the donkey-boys expect something after the rides to the —

> "Temples, palaces, and piles stupendous,
> Of which the very ruins are tremendous."

The other method of making the excursion to the First Cataract, or farther if desired, is by dahabeah, if one has two or three thousand dollars to expend on the enterprise, which may be divided among the excursionists; and the greater the number the less the expense. These boats comfortably accommodate from four to eight persons, according to their size. An arrangement is usually made with a dragoman for everything required for the trip; and an iron-clad agreement must be made with him, put in writing, and attested by the consul of the voyager; for even if the contractor be entirely honest, which is not always the case, there are such a multitude of details that differences are liable to occur.

There are plenty of dragomans in Cairo; and as soon as the tourist lands at Alexandria, they will begin to put in their appearance. They are Arabs, Egyptians, Turks, Syrians, Maltese, and usually speak English, French, or Italian, or some of these languages. Some of them are honest, honorable, and high-toned men; but the voyager finds it necessary to examine into their character and qualifications if he is well informed.

Looking at a contract for an actual trip made, we find that the price was £400, not far from $2,000; and the tourist added $150 to this sum because the contractor was "out of pocket" at the end of the trip. The steamers are therefore much the less expensive for making the excursion. But the dahabeah has its advantages as well as its outweighing disadvantages. One can select his company, and have the pleasure of enjoying it for two to four times as long as in the steamers. He can regulate his table to some extent, though the markets on the Nile are not equal to those of New York.

A dahabeah for five persons, and having this number of berths, is a craft seventy-five feet long, sixteen and a half wide, and draws thirty-three inches of water. The after-half contains the cabin, the floor of which is two feet and a half below the forward deck, so that a height of six and a half feet is obtained for the interior. The saloon, used as a sitting and dining room, is about thirteen feet square, with a divan on each side, and a table in the centre.

There is another saloon in the after-part of the boat, with divans in an alcove, and with a berth on each side. There are three staterooms and a bathroom, with other needed conveniences. The flat roof of the cabin becomes the promenade deck, over which an awning is spread. Seats are provided there, and deck-chairs may be used in addition. The forward deck is occupied by the crew, ten or a dozen of them, besides the dragoman, reis, or captain, and the pilot. The galley, or kitchen, is in the bow, and two cooks prepare the meals.

The dahabeah is a sailing-craft having a short mast near the bow, on which an immense lateen sail is spread, the peak being more than double the height of the mast. At the stern a shorter mast is stepped, and on it is carried another sail like the one forward, not quite half its size. The wind does not always blow on the Nile, and when it blows it sometimes comes from the wrong direction; and the large crew for a craft of this size have to "track," her or drag her with ropes from the shore. The river is full of this class of boats in the season, and even a hundred of them may be in sight at once at points of special interest.

Visiting from one dahabeah to another is very common when they are moored near each other for the night; for even the steamers do not run in the darkness. The party oftener than otherwise consists of not more than three or four, and they have the means of making the days pass very pleasantly. With an unlimited letter of credit, and the whole season before him, the wealthy tourist may make a good thing of it, especially if he has an ambition to become an Egyptologist.

On the other hand, for the ordinary traveller engaged in simple sight-seeing, the journey may become monotonous; and after one gets used to the natives, there is not much that is exciting or sensational in the trip. Some become positively wearied with the sight of pyramids and ruins, and find they all look alike. Even three weeks on a steamer, with the tramps and donkey-rides, require some degree of interest in Egyptian history and archæological research to render touring on the Nile agreeable, and to some it may become intolerable.

But the "round-the-worlders," as Felix christened the party from the Guardian-Mother, with hardly an exception, were educated people, and were capable of enjoying the wonders of the past that were to be revealed to them on their excursion up and down the Nile. They were to combine the advantages of the dahabeah and the steamer; for they had only their own company, and the means of going ahead at all times when the boat was not aground, and they did not care to continue in the night.

The baggage was sent to Bûlâk, and the party followed in carriages, though the boys went over with the sailors on donkeys, leaving the hotel an hour sooner. They were full of frolic, and the streets were still interesting to them. They had plenty of time, and they made a run around the Ezbekiyeh for the last time for the present, taking a diversion into the Muski, which was their favorite resort. As they were about to return, Louis saw something in a shop-window that attracted his attention.

It was a little Greek cap, or fez, made of crimson

velvet, and ornamented with silver. Whether he was
thinking of Miss Blanche or not, as he rode along the
Muski, picking his way through the crowd of camels,
donkeys, dogs, and foot passengers, there is no means
of knowing; but it occurred to him that this particular cap would become the beautiful maiden of the
party. He had seen them on the heads of pretty
Greek girls in Athens and elsewhere, and he believed
that with this cap Miss Blanche would be a miracle of
loveliness.

"Hold on a minute!" he called to his companions.
"There is something in a shop here that I want to
buy. Go down the Boulevard Clot Bey to the bridge,
and I will overtake you in a few minutes."

"Take Don with you to do the talking," suggested
Scott.

"No, they speak French in the place, for the sign,
'*Ici on parle Français*' is on the window," replied
Louis, as he rode back to the store.

He entered the place, and asked to see the cap in
the window. The man in charge was a Frenchman,
and was exceedingly polite, even for one of his
nationality. He took the cap from the window, and
then he fussed over it for a long time to put it in condition to make a sale. Louis was impatient to rejoin
his companions, and he told the shopkeeper he could
wait no longer. He looked at the man, and he could
not help thinking he resembled Monsieur Ulbach.
He was a little startled when he first discovered this
similarity. But he had a scar on his forehead, and

was not as tall by two inches at least as the French
detective.

Louis was satisfied that the shopman was not the
companion of Captain Mazagan, and he dropped the
subject from his mind after a critical examination of
the man's face. He told the Frenchman that he was
in a hurry, a second time, and began to move towards
the door.

"Here it is," he said, when he saw that he was in
danger of losing a possible customer.

With the dust brushed off, and arranged with
French taste, Louis thought the cap was even prettier
than when he had seen it in the window. He could
imagine just how Miss Blanche would look with it on
her head. He turned it over and over many times
with the picture of the fair girl in his mind; and
while he was doing so he heard a whistle, which
seemed to come from some apartment in the rear of
the store, and from which the Frenchman had issued
at his entrance. It was rather early in the day for
shopping, and there were no other customers in the
shop. Louis heard the whistle, but it meant nothing
to him.

"What is the price of this Greek cap?" he asked,
after he had decided to purchase it at any price.

"One hundred francs; and it is very cheap at that
price," replied the salesman, who seemed also to be
the proprietor.

"One hundred francs!" exclaimed Louis, dropping
the cap on the counter as though that was the end of
the negotiation.

He understood the "tricks of trade" in Cairo, and knew that the Arabs and Egyptians were not the only sharpers. He saw that the salesman had just doubled the price at which he would have been glad to sell the cap. He had priced a similar though not the same article a few days before, and it was only thirty francs, with all the leeway between the asking and the selling price; but it was far from being as elegant as this one, and he had been afraid to offer even half the sum demanded.

"It is very cheap; but you belong to the party of rich Americans, and you will recommend my shop to your friends if I sell it to you for four Napoleons," persisted the Frenchman, beginning his descent.

"I will not give eighty francs for it," protested the customer.

"It is very cheap; but the ladies of your party will come to my store, and you shall have it for seventy-five francs.

"No; I had one offered to me here in Cairo for thirty francs."

"Never! Not like this cap! It could not be!" exclaimed the salesman. "But your people are very rich. I was told that one young man in your company had one hundred million francs; and I shall sell this cap to you for seventy francs."

"No, you won't," replied Louis very decidedly.

"What will you give for it?" demanded the Frenchman, as Louis heard another whistle in the rear room.

" Forty francs; it is prettier than the one offered me for thirty," replied the intending purchaser; but he thought the boys would get to Bûlâk before he overtook them.

"Forty francs! St. Genevieve! I should be ruined if I sold it for that!" groaned the shopman. "Forty francs? Oh, never!"

"Very well; perhaps I will call when we return from the First Cataract;" and he started for the door.

"Your party are rich by a thousand million francs," said the salesman, "and I must sell my merchandise to them. You shall swear not to mention it to any person, and I will let you have it for fifty francs."

"I will not swear or even promise, but I will take the cap at that price," said Louis, producing his purse.

"It is ruin, but you shall have it," replied the Frenchman, shrugging his shoulders as though he was intensely dissatisfied with himself, as he made a neat package of the cap, which the purchaser put in his pocket after he had paid for it.

"I beg your pardon, sir; but you say you had a cap offered you for thirty francs. I sell you one like that for twenty francs. Come in my back shop, and I will show you a dozen of them; but they are not like the one you have bought."

Louis wanted to know whether he had been cheated or not, and he followed the Frenchman into the rear room. There was no person there, and it appeared to contain nothing but goods. The man took several caps from a shelf, and the visitor proceeded to examine one of them. A moment later he found himself on the floor, with two men holding him down. One of them was Monsieur Ulbach, and the other wore a white handkerchief over his face.

The sailors and the boys reached the steamer which was waiting for them, but Louis had not overtaken them. They reported that the absentee had gone into a shop in the Muski for something and was to overtake them. They waited an hour for him, but he did not come, and Captain Ringgold began to be alarmed about him. The ladies were putting their staterooms in order, and did not hear the report. The commander sent the entire party back to look for Louis, and then started himself.

CHAPTER XXXI

THE ADVENTURE IN THE MUSKI

Louis Belgrave understood the situation as soon as he obtained a sight of Monsieur Ulbach ; and it was hardly necessary for the other conspirator to veil his face, for the victim quite as readily fathomed his identity. No great violence had been used, for it was not the policy of the villains to injure him ; but it was not in the nature of the young millionaire to submit like a lamb to such an assault as had been made upon him.

At the moment he had been attacked he had been busily engaged in examining one of the Greek caps, and the actors in the scene had crept up softly behind him, so that all the advantage was with them. But no sooner was he on the floor of the back shop than he realized the full meaning of the transaction.

He had listened to the recital of the details of the intended conspiracy in a *café* at Gallipoli, when Ali-Noury Pacha gave his instructions to Captain Mazagan, and several attempts had been made to carry them out. But the vigilance of Captain Ringgold had defeated them, though Louis and his companions had fought quite a battle with the brigands at Zante, and caused the capture of the villains, with the exception of the principal, who was a prisoner at the time on board of the Guardian-Mother. Ulbach had been wounded by a shot from the revolver of Felix, and must have spent a considerable portion of the preceding three months in the hospital of the prison to which he had been sentenced. How he had made his escape before the expiration of his sentence was unknown to all but his confederates.

As soon as Louis saw the conspirators who were holding him down, he found that both of them had removed their shoes, and he understood in what manner they had come upon him when he had no suspicion of their presence. One of the two men held him by the collar of his coat, and this one was Mazagan; while Ulbach had seated himself on his knees, and appeared to be gradually transferring his weight in the direction of the head, as if he intended to plant himself on the chest of the victim.

Louis kicked and struggled to shake him off. Then he attempted to utter a cry loud enough to be heard in the Muski, where his donkey-boy was waiting for him. But Mazagan promptly checked this movement by tearing the handkerchief from his face and stuffing it into the mouth of the young man. The conspirators evidently found they had taken a larger contract than they supposed, for Louis did not give them an instant to proceed with the plan, whatever it was.

They were better satisfied on this point a minute later. Louis did not confine himself to any one form of resistance; for while he was struggling to shake off his assailants, he had worked his right hand into his hip pocket, where he always carried his revolver. As he made a desperate attempt to free himself, he had drawn out the weapon. Ulbach was in front of him, and he fired at him first. He had been thoroughly trained by an expert in a shooting-gallery for just such practice as he needed at this moment, and he discharged the pistol on the instant. Monsieur Ulbach tumbled over backwards, and Louis feared he had done more than he intended, for he did not mean to kill the ruffian.

But the detective immediately sprang to his feet, and thus relieved the victim from all anxiety on that point. He would not have taken the life of the villain, even to save himself. The Frenchman placed his left hand on his right shoulder, and began to squirm and wriggle, dancing about the room as though the floor was composed of red-hot plates.

"He has shot me!" he exclaimed in his own language. "I am ruined now! I shall never be able to use my right arm again!"

Mazagan, though he was plainly disconcerted by this turn in the adventure, did not release his hold upon the victim; and Louis had ceased his struggles for the moment in his effort to measure the mischief he had done to the detective. For a few seconds there was a calm, and the shopkeeper became the principal actor in the scene. He absolutely tore his hair with rage and excitement.

"I am wounded, Jules!" groaned the detective.

"Served you right!" exclaimed the shopman. "You have ruined me! I shall be arrested! I shall lose my shop! My brother is killed!"

"Your brother is not much hurt," interposed Mazagan. "Take hold of this young man's feet, and hold him while I tie his arms behind him."

"No, I will not! You have ruined me!" persisted the shopkeeper, still tearing his hair.

Louis thought his time had come to make another effort to escape, while the conspirators were fighting his battle for him by quarrelling among themselves. Mazagan did not appear to have considered that his victim might be armed with a dangerous weapon; and, as he was a sea-captain, he was probably aware of the stringency of the custom-house regulations against the introduction of fire-arms into the country, with the exception of guns for hunting.

The victim attempted to shake off the hold of Mazagan as soon as the shopkeeper refused to assist him in securing the prisoner. He adroitly threw up both of his feet, so that he kicked the conspirator in the head as he bent over him. Then a new distraction came, for Pierre Ulbach, the one who kept the store, suddenly closed the door of the back room, and announced in the utmost consternation that three men were entering the shop.

By the side of Louis there was a trap-door in the floor, with stairs leading to a cellar, where the conspirators had doubtless been concealed while Louis

was bargaining for the Greek cap; and the whistles
were probably intimations that they were ready to
receive their victim. The announcement of Pierre
had its effect upon Mazagan, for he hastily rolled his
prisoner over into the opening in the floor. Louis
struck the steps; but he was out of the grasp of his
stalwart captor, and he promptly gathered himself up,
and descended to the cellar.

The revolver was still in his hand; for in the confusion Mazagan had not attempted to gain possession
of it. The cellar was not utterly dark, for the prisoner found a window about eighteen inches high in
the rear of it. The trap-door had been hastily closed,
and the light was not increased from that direction.
Louis seated himself on one of the steps, and proceeded to consider the situation as it was at that
moment. His first thought was that Mazagan had
thrust him into this den with the expectation of find-
ing him there when he was ready to take the second
step in the drama.

As he reflected in regard to his next move, he heard
footsteps in the back shop above him. Then he heard
voices, and it was evident that the three visitors, whoever or whatever they were, had invaded the privacy
of Pierre's back shop. Louis listened attentively with
his ear close to the trap; but the language used was
neither English nor French, and he could not understand a word of it. For a full hour he listened to
these incomprehensible sounds without being any the
wiser for them. At times the conversation was
stormy and even violent.

Louis wondered whether or not his companions had not got tired of waiting for his appearance, and returned to ascertain what had become of him. Don John was with them, and knew Mazagan by sight. Possibly the talk was between him and the chief conspirator. He judged that at least an hour and a half had elapsed since he parted with his friends, and they could hardly have given up his return before they reached the steamer landing. He concluded, therefore, that the angry conversation had no relation to him.

When he had arrived at this conclusion, expecting no relief from that direction, he descended the stairs and made a survey of the window. It was not hung on hinges, but appeared to be nailed into the frame. He spent another hour in various attempts to remove the sash; but he had no tools of any kind, and he did not succeed. The state of things seemed to him to become desperate, and he finally tore up one of the steps, the risers of which were simply nailed to a plank frame.

With this board he proceeded to smash the glass in the sash, at the time when those above were talking the loudest. In a moment, as it were, he had broken out the sash and the glass. Mounting a barrel he sprang through the aperture thus made, and found himself in an alley full of filth and rubbish, just as he heard the trap-door in the back shop open. He started at the best speed he could make in such a place, and came out in a narrow back street.

He brushed his clothes as well as he could, and then joined the passers-by, who presently brought him out at the Rosetta Garden, and he knew where he was. He made his way around to the Muski at once. In the square he met a bootblack, and he gave him a piastre in advance to brush his clothes, and he was as good as new then. When he reached the store where he had bought the cap, he found it closed. Monsieur Pierre must be in some kind of difficulty; but the donkey-boy was still there, and Louis immediately gave him a silver coin of the value of half a dollar for his fidelity, which made him rich, and he returned bows and *salams* enough for a viceregal reception.

Louis had not even lost his Greek cap in the encounter with the enemy. He looked himself over very carefully; and though he was a little sore in one of his hips, probably where he had struck the stairs, he was not otherwise damaged, and was willing to believe that he had escaped "by the skin of his teeth." Mounting the donkey he hastened to the landing-place of the steamers at the great bridge, and the boy soon found the Karnak, which had been engaged for the use of the party. He paid the boy his full fee for the time he had employed the donkey, and the recipient perhaps believed he was the Khedive in disguise.

The first person he discovered on the deck of the steamer was Mr. Hornbrook, who did not seem to be aware of the cause of the delay of about two hours, though he was very impatient on account of it. He conducted the young millionaire to his stateroom, but he asked no hard questions.

"This is very bad, Mr. Belgrave," said the conductor, when he had ushered Louis into his room.

"What is very bad?" asked the young man.

"We are more than two hours late, and we ought to be at Bedrashen by this time, for we have to see Memphis to-day, and then go on towards night to Ayat," replied Mr. Hornbrook. "The longer we are delayed, the less we shall see of the ruins of the city."

"The steamer is engaged by the day, and we are in no hurry, Mr. Hornbrook, and we can give a whole day to Memphis if so disposed," replied Louis.

"You can take three months for the trip if you like; but it was my desire to make the trip cost you as little as possible."

"Don't trouble yourself about that," said the young tourist, rather magnificently for him. "Where is Captain Ringgold?"

"I don't know; the movements of this party are inexplicable to me," replied the conductor. "All the young men and the sailors came down on time. Then we waited an hour, and the commander with all the donkey party set off for Cairo again. They have not yet returned, and I don't understand it."

"I think I will go and see what has become of them," added Louis, who did not intend that the conductor should know what had occasioned the delay, for the operations of Captain Mazagan were to be a profound secret still to all except the three who had been taken into the confidence of the commander.

The donkey-boy whom the young millionaire had so munificently rewarded was still on the shore, and he almost leaped out of his skin when his customer shouted " *hammar* " to him.   Louis mounted the little animal; but he had proceeded only to the bridge over the Ismailiyeh Canal, when he discovered the party approaching, led by the commander in a carriage.

"Where have you been, Louis?" demanded the captain, who was evidently laboring under more excitement than usual.

"I have had an adventure; and fought my way out of it.   Monsieur Ulbach got a bullet through his shoulder.   No more at present from yours truly," replied Louis, as the rest of the party came up with the carriage.   The searchers began to cheer as soon as they saw Louis, and nothing more could be said.

" Discharge your donkey-boy, and get into the carriage with me," said the commander.

Louis complied with the request, and again paid the boy his fee and his liberal *bakshîsh*.   On the way to the Karnak, Louis briefly related what had occurred at the shop, and in what manner he had effected his escape.   It was evident to both of them by this time that the difficulty into which Pierre Ulbach had fallen, and which had caused him to close his place, had assisted in the plan of the victim.

In another half-hour they were all on board of the steamer, and she cast off the fasts for her voyage up and down the Nile.

CHAPTER XXXII

THE FIRST DAY ON BOARD A NILE STEAMER

THE Karnak was under way, and Louis Belgrave was trying to forget the disagreeable adventure through which he had just passed. It seemed to him, and still more to Captain Ringgold, that he had escaped by a miracle; but both of them agreed that it had been only by a lucky chance. The visit of the three men, whether they were officers of the law or creditors, had turned the tide in his favor; though if the victim had not "taken the bull by the horns" when he disabled the French detective, he might have been bound and hurried away to Rosetta.

Ali-Noury Pacha was thirsting for his revenge at the present time. The commander of the Guardian-Mother, in protecting the beautiful girl from his approaches, had mortally offended him; he had treated him precisely as though he had been a common man, and not an Oriental magnate. He had spoken plainly and even bluntly to him, telling him that his character was so bad he could not permit the ladies under his charge to receive and associate with him. Mazagan had been instructed to capture the "houri" if possible; if not, the young millionaire.

While all on board the ship were aware of the attacks of the Moorish captain and his agents, they had, with the exception of the commander and the three young men, no suspicion of the cause of these assaults, and attributed them to brigands and pirates. The captain was entirely confident of his ability to protect his passengers; and to have had the actual situation known to some of them, Mrs. Belgrave and the Woolridges especially, would break up the voyage. The captain had no time to talk with Louis, and the steamer proceeded on her voyage.

The party had not visited the steamer before, and they were interested in looking over their home for the next three weeks or more. Most of the tourists had done this while they were waiting for Louis; and when he came on board, they were all busy in unpacking their trunks, and putting things in order for the voyage, so that the absentee had not yet met them. He was much interested in the vessel, and he made an examination of her as soon as she was under way.

Captain Ringgold had assigned the staterooms himself. The Karnak had a main and an upper deck, the latter covered by an awning, so that it made a delightful promenade, and it afforded an excellent opportunity to see the shores and the boats on the river. On this deck were two structures containing apartments, the forward one being the dining-room, large enough to seat the entire party. The after one contained the ladies' saloon and four staterooms, which had already been assigned to the four of them on board.

On the main deck was the principal cabin, with a saloon and four staterooms, each of the latter having two berths, not one above the other, but one fore and aft, and the other athwartships. The saloon, abaft these rooms, was about twelve feet long, and the broad divan could be occupied by four berths at night. Forward of the engine was another house in which were four staterooms, and the captain had assigned these to the seamen, as they were apart from the other accommodations.

The Karnak was a side-wheeler, and fore and aft the paddle-boxes were the offices of those in charge of the steamer, together with conveniences for the passengers. Captain Ringgold showed Louis over the steamer, and they came at the end of the survey to the stateroom they were to occupy together. They seated themselves, and began to talk over the adventure of the morning.

"You have had quite a number of just such affairs as this; and since I have been connected with you, this makes the third time you have put a ball from your revolver into a human being," said the commander.

"Human as they were, they were all demons, and I never used my revolver till my life or liberty was at stake," replied Louis.

"You were perfectly justifiable in firing when you did in every instance, as I told you at the time; and you did quite right to defend yourself this morning," added the captain.

" But I may be arrested by the authorities for what I have done," suggested the intended victim.

" You will not be arrested; I am as sure of that as of my own existence. I am only sorry you had not shot Mazagan."

" He was behind me and holding me down, so that I could not see him; for I should certainly have chosen him as my target if I could have taken my choice."

" You did very well as it was. So far from being arrested, your assailants are in vastly more danger than you are, Louis; for if anyone is taken up the whole truth must come out, though a Mohamme-dan country is not the best for the trial of this case. This attack follows your refusal to pay the blackmail levied upon you. You have disabled the detective for the present, and I think we shall have peace now for a few weeks," continued the com-mander, as they left the room to join the party on the upper deck.

The entire company were seated in the space be-tween the two houses on deck, and every one agreed that it was a delightful trip the tourists were hav-ing. The weather was beautiful, with no danger of rain in the present or the future. The Karnak was passing the island of Roda on one side, while the Pyramids of Gizeh were in sight on the other. On the left, or east bank, the Arabian Desert ex-tended nearly to the river. On the west bank was a tract of fertile land, covered by the inundation, about a dozen miles wide in this section.

The steamer was running between two deserts; and sometimes the hills that bordered the one on the Arabian side extended close to the river, with an occasional elevation of a thousand feet. It was early in the season, and there were but few steamers or dahabeahs to be seen, though it was now the middle of the month of December, at which time the Gaze line begins its regular excursions.

" Ladies and gentlemen," said the commander, after they had taken the gauge of the scenery, "I have looked forward to the leisure we shall have on this voyage up the river to listen to the discussion of the subjects assigned to various members of the company. I have not been able to call upon many of them so far, we have been so fully occupied with sight-seeing. Mr. Woolridge enlarged his topic from horses to the animals of the country, and he has already told you about the camel. I shall call upon him now; but it is to be understood that Mr. Hornbrook may interrupt the speaker at proper times, when it is necessary to point out objects of interest on the river and its shores."

" 'The horse is a very noble animal; he has four legs, one on each corner.' That is the way the schoolboy began his composition on the horse; but it is not necessary for me to describe the horse, for most of you have seen one of them at least. He dates back to the early periods of the world, and those of you who read your Bibles are aware that he is mentioned in the Scriptures, though he comes in only in connection with war. It does not appear that the horse was in use in the earliest days of Egypt; but just now he is common enough in most parts of the country.

"But Egyptian horses would not take with English or American sporting gentlemen. They have not cared for and cultivated the animal so as to bring him up to a high standard. Most of you have had some experience with Egyptian donkeys, and all of you have seen him in profusion. The donkey-boy is not included in my subject; and I will only say that I think he is a smart fellow, and, with the proper facilities, I am confident he would compare with the newsboy and the street Arab of New York City.

"The mule don't seem to have much to do with this subject; and though he is sometimes imported from Spain and other countries, they don't make a business here of raising him, useful as he would be. I have told you all you ought to know about camels before, and they don't have camelopards here. Though he is a tall subject, I must omit him. They have the buffalo here, but he is not the fellow I have shot on our Western Territories. His beef is not first-class, but he is good as a draught animal, and the cows don't give butter, but they do milk, from which they make it.

"They have cows here with their progeny, and

consequently bulls and oxen, whose pictures you will find on some of these monuments, but they are not photographs. The cows are as useful here as in Vermont and New Jersey. They have a curious churn here for making butter, which is a leather bag, held up by a rope, and shaken. The goat does duty in all these villages, and at the tents in the desert; they make water-bags of his skin; also churns. They raise plenty of sheep in Egypt, but the wool is coarse and wiry. In the desert it is about the same as the covering of a hog.

"Pigs are not thought much of in Egypt. The ancients of this country had a multitude of gods; Osiris was the principle of light, while Typhon was darkness, and the grunter was his particular emblem. A Berkshire hog is black, and might have filled the bill. The pig is an unclean beast to the Mohammedans: they don't eat him, and they don't keep him. Dogs are a nuisance here, and not one of them has a master, though the people will not kill or abuse them. The cat is as common as in other countries, and was one of the sacred animals of the ancients. There is a superabundance of mice here as elsewhere, and what the cats can't dispose of the weasel assists in removing. All kinds of poultry are kept here, though the hens are small. Machines for hatching out chickens were used by the ancient Egyptians.

"There are no game-laws here, and a sportsman may shoot anywhere he pleases; but a man must have a license to carry a gun, or any fire-arm. Game animals are not plenty, only antelopes, wild goats, and game sheep in the hills, very rarely a wild boar or a striped hyena. Game on the wing is plenty, such as ducks and grouse.

"The crocodile of the ancients was an ugly customer, sometimes thirty feet long. Once in a while smaller ones are seen on the river, but, as in Florida, they have nearly disappeared before the filling up of the country with settlers; but the crocodile is not the same fellow as our alligator. The three snakes of the worst reputation are the cobra-de-capello, the horned viper, and the echis, all of which are very venomous, and I advise you not to make their acquaintance.

"The fish of the Nile are the most abundant during the inundation, when they emigrate from the upper region; but the water is warm, and they are not nice, though salmon, perch, carp, and many fish which are strangers to us, are caught. You have heard something about the scarabæus, the beetle, and he is as common as his picture on the monuments. Wasps are very large, and have a 'business end,' which makes them an undesirable companion to fool with. You have been introduced to the house-fly: I need not enlarge upon his facilities for botheration. Mosquitoes bite just the same here as in New Jersey, and in some places are quite as abundant. Other cheerful companions when you want to read, rest, or sleep, are fleas, bugs, lice, and at other times scorpions, tarantulas, and centipedes may make things pleasant for you;

and I will now cease to make things unpleasant for you," said the gentleman as he seated himself.

A very hearty round of applause followed the talk of the sporting gentleman, as he had once been, but was no longer, in which Don and the sailors, who had seated themselves on the rail, took an active part. The party gave their attention to the shore. The conductor named the villages they passed, but the commander declared again that names meant nothing in Arabic to the Americans.

"All right; I will not bore you with names, but I will tell you about them where there is anything worth telling," replied Mr. Hornbrook. "Here are some military establishments, and beyond them you see the palace of the Khedive's mother, which is connected by rail with Cairo. In a few minutes more we shall make a landing."

"There is a drove of donkeys there!" exclaimed Mrs. Blossom. "Do they raise them here?"

"We raise them in Cairo, and have them sent down here for your use; for this afternoon we visit the site of the ancient city of Memphis, and Sakkara, which was the graveyard of the city, on the same elevation as the Pyramids of Gizeh, where the overflow could not disturb the tombs. But there is the bell for lunch, and we must attend to that first. You will be hungry enough for your dinner after your return."

The Karnak came up to the bank of the river, and was moored there for the rest of the day. The lunch proved to be first-class, somewhat to the surprise of the tourists, who had not expected much. It was disposed of with hearty relish. The sailors were served like princes, as they thought, in the forward saloon, for they were to attend the party.

CHAPTER XXXIII

THE NECROPOLIS OF ANCIENT MEMPHIS

THE party landed near the village of mud huts called Bedrashen, which is a railroad station. Not only the donkeys which had been sent up from Cairo were in waiting for the visitors, but as many more had gathered from the vicinity, whose drivers were exceedingly persistent to obtain employment; but Mr. Hornbrook simply shouted "*Imshi!*" to all of them, and the tourists mounted those provided for them.

Four of them had side-saddles for the ladies; and as not one of them had ever mounted such a beast before, the operation caused some amusement to the spectators. Three of them were experienced horse-women, though they declared that it was like getting on the back of a large dog. Mrs. Blossom made some objection, and declared that she would walk; but it was two miles to Memphis, and two more to Sakkara, and she finally took her seat in the saddle.

Don and the sailors were supplied with donkeys; and as they understood their mission, they had provided themselves with sticks on board of the steamer. The vagrants about the place, who seemed to include the greater part of the population, were assembled in force. The commander arranged the procession as he had on the trip to Gizeh, and the sailors and the boys, who joined them for the fun of the thing, rode on the flanks, and would not permit one of the beggars to get within hail of the adults of the company. The flankers brandished their weapons, and this was enough. They were soon dispersed, and Louis took his usual position by the side of Miss Blanche.

"Now look about you, friends," said the conductor with a smile.

"I don't see anything but rubbish," replied Mrs. Belgrave. "Here are a few palms, which are pretty enough ; but we have seen plenty of them in the last year."

"But you can also see blocks of granite, bits of brick-work, and broken pottery."

"Have we come out here to see this rubbish ? " inquired the lady.

"But this is the site of the ancient city of Memphis, the capital of Egypt in the early ages of the known world, founded by Menes, the first king of the First Dynasty. The monarchs before him were considered as gods. According to Mariette, he reigned 5004 before the Christian era," continued Mr. Hornbrook ; but the commander gave him a hint that the party had already been over the history of the dynasties.

"But there is nothing here to see," suggested Mrs. Belgrave.

"You will see something before you return, and we will go on now."

In the centre of the site of the lost city was a considerable tract of low ground, which was covered with water during the inundation, and cultivated in the summer. Near this the conductor halted the party, and they dismounted, and followed him into a hollow, where they discovered a huge mass of stone that seemed to have been fashioned into some shape.

"This is the colossal statue of Ramses II., the mightiest monarch of his age," said Mr. Hornbrook. "It was found seventy years ago, and presented to the British Museum; but they could not move it, and it remains where it originally stood. It was forty-two feet high, though now it is partly dismembered. He is the Sesostris of the Greeks, and lived about twelve hundred years before Christ.

"It is said, though I do not vouch for the truth of the story, that when Ramses II. reached the frontier of Egypt on his return from a victorious campaign, he was invited with his wife and children to a banquet at the house of his brother, who was a bad man, and desired to assassinate the king. He employed men to surround his brother's tent with combustibles, which were set on fire. The servants were tipsy after the banquet, and failed to render needed assistance to the wife and children of the monarch, and Ramses himself, with a prayer, rushed into the flames, and succeeded in saving them. In gratitude for their preservation, he erected this statue.

"THIS IS THE COLOSSAL STATUE OF RAMESES II."   Page 312.

"The figure when it fell came down upon the face. A great deal more might be said of these surroundings; but the commander has so often more than hinted that the party are not antiquarians, that I will spare you any further remarks, and we will proceed to Sakkara, which was the cemetery of Memphis, not quite two miles distant; but it was the nearest ground not visited by the inundation, on the border of the desert."

The company mounted the donkeys again, and resumed the march. This was the route by which the mummies were borne to their final resting-place in the rock-tombs. The ascent to the plateau began at once, and they soon passed the ruins of a village, possibly inhabited by the embalmers of the mummies. On one side were caves which had been used as tombs; and near them the remains of preserved human beings and of cats had been dug up. In one of the grottoes was the figure of a cow, representing a goddess, hewn out of the solid rock.

After passing through a low place of cultivated land, the party ascended to the necropolis, as the burial-place is called. Having passed the wall and reached the higher ground, they halted to have a view of the region below them, taking in the green valley of the Nile, flanked by the ranges of hills separating it from the two deserts. They enjoyed the prospect; but the business of the afternoon was to see the wonders of Sakkara. Half a dozen pyramids were in sight near them, and they proceeded to the most noted of them.

"On your right, with a wall of bricks made from Nile mud, is the cat cemetery; for these animals of the house had a sacred meaning to the ancient Egyptians, and they embalmed and buried them as they did human beings," said the conductor. "You see around you the ruins of several pyramids; and perhaps their destruction was partly caused by the operations of treasure-seekers as well as antiquarians. This is what is called the step pyramid."

At this point the party halted. This pyramid, though a near view makes it appear quite different from others, is really the same; for all of them were covered with stone slabs, which smoothed down their sides; but time has removed this veneering from many of them. The step pyramid is one hundred and ninety-seven feet high, and it consists of six stages, or "treads" as the carpenters would say, of unequal height, with an average of thirty-three feet. It dates from the Fifth Dynasty, nearly four thousand years ago; and some claim that it is the oldest existing structure in the world.

A troop of Bedouins had followed the party, and offered their services to assist in the ascent of the pyramid, which is practicable in spite of the height of the several steps; but even the boys did not care to mount it. The study of the hieroglyphics has failed to inform the inquirers in regard to the use of this monument, though it is believed to have been built for a different purpose from those of Gizeh. From this point the company proceeded to the house of

Monsieur Mariette, where he lived while conducting his explorations.

"On the left of you," said the conductor, pointing, as the party stood by the house, having left the donkeys to the drivers, "was the Serapeum."

"Who was he?" asked Mrs. Blossom.

"Not a man, but a temple," replied Mr. Hornbrook rather impatiently. "The word comes from Serapis, an Egyptian god, who was first the symbol of the Nile, but afterwards an infernal deity. Apis was the chief god, sometimes considered the same as Serapis, and was worshipped in the form of a bull, which accounts for the figures of this animal seen on the various structures. Osiris, represented in the form of an ox, was the source of life. The mythology of the Egyptians is so complicated that it requires a great deal of study to understand it."

"I have read an account of the Sphinx in the 'Age of Fable' in which the figure is described as we saw it," added Louis. "It is the old Œdipus story."

"The Serapeum is the mausoleum of Apis, the sacred bull. He lived in the Temple of Apieum at Memphis, and when he died he was buried here," continued the conductor, as he led the way to the subject of his remarks. "The subterranean portion of this institution, which we will now enter, consists of long underground vaults, hewn out of the solid rock."

The tourists were astonished, not to say confounded, by the magnitude of these vaults. Mr. Woolridge declared that the principal one looked like a wine-cellar, big enough to hold all the wine in Europe. Some of the bull tombs were seventy feet below the average level of the ground. On both sides of the main vault, which is three hundred and thirty feet in length, were cells or chambers, each for the interment of a particular bull; and not less than three thousand of them were buried here and in this vicinity.

Each of these chambers contained a sarcophagus, hewn from granite, twelve feet five inches long, by seven feet six inches wide, and seven feet eight inches high, on the top of which was a convex lid. Every one of these had contained the body of a mummified bull. The weight of these coffins was sixty-five tons. The explanations of the conductor, in connection with what the party could see, were astounding; and they obtained their best idea of the magnitude of the works of the ancient Egyptians. The hieroglyphics had told a wonderful story to those who could decipher them.

In the course of his explorations, Mariette found a vault which by some unaccountable chance had escaped the attention of all previous searchers for the secrets of these tombs. It had been walled up, according to evidence obtained, in the thirtieth year of the reign of Ramses II. By the finder's chronology it had been tightly closed for thirty-seven hundred years. Everything within it appeared to be in its original condition. The marks of the fingers and the feet of the workmen who had done the last duty there were to be seen in the mortar and the sand.

But there was more to be seen, and the party left the cavern, though there was nothing to be compared with what they had just visited. Not far from Mariette's house, they came to the tomb of Ti. The burial places of the necropolis are of two kinds, the rock-tombs which they had seen, and the mastaba, which is above ground. That of Ti was of the latter description, but the exterior had decayed; though the interior decorations exhibited a wonderful knowledge of art for the period in which they were made. In places the painting was in condition to be made out, and many of the subjects which adorn books on this country came from this place. The visitors examined them with interest, and some of them were able to understand what they meant, though they had taken no lessons in hieroglyphics.

Although there was enough to occupy the tourists for several hours more, the night was coming on, and they hastened back to the Nile in the same order they had come. On their arrival, breaking through the crowd of vagrant *bakshîsh*-seekers, they found two dahabeahs moored near the Karnak. One of them was the Gazelle, with a party of four Americans, including two ladies, on board. The party were seated on the upper deck, enjoying the evening air, but they politely saluted the Karnakers as they came to the shore.

The stars and stripes which floated at the stern indicated their nationality, and the commander hastened to invite them to dinner, which was waiting the return of the voyagers. The invitation was accepted, and it was a very pleasant party which surrounded the table on the hurricane deck of the steamer. Each had a story to tell of his experience, and Louis was introduced as the owner of the Guardian-Mother.

It was a very pleasant occasion in the evening; as soon as conversation began to flag, singing was introduced, and it was ten o'clock before the guests returned to their dahabeah. Both parties hoped they might meet again; for this social intercourse is one of the pleasures of a Nile voyage.

As soon as it was light in the morning, the Karnak was under way; but most of her passengers were on deck very soon after. Mr. Hornbrook, who occupied the main cabin with Don and Felix, was on hand, early as it was, and began to describe the objects to be seen on the shore. But there was nothing which was important enough to be recorded till nearly breakfast time, when he pointed to a pyramid on the border of the desert.

"The village on our right is Rikkah, where parties land who wish to visit that pyramid; but we don't stop here," said Mr. Hornbrook.

"I am glad you don't!" exclaimed Mrs. Belgrave. "If I could come out here, and spend years, I might get some idea of all these things."

"If you have anything more like the Apis tombs, trot it out," added Scott.

"You will see some things more wonderful than those. That is the pyramid of Medum, and it is believed to be the oldest monument in the world."

" Another ! " exclaimed Felix. " You have lots of the oldest things out here."

" Three different chronologies," replied the conductor with a smile. " This pyramid is so different from others that the Arabs call it the ' false pyramid,' and that is the name it goes by. There is a mastaba near it, which was opened by Mariette. Now we are coming to Wasta, where a branch of the railroad has been extended to the Fayûm."

" Is it a pyramid ? " asked Mrs. Blossom.

" No ; it is an oasis," replied the conductor. " I must tell you something about it."

The party seated themselves ready to listen, while the good lady wondered what an oasis could be.

CHAPTER XXXIV

RUINS OF TEMPLES AND PILES STUPENDOUS.

"THE Fayûm is generally visited directly from Cairo, for there is a railway the entire distance, with one change at Wasta, which we are now approaching on the east bank. The distance is seventy-five miles, which is made in four hours. There is a fair hotel at the principal place.

"The most of the territory is in a depression of the great plateau in the eastern part of the Libyan Desert, 300 to 400 feet above the level of the sea. The Fayûm is celebrated for its extraordinary fertility. It has an area of 840 square miles, with a population of 200,000. It is abundantly irrigated naturally and artificially by a stream 207 miles long, from farther up the Nile, which has been improved and adapted for this purpose, so that the water is distributed all over the oasis.

"This region formerly contained Lake Moeris of ancient fame, now entirely dried up. It was thirty-five miles long, and the income from its fisheries kept the wives of the Pharaohs in pin-money. Another lake has taken its place, not on the same area, Birket el-Kurûn, thirty-four miles long, and six and a half wide. Its fisheries are important, and some tourists explore its shores, where the shooting is good.

" Medinet-el-Fayûm is the principal city, and has 40,000 inhabitants. The ancient capital was Crocodilopolis, of which only the ruins remain. If you go there you will find an ancient labyrinth, full of columns and apartments.

Mr. Hornbrook was shrewd enough to perceive that some of his party had become weary of too much sight-seeing, and he made his remarks very brief, and did not allude to the pyramids and other objects of interest. He saw that the tourists were enjoying themselves very much ; but they had not much fancy for excursions to see the wonders of the country at a distance from the river. He was disposed to adapt himself to the tastes of his charge, and he did not insist that the ordinary programme for antiquarians and scientists should be carried out.

On the third day the conductor pointed out everything on the shore, but his remarks were very brief. He told about tombs and ruins without exciting any desire on the part of the listeners to visit them. They preferred to hear about them, making constant use of the guide-books. The evening was cool, and the company were driven to the saloons, and even there wraps were in demand. At Beni-hasan, where the steamer remained over night, there were several dahabeahs, and social relations were established. On the fourth day the conductor followed the same plan, and the volumes were in use all day.

At night the Karnak arrived at Assiut, one of the most important towns on the river, 252 miles from Bûlâk, with a population of 32,000. There was an American mission here, which had many schools, churches, and stations, and had made a decided impression. Mrs. Belgrave was interested in such matters, and gave the party some account of them. She had been appointed to look up the religious matters connected with Egypt.

The following day was Sunday; and when she was asked about the Copts, several convents belonging to the sect having been pointed out to them by the conductor, she gave a brief talk about them.

"The Copts are descended from the ancient Egyptians," the lady began. "They are nominally Christians, but I am sorry to say that they dislike other followers of Christ even more than they do the Mohammedans. There are 300,000 of them in Egypt, about one-twentieth of the whole population. Most of them live in Cairo, for they are employed as clerks and accountants, having a taste and talent for figures, and in the higher grades of mechanical occupations, such as smiths, jewellers, watchmakers. Some of them work on the land, but this is not generally their pursuit.

"They have a religious organization, with a patriarch, and bishops. They have seven sacraments, like the Catholics, and many of their rites are the same. Wednesday and Friday are fast days with them, and they have other long fasts, one of nearly two months, during the year. They have an ancient language of their own, and they keep up the earliest forms of worship, which are very ceremonial."

It was a busy day in Assiut; for Sunday is the market-day, when the people come from the country to sell their produce, mostly lentils, with a variety of other vegetables. Those of the party who were not as particular in the observance of the day as the commander and Mrs. Belgrave, who attended service at the mission, engaged donkeys and rode about the town. There was much that was interesting to be seen, especially in observing the manners and customs of the people.

As in Cairo, they were especially struck with the appearance of several funeral processions, with the distributers of water and wailing women, who seem to take the part of mutes formerly employed in England on such occasions to assist in the mourning. The chants of these women were more solemn and impressive than at the capital, where the crowd in the street robs it of a portion of its effect. They found also some very fine mosques in the city.

"The ancient city on this site was Lycopolis," said the conductor, as the tourists finished their lunch; "and the necropolis contains some tombs, grottoes, and catacombs, which are visited by many tourists."

"I think we will not go to them," added the commander with a smile. "We have seen many specimens of these tombs, and we don't care to see any more of them at present, for they are likely to become monotonous."

"There is nothing very different about the tombs
of this necropolis from what you have already seen;
but the mummies of jackals, kittens, and birds of prey
have been found here," said Mr. Hornbrook. "If
you wish to visit them, you can crawl through small
holes, dirty and dusty, and pick up the bones of these
animals."

"Have us excused," replied Mrs. Woolridge.

On Monday the members of the party felt very
much refreshed by their rest, and the steamer proceeded as far as Balianeh. This was the landing-
place for tourists visiting Abydos, which contains
some extraordinary relics of antiquity, and the party
decided to visit the site of the city the Arab name of
which means "the buried." Abydos was second only
in importance, and was a sanctuary where the great
and the rich caused their mummies to be conveyed,
in the belief that burial within its sacred precincts
would procure a favorable judgment for them in the
next world.

Seti I., the father of Ramses II., built the Memnonium here. Mariette made extensive explorations
about this building, and removed the sand which covered a large portion of it. It is not a religious temple,
but a group of sepulchral sanctuaries. The presence
of the sacred tomb of Osiris was supposed to impart
a blessing to the magnates buried here.

The temple contains many inscriptions, and the
columns were set up in great numbers. The burial
temple of Ramses II. is in a very ruinous condition.

Some of the monarchs appear to have had several burial-places. A few of the structures formerly had metal doors, which have all disappeared. This visit was quite satisfactory to the party, for it was, to some extent, different from what they had seen before.

On the seventh day of the trip the steamer proceeded to Keneh, a town of 16,000 inhabitants, and noted for its pottery, extensive enough to supply the whole country. The ladies were interested in this art; and the conductor afforded them every opportunity to gratify their taste in witnessing the moulding, and in purchasing specimens, a large number of which were packed and sent to the Gaze agent in Alexandria.

"This is the place where the caravans carrying goods to the Red Sea set out," said Mr. Hornbrook. "The distance to Koser, a port on that sea, is one hundred and ten miles; and if any of you wish to make a camel journey over the Arabian desert, you can accomplish it in four or five days."

"We prefer to visit Koser, if at all, from our steamer," replied the commander; but some of the " Big Four" thought they should like to make the journey, for it would be a novel experience.

Instead of crossing the desert, the party crossed the river, and soon found themselves seated on better-equipped donkeys than they had usually found, on their way to the great temple of Dendereh, two miles from the shore. They passed through groves of palms and well-tilled fields, and occasionally by a dwelling guarded by noisy dogs. The temple was dedicated to Hathor, the Egyptian Venus. The portico is one hundred and thirty-nine feet wide, and supported by twenty-four columns, the capital having four heads of the goddess with cows' ears.

The main building contains a multitude of apartments, devoted to various purposes in the ceremonials in honor of the divinity. Connected with it are twelve crypts, some above and some below the floor of the structure, which seem to mingle the solemn with the festive in an odd manner to modern observers. The grandeur of these remains of former splendor made its due impression on the most of the tourists. But it was only the beginning of the series of mighty works which were to be presented to their view within the next few days. They returned to the steamer, and passed the evening in talking over what they had seen during the last two days.

The party were tired when they retired, and they did not "turn out" till late; but the Karnak had been making her best speed for three hours. The conductor was full of information, as usual; and Mrs. Belgrave gave quite a lecture on the Mohammedan religion, in which even the boys were deeply interested. At noon Mr. Hornbrook began to point out the temples of Thebes and Karnak, of which "the very ruins are tremendous;" but they saw nothing of "the hundred gates, as sung by Homer." The steamer went up to the landing, and the entire party, bag and baggage, proceeded at once to the Hotel Thewfikieh, as they persist in spelling it.

It has a veranda in the front, and another in the rear; attached to it is a garden for the production of the vegetables consumed in the hotel, and with plenty of palms in the vicinity. Accommodations for the tourists were reserved, and they went to their rooms at once. A very substantial and palatable lunch was soon served, and the company were ready for the business of the afternoon. They were to remain three days at this hotel.

"A word before we start," said the conductor. "You will wish to purchase antiquities, which will be constantly thrust in your faces, unless the sailors keep the Arabs off, as they have done on former occasions. You can buy these articles if you wish, but the chances are that they will be spurious, for they manufacture them here, as they do nails from the true cross in Europe; and they do it so well that even experts are sometimes deceived. Your donkey-boys are very good fellows, as a rule, and they will render you every assistance you require. Now for the Temple of Luxor."

But the commander interfered, and insisted upon knowing the points of the compass, as he termed it. He wished the party to understand what was on the right bank of the Nile, and what on the left. Mr. Hornbrook explained that Luxor and Karnak were on the right bank, and the necropolis on the left.

"But which is the right bank?" asked Felix. "I have been mixed about that, and it seems to me everything is hind end to here. When I went to school the master made us study our maps with the top to the north; and here I keep thinking we are running to the north instead of the south. The right bank is on your right going with the current, and that makes it on the east side."

"Quite right, Mr. McGavonty," laughed the conductor. "We are on the east side now, and so are Luxor and Karnak."

"Heave ahead, my hearties," added Scott.

The party arrived at the Temple of Luxor, and proceeded to make a survey of it. The foundation of Thebes is said to date back to the time of the First Dynasty, the average date of which is nearly four thousand years before Christ; but nothing has been found among the ruins to indicate an earlier period than twenty-five hundred years before our era. Its most flourishing period was from 1600 down to 1100 B.C., when it was thrown into the shade by Memphis, the capital of the Pharaohs.

The temple is a very long building, with an imposing pylon, or portico, with obelisks and colossal statues in front of it. The interior is filled with hundreds of columns. It was difficult for the party of visitors to "take in" so extensive a structure. The great Peristyle Court is one hundred and eighty-five feet long by one hundred and sixty-seven feet wide, with two rows of columns. Beyond this, leading to the middle court, is the Colonnade, one hundred and seventy-four feet long, with seven pairs of pillars forty-two feet high. The second Peristyle Court is similar to the first.

It is an immense building, and it was several times enlarged by different monarchs. The party paused at the entrance to the temple they had visited to examine the obelisk near it, and to see if they could make anything of the quaint figures sculptured on the walls; but the hieroglyphics were as uncommunicative to them as they had been to all the learned of the world before the time of Champollion. The company were much interested in this temple, and were rather sorry to be called away from it to visit Karnak.

CHAPTER XXXV

KARNAK, THE COLOSSI, AND PHILÆ

THE distance from the Temple of Luxor to Karnak is nearly a mile; but in the days of the Ramses the avenue leading to it was bordered with sphinxes, and there are several roads of this description near these vast structures. A few of these figures remain in a very ruinous condition. The party mounted the donkeys, for they were tired after the walks in the Temple of Luxor.

Though the members of the company were not much given to gushing, and had become accustomed to magnificent and wonderful sights in their travels, they could not restrain some expressions of wonder and admiration as they approached the Temple of Ammon at Karnak. Most of them had read something of the marvellous structures of Upper Egypt; but they were not prepared for the reality as they found it.

" But who was Ammon, whose name was given to the temple? " asked Miss Blanche, whose devoted knight was at her side as usual when he could obtain this desirable position.

" He was the chief of the Egyptian deities, and the

Greeks and Romans identified him with Jupiter, or Zeus. There is what is left of one of the sphinxes that formerly lined the avenue," replied Louis.

"It has the head of a goat," added the maiden.

"Hardly; it is the head of a ram. The god was given the form of a ram with a human head; and you will see no end of this symbol among these ruins, though I find it quite impossible to keep the run of the various animals that figure in the mythology of the ancient Egyptians."

"Did Ramses II. take his name from this symbol?" asked the fair maiden innocently.

"Not at all," laughed Louis, though he saw that his companion did not intend to make a pun. Ramses was hardly his name when he was living. He was the Pharaoh of the Bible, and the Sesostris of the Greeks; but I don't know what his name was when he was in the flesh, in the living flesh I mean, for his mummied form is still preserved."

"Of Ramses II.!" exclaimed Blanche.

"The successor of Mariette in charge of the antiquities of Egypt, suspected from the appearance of relics in the hands of travellers, that an Arab had discovered a tomb from which priceless treasures were obtained and sold. It was a mystery; and Professor Maspero, who succeeded the great Egyptologist, determined to solve it. He came to Luxor at once, and had the Arab arrested; but he was as silent as a martyr, and remained in prison two months. A reward of $2,500 was offered for the secret, and the brother

of the robber obtained it. He conducted the authorities to a desolate spot in the Great Necropolis. They
descended about forty feet, and found a long gallery
and vault, both of which contained thirty-six mummies, over twenty of which were of royal personages.
Among them were the remains of Ramses II., which,
with others, is now in the Gizeh Museum, to which
they are this year removing the antiquities of that at
Bûlâk."

"I heard something about that museum, and we
are to visit it on our return to Cairo," replied the
young lady.   "But what is this in front of us ? "

"That is the propylon, or front gate, of the great
Temple of Ammon. Here is a plan of the whole
thing," said Louis, opening his guide-book.

This structure is three hundred and seventy-two
feet wide, and one hundred and forty-two high. As
it stands now it is something like the triumphal arches
one sees in Paris and Rome. There are six of these
stupendous gateways, all of them ornamented with
historical or mythological sculpture. The buildings
contain a series of gigantic courts and halls, most of
them filled or surrounded with immense columns which
filled the beholders with wonder at their size and
admiration of their fine workmanship.

The young men of the party mounted to the top of
the pylon by available stairs, and had a wonderful
story to tell of their visit and what they had observed,
on their return. They mentioned the smaller temples
they had seen, and some of these were visited, each of
which was explained by the conductor.

The Hypostyle Hall, as it is called, seemed to be the crowning wonder. It was built about 1500 B.C., and is three hundred and thirty-eight feet long by one hundred and seventy wide, is therefore big enough to take in the Church of Notre Dame in Paris, or any church in the United States. It is literally packed with columns, one hundred and thirty-four in number, which support the roof. The two rows which extend down the centre are higher than the others, sixty-nine feet. Those on the two sides are forty-two feet high. These pillars are square, and over eleven feet deep, or as large on the floor as a fair-sized chamber.

The party followed during the rest of the day the leading of the conductor through avenues of columns, some square like those described, and some round, with capitals, in imitation of the calyx of a flower, the bud of the papyrus generally; and then they had enough for the first day. The dinner at the hotel was excellent; and the tourists were tired enough in the evening to rest, though they had a visit from the American vice-consul, a native. Similar officials remain at the large places on the Nile to assist travellers from the United States.

Early the next morning the company crossed the river in boats to the necropolis of Thebes. On their way up the river they had observed many contrivances, some worked by steam, others by oxen, and a greater number by hand, for irrigating the land; but here they had an opportunity to examine more closely one of these "shadufs," as they are called. It was on the principle of the old-time well-sweep, consisting of a long pole, pivoted in the centre, with a weight at one end and a perpendicular pole at the other, to which the bucket was attached, and lowered into the water. It is drawn up when the pail is filled, and the contents emptied into a trench, or reservoir. Where the height was too great for one sweep, another was fixed above it.

Donkeys were in readiness, and the tourists proceeded to examine the city of the ancient dead. The first point reached were the Colossi of Memnon. These two immense statues have suffered a great deal from the lapse of time, and an artist need not go into rhapsodies over them except as representatives of bygone ages. The figures are seated on their thrones, and were set up in honor of Amenhotep III. This king was a Memnon, but not the same as the Greek of Homer. These Colossi formerly stood in front of a Memnonium, or temple, entirely destroyed.

The height of the figures, including the pedestal, is sixty-four feet. Each foot is ten and a half feet long, and the leg below the knee not quite twenty feet. It is about the same across the shoulders, and the middle finger is four and a half feet long. The northern of them is the noted vocal Memnon, "which at sunrise played." This was doubtless a trick of the priests, as the poet suggests. It refused to give any utterance for several days when kings and princes came to it to hear the wonderful sounds; but it played twice when the Emperor Hadrian visited it one morning, after a long silence; and the people reverenced the monarch on account of the special favor granted to him. Give a franc to an Arab, and he will reproduce the sound by striking a certain stone with a hammer.

During the inundation the water rises to the toes of the statues, and they seem to be holding court in a lake. The Ramesseum, commonly called the Memnonium of Ramses II., was next visited. It is a vast building, but age has left many marks upon it. It was originally two hundred and twenty feet in width, but it is not all there now. It contains courts, peristyles, and columns, and especially the fallen statue of Ramses, the most gigantic stone figure in Egypt, which is saying a great deal. It was twenty-three and a half feet across the shoulders.

The party spent the rest of the second day at Luxor in visiting and revisiting both the temples of Karnak and those in the necropolis; and the more they saw the more their wonder increased at the magnitude of the enormous structures. Many volumes have been written about them, and additional information is obtained from time to time, and added to the vast store of knowledge accumulated. The mysteries of the present may be made plain in the future.

On the twelfth day of the excursion the steamer proceeded to Edfu. It was Sunday, and the commander insisted that it should be made strictly a day of rest, which all needed. But the next morning the party went to the Temple of Edfu, which was a vast structure, though they visited only a few of the principal halls. The voyage was renewed, and the quarries from which most of the stone for the wonderful buildings had been brought were pointed out to them. At Kom Ombo the steamer moored for the night, and the next morning proceeded on her trip, arriving at Assuan at noon; and this was the termination of the upward voyage of the Karnak.

Three days were passed here; and after dinner the tourists went over to the island of Elephantine, glad to escape for the time from the Arab and Egyptian pedlers who surrounded them as soon as they appeared. But the ladies were pleased with the black and gray ostrich feathers shown to them, and intended to purchase some of them later, for they were very cheap here.

There was formerly a temple on this island, the conductor informed the company; but some of them were glad that Mohammed Ali had caused it to be removed to make room for the palace he erected in its place. They looked at the Nilometer here; but it was similar to the one they had seen at Cairo, and they were not greatly interested. There were plenty of blocks of stone on the island, which had occupied places in buildings that had now disappeared.

There is a railroad from Assuan to the shore opposite the island of Philæ, and the travellers were glad of a little change of conveyance. It was too far from the river to permit them to see the First Cataract from the windows as they passed it. The Nile is filled here with islands for about five miles, most

RUINS AT PHILAE.   Page 337.

of which are inhabited. The party were ferried over the river to the island, which was sacred to Isis, as well as the temple on it.

"If you will take a seat here on this ruin, under the date-palms," said Mr. Hornbrook, "I will tell you a story about Osiris, one of whose graves was on this island."

"How many graves did it take to hold him?" asked Scott.

"Fourteen; but hear the narrative from mythology," replied the conductor. "Osiris and Isis, to the latter of whom the temple yonder was erected, were brother and sister; but they married, after the ancient custom, and had three children, one of whom was Typhon, a bad character. His parents had a happy reign, and the realm became very prosperous. The wicked son conspired against his worthy father, and at a banquet induced him to lie down in a curiously prepared chest.

"The conspirators closed the receptacle, and then threw it into the Nile. It floated down the river, and went ashore in the Delta. Isis wandered about in the greatest distress, seeking her missing husband. At last she found the strange chest, and concealed it. While engaged in a boar-hunt, Typhon found the body of the god, cut it into fourteen pieces, and scattered them over the country. Isis learned what had been done, and she gathered up the parts. As fast as one was found, she buried it, and erected a monument to her husband. This is why it required fourteen graves to bury him. Osiris, however, was not dead, but continued his reign in the lower regions. He trained his son Horus for battle, and the latter waged war against Typhon, whom he defeated, but could not destroy. Now Osiris is the principle of light, and Typhon of darkness."

"That is very good mythology," said the commander, as he rose from his seat. "Now we will see the Temple of Isis; but I doubt if we find the grave of Osiris."

The temple was on the east shore of the island, and it was interesting enough to occupy them for several hours. It contained the usual courts, chambers, and columns, more beautiful and impressive to look at than to read about. But they were more delighted with the beautiful scenery of the island, though the temples added to the picturesque prospect. Boats had been sent up as far as the cataract to convey the travellers back to Assuan.

They were obliged to walk about a mile to reach a safe place for the embarkation; but the path was along the bank of the river, which afforded them a good view of the islands and of the cataract, so that the time was not wasted. The young men did not consider it as of any great account as a waterfall, and thought it was honored with a title it hardly deserved.

"I should call it the rapids, for that is all there is of it," said Morris. "You could make a hundred such out of the river above the falls at Niagara."

"But they make a big thing of it here, and I

should say it would be a difficult matter to work a
dahabeah against the current," added Scott.

"If you were in one you would find it so," suggested the conductor. "Before the English took a
hand in the affairs of Egypt farther up the Nile,
many dahabeahs used to go up to the Second Cataract;
but they don't do it now, for the country is not always
safe there. It used to take from sixty to a hundred
men to haul one of these boats up the rapids. The
Arabs magnified the difficulties in order to increase
the price."

"But what do all these boys want?" asked Louis,
when a squad of nearly naked young Arabs presented
themselves.

"*Bakshîsh*, for which they will make the descent
through the rapids on a log, or without one," replied
the conductor.

The young men were more anxious to see this feat
than to gaze upon the ruins of past ages, and three of
the Nubians were feed for the purpose. The sight was
not very exciting, but it amused the party for a time.
The sailors drove off the beggars, and the company
proceeded on their way. Mr. Hornbrook gave the
names of the islands; but the trip was rather tame,
perhaps because the party were tired of sight-seeing
for the present. But that did not prevent them from
visiting the Arab cemeteries in the vicinity after they
landed. The graves were in the midst of the desert,
each with a rectangle of rough stones on it, with a
slab bearing an inscription, the date of some of which
went back to the ninth century.

Making their way from the cemetery through the vagabonds that beset them, they reached the steamer. The conductor announced that the trip, so far as sight-seeing was concerned, was practically finished. On the fifteenth day of the excursion, the Karnak was headed down the river, and moored at Edfu for the night.

zi

CHAPTER XXXVI

THE HALL OF THE ROYAL MUMMIES

THE stupendous monuments of antiquity had largely occupied the attention of the party from the Guardian-Mother for fifteen days; and they found the time allotted to seeing these wonders by the Gaze managers amply sufficient for persons unlearned in Egyptology. They had looked upon them simply as sight-seers, gathering what information they could as they went along.

But the visits to pyramids, temples, tombs, and colossi were not the whole of the trip up and down the Nile. The social features of the journey had been greatly enjoyed. They were rather early in the season; but they had fallen in with quite a number of private parties in dahabeahs, and had made some very pleasant acquaintances. Those whom they met were naturally very much interested in the voyage around the world, which had to be related many times, and the evening meetings with English and American parties travelling over the same route were very delightful.

Mrs. Belgrave had taken care that the "Gospel Hymns," containing the music, should be brought along; and the singing was apparently enjoyed quite as much by the visitors to the Karnak as by the "Karnakers" themselves. Then there were no troublesome calculations about the weather when they were going on an expedition to a tomb or a pyramid. It was always practically pleasant. Uncle Moses was the weather prophet of the tour, and he kept a record of it. Not a drop of rain had fallen since the company left Cairo; and though the travellers had journeyed to the verge of the Torrid Zone, the heat had never been oppressive.

"I had an idea that the Cupids of this excursion would have been about melted by this time," said Uncle Moses, after the Karnak had moored at Edfu, and the party had seated themselves on the promenade deck just before dark. " I expected that Brother Adipose Tissue would have parted with twenty pounds of flesh by this time."

"On the contrary, I think I have added another quarter of an ounce to my weight," chuckled Dr. Hawkes. "Brother Avoirdupois does not appear to be a particle more shadowy than when we left Alexandria, and neither of us had ever mounted a camel."

"What are the weather figures you have noted, Uncle Moses?" asked Captain Ringgold.

"I was looking them over just as we left Assuan, and I found that the glass has gone up to 80 only on two days during the voyage," replied the weatherman. "The sky has been clear most of the time, and I could not find a day on which the wind had been

either east or west. It was always either north or
south. We had it south south-west for four days beginning with the third of the trip. On five days it has
been a little cloudy. We' had one foggy morning
only. The prevailing winds were from the north."

"But the wind is west now," said the commander.

"I see that it has changed from the north," added
Uncle Moses ; and it continued in that quarter for the
next six days, so that his deductions were materially
changed when the Karnak arrived at Bûlâk.

It is unnecessary to give the details of the return
voyage down the Nile of the Karnak, for the novelty
of the trip was gone. But the time was not wasted,
for several points of interest were visited which had
been left on the upward passage. Christmas was
properly celebrated with an excellent dinner, and
Santa Claus paid a visit to the steamer, though he
must have found it hard sledding where not a flake
of snow had ever fallen. The stockings were not
hung up, but there was an exchange of gifts among
the younger members of the party.

Louis engaged Chloe to pin the Greek cap he had
purchased in the Muski, on the occasion of his unfor-
tunate visit to the shop of Pierre Ulbach, to the
pillow of Miss Blanche's bed after she had gone to
sleep. He had been so mortified by the adventure
that he had kept the cap out of sight after he went on
board of the Karnak. But the beautiful young lady
appeared at breakfast wearing the pretty headdress ;
and it produced a decided sensation, for she could

have worn nothing that added so much to her native loveliness.

Louis was positively enraptured at her appearance, and Dr. Hawkes declared that Cleopatra must have been tame in her beauty compared with the belle of the Karnak. The young lady was very much puzzled to know who had been the donor of the gift, though others had not the least difficulty in determining who he was. But the point was not settled at the table; and her mother whispered to her that she had better say nothing more about it, for everybody else knew from whom it came.

"It was either papa or Morris," said she after breakfast.

"Of course it was Louis Belgrave, child," replied Mrs. Woolridge. "How dull you are!"

She did not believe it even then, and she asked Louis about it. With a heavy blush he confessed that he was guilty, and explained in what manner he had happened to purchase it, though he was careful not to add any of the attending circumstances of his visit to the shop. The steamer continued on her voyage down the river during the day, which was given up to fun and frolic.

"I don't know precisely where we are going when we have seen all we desire of Egypt," said Louis, on the following day, when the party were gathered on deck. "I suppose we are going somewhere."

"No doubt of it," replied Captain Ringgold. "We shall go through the Red Sea on our way to India;

but there is something more of Egypt to see if we choose to see it, and that question is still to be decided. There are two more cities on the north, Rosetta and Damietta, though it would hardly pay to visit either of them."

"I believe the Rosetta Stone is in the British Museum," added Louis.

"It is; I have seen it there," replied Mr. Hornbrook. "The Tablet of Tanis, now in the Museum of Bûlâk or Gizeh, confirmed the discoveries of Champollion."

"Like Mariette, Champollion was a Frenchman, born in 1791," added Professor Giroud. "He devoted himself from his boyhood to the study of the Oriental languages, especially the Coptic. He became a professor of history in Paris, but was dismissed for his Bonapartism. He wrote several works on Egyptian subjects. His study of the languages prepared him for his special work. Up to his time no one had been able to make anything of the Egyptian hieroglyphics.

"In 1824 this diligent student arrived at the conclusion that these symbols you have seen on temples, tombs, and pyramids were the representatives of either sounds, like the characters used by a short-hand writer, or the signs of ideas, like words. He made an alphabet of twenty-five letters, representing sounds. But these were only a portion of the resources of the Egyptian language, for the symbols representing ideas were practically unlimited, and 1700 of them were in actual use.

"As among the American Indians and the Aztecs, ideas were sometimes represented by pictures, as gladness was shown by a woman beating a tambourine, or a man dancing; a jackal meant cunning or trickery, and so on. With hardly anything to work upon, Champollion solved the mystery in the Rosetta Stone, which Napoleon's engineers discovered in 1799, and which the English carried to London. The subject is too difficult and complicated to be explained here; but in the library of the ship something may be done in that way."

"But what is the inscription about?" asked Mrs. Belgrave.

"That is of far less consequence than the service it rendered learning through Champollion, which Niebuhr, the distinguished geographer, said was the greatest discovery of the century. The stone contains the record of a resolution passed by the priests setting forth the glories of Ptolemy V., though he was a boy of only fourteen. The Tablet of Tanis, which you saw at Bûlâk, or may see, records the Decree of Canopus, a sacred city about fifteen miles east of Alexandria, in honor of Ptolemy III., and also to the Princess Berenice, who died young and unmarried, and was called 'The Princess of Virgins.' This stone, like that of Rosetta, was to be set up in the highest temples."

It would be impossible to report all the instructive conversations that took place on the deck and in the cabins of the Karnak. On the third day of January the steamer arrived at Bûlâk, and the excursion was finished. The officers and servants on board were liberally rewarded by the commander, for they had been all that was required of them.

As soon as the party reached Cairo and were again installed in the hotel, Louis took Don with him, and made a visit to the Muski. The shop of Pierre Ulbach was closed, and he set the engineer to inquiring what had become of him. It appeared he had failed in business, after robbing his creditors. A policeman gave this information, and he spoke French. Louis asked him what had become of the brother of the shopkeeper and another man who had been with him. They had left together, and gone to Rosetta. One of them had been hurt by falling down the trap-door steps.

Louis was satisfied with this information, and it fully justified the prophecy of the commander that nothing would be done about the shooting. The party spent another week in Cairo, and made three visits in this time to the Citadel, with its magnificent view. They spent three days in exploring the museum, both at Bûlâk and at Gizeh. In the latter they saw what some of them considered the most wonderful sight they had seen.

In the "Hall of the Royal Mummies" they saw the remains of the kings and queens, which had been discovered, as before related, as late as 1881, hardly more than ten years before their visit. They looked them over with especial interest, and all the rest of the museum seemed to gather interest from their presence. These emblems of mortality appeared to make the past more real to them than tombs and temples.

"This is the mummy of Ramses III.," said Mr. Hornbrook. "He was the Rhampsinitus of the Greek, and reigned over 1200 years before the time of Christ. The inscriptions on the coffin record that this body was moved twice. Here also are the coffin and mummy of Ramses II., sometimes called Ramses the Great, for he was the most powerful king of his time. He was also, as you have been told before, the Pharaoh who oppressed the Isralites, and tried to follow them across the Red Sea, as you read in your Bibles."

"That the body of Pharaoh!" exclaimed Mrs. Blossom, with an attitude that was almost tragic. "I can hardly believe it!"

"I have no doubt about it," added the commander.

"The most learned men of the age have proved it," said the conductor. "As you don't read hieroglyphics yourself, you will have to take the word of the scholars for it. But the Hebrew in which the Old Testament was written is just as intelligible to you as the inscription on this mummy case."

"I suppose I must believe it," replied the good lady. "But how strange that I, Sarah Blossom, should be looking at the dead body of old Pharaoh!"

"I suppose you are sure he is dead, are you not?" asked Mr. Hornbrook.

"What a question! How long has he been dead?"

"Over three thousand years."

" Good gracious ! "

The entire day was spent among these royal mummies, and there was enough to occupy the attention of the party, even including the boys. Two other days were used up among other curiosities. On another day the company went to a mosque again for the purpose of obtaining a better idea of the worship of the Mohammedan religion, which was explained to them by Mr. Hornbrook.

At the end of the second week the tourists proceeded to Alexandria, and went on board of the Guardian-Mother, still attended by the conductor. One of the first vessels that attracted the attention of the commander, when he came on board, was a steamer of four hundred tons, anchored nearly a mile from the ship. Glasses were soon brought to bear upon her, and it was soon settled beyond a doubt that she was the Fatimé.

" I have no doubt Mazagan has brought his wounded companion on board of the Pacha's steam-yacht, and her presence here indicates that they have not abandoned their plan," said the commander. "That treacherous Moor now in command of the Fatimé evidently has some other scheme to carry out, and we shall not know what it is till he develops it in his actions."

" It is a question of so much money with him," replied Louis, to whom the captain had pointed out the vessel. " I don't see that we can say or do anything to prevent him from following the Guardian-Mother."

" Perhaps we can," added Captain Ringgold thought-
fully, " I will do what I thought of in Cairo."

" What is that, sir ? "

" I may write to Ali-Noury Pacha, and inform him
of the manner in which Mazagan offered to sell him
out for half the price he was to pay him, and collect
the other half of his employer."

" I am afraid the Pacha will not believe you," suggested Louis.

" I have not entire faith in the plan; but in the
meantime we can be as vigilant as ever in the protection of our passengers. If it were not for the Maud,
we should have no difficulty in running away from the
Fatimé. I suppose her ship's company still desire
to navigate her over the Red Sea and the Indian
Ocean."

" Do you think of disposing of her ? " asked Louis,
somewhat startled by the idea.

" We have kept the Maud in the water much longer
than I supposed we should when she was purchased,"
replied the commander, closely observing the expression of the young owner. " As you are aware, I had
the upper deck strengthened, and everything prepared
to take her out of the water, and carry her on board
like any of the other boats. We can hoist her up at
any time ; and the question comes to me now whether
it ought not to be done."

" That would break the heart of Captain Scott and
some of the rest of the Maud's ship's company,"
added Louis with a smile.

" We will not decide the question now, for I should not like to break anybody's heart; we may have rough seas, and it is evident that we have a new battle to fight with the Fatimé. It would be safer for you and the others to be on board of the Guardian-Mother."

" When shall we sail, Captain ? " asked Louis.

"To-morrow, I think. All the accounts are settled, and there is nothing to detain us here any longer. Our next point will be Port Said, and we are not yet quite done with Egypt. Your mother and Mrs. Blossom will certainly desire to see Mount Sinai, which is in Asia. After dinner we will meet and settle all pressing questions," said the commander, as he glanced at the Pacha's steamer, which appeared to be a standing threat.

Before they retired that night it was decided that the Maud should not be taken out of the water at present, though the question would come up again at Suez. On the following day the Guardian-Mother sailed from Alexandria, closely followed by the Maud. The Fatimé had disappeared in the early morning, but she was discovered again; headed to the eastward, off the Bay of Abukir; and it was evident that she was ready for business in the hands of her present reckless and unprincipled commander. It was apparent to Louis Belgrave that the "Big Four" were to be more abundantly supplied with adventures during the next two or three months than they had been in " The Land of Egypt."

If Captain Ringgold was still cool and self-possessed, he was more anxious than he had been before for months, for the seas and the countries the All-Over-The-World excursionists were yet to visit were more favorable than before to the operations of such a pirate as Captain Mazagan.   It was watch and wait, always ready, with him.   What fortunes and misfortunes awaited him and the " Big Four," with what the party saw and what they learned, will be duly chronicled in " Asiatic Breezes; or, Students on the Wing."

www.ingramcontent.com/pod-product-compliance
Lightning Source LLC
Chambersburg PA
CBHW021710110726
47902CB00005B/1138